DEADLY TROUBLE

TROUBLE

VEGAS VIXENS BOOK TWO

J.L. HAMMER

Entangled Publishing, LLC
2614 South Timberline Road
Suite 109
Fort Collins, CO 80525
Visit our website at www.entangledpublishing.com.

Select Suspense is an imprint of Entangled Publishing, LLC.

Edited by Laura Stone
Cover design by Fiona Jayde
Cover art by iStock

Manufactured in the United States of America

First Edition August 2015

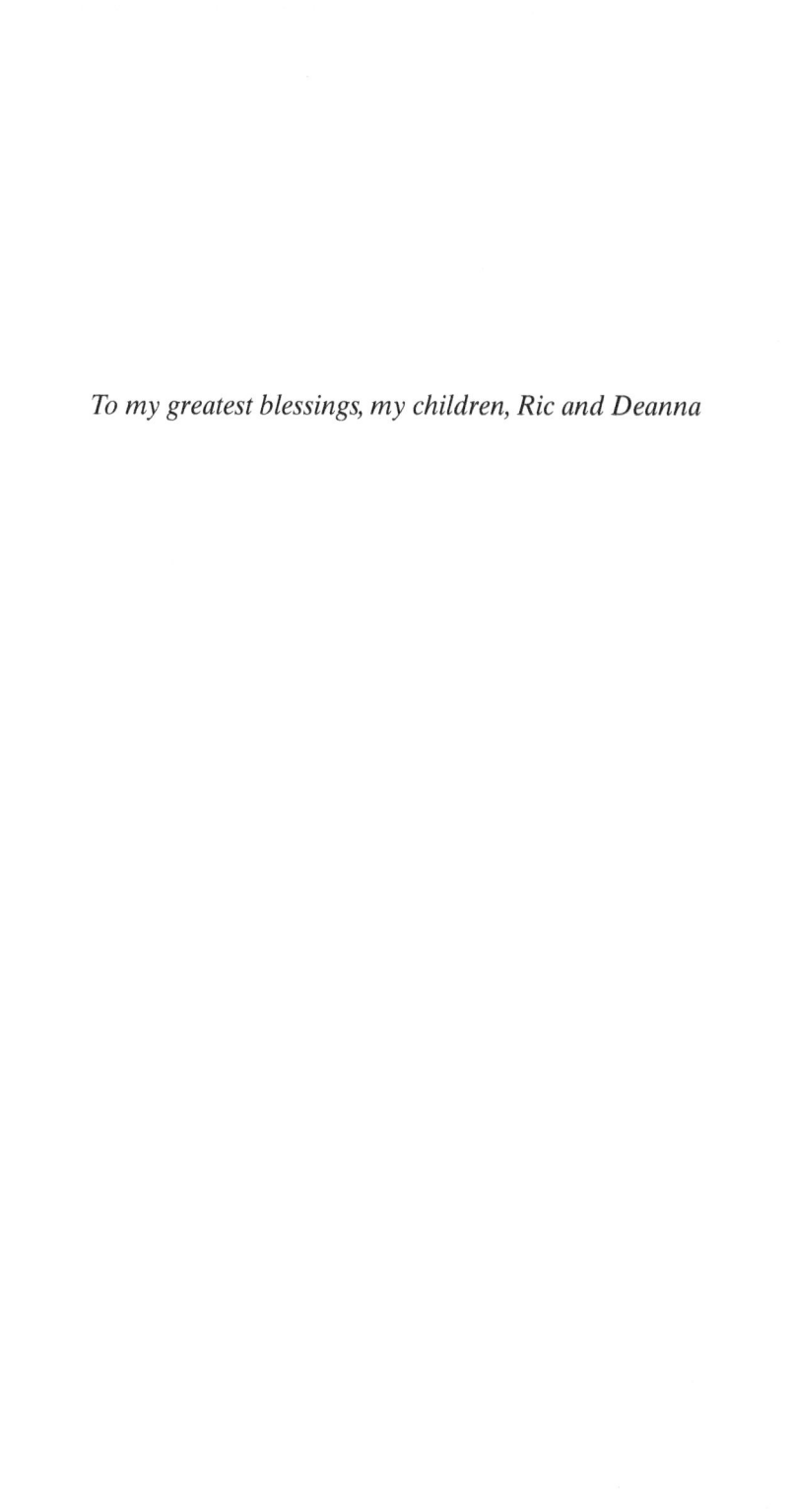

To my greatest blessings, my children, Ric and Deanna

Chapter One

Lily Sanborn adjusted the towel to cover the lower portion of Sal's unclad body and refocused on massaging the stiffness from her client's massive shoulders. "For an old guy, you sure are built. I bet you used to be a weight lifter." She thought for a moment and ventured, "No wait, make that a linebacker in college football."

She tossed back her waist-length ponytail threatening to slip over her shoulder and leaned the weight of her petite body into him to apply more pressure. Air expelled from his throat and created a deep moaning sound. Without missing a beat, her fingers kneaded one ham-sized arm then the other. Exhaustion from way too much overtime hovered nearby, and she blinked away the blur threatening to impede her vision. Sometimes she worked for so many hours straight that the bland walls of the ten-by-twenty room started to close in on her.

Although the rhythmic pace of her hands never ceased, her mind drifted outside of these walls to a white stretch of sandy beach that met a cloudless blue sky. She could almost taste the fruity, alcoholic beverage against her lips and feel the salty, warm breeze touching her skin. *Time to work, not to daydream.* "Your wife will arrive later this afternoon. We need to get you dressed."

Sal didn't respond, but she hardly expected him to. Finally his muscles relaxed enough, and she brushed her hand over the bulk of his bicep. His skin held a rosy hue and felt firm to the touch. Perfect. She glanced over her shoulder at the gauge in the glass cylinder of the embalming machine, the level of pinkish-red fluid barely noticeable. "Almost done."

Lily always liked to think of her clients as alive rather than corpses lying on cold slabs. Peaceful Memories Mortuary was their last stop, and she wanted to send them off looking their best. Their souls had either taken a one-way ticket to Heaven or went the opposite route to go pop and sizzle in Hell's eternal wok. "No devil for you, Sal; you were a good man. You have a wife and grown children who are eager to kiss you good-bye."

Unlike my own father whose roaming eye left only bitterness, and nobody, not even his children, would bother to kiss him good-bye. An American gigolo, her maternal Chinese grandmother called him, with his handsome, Anglo features. She shook her head at the unwanted thoughts. After removing the embalming fluid tube, she dried off and powdered the nearby skin. Once the incision was sutured, she flexed her cramping, gloved hands. Lily's stomach growled, but at this point, her schedule was far too busy for a lunch break.

Maybe after Mr. Salazar left.

"Ms. Viv, you're up." She strolled over to another client on a hydraulic, stainless-steel table, her protective scrubs swishing with her movements. She maneuvered the freshly washed body into a floral dress. The ventilator that hovered above her head whispered as it removed the toxic fumes and provided clean air.

The double doors opened, and Rae, the receptionist, stepped in. Her black, shoulder-length hair—almost as dark as Lily's—gleamed from the overhead light. "Is Ms. Vivian Thorndike ready?" Her bold gaze assessed the bodies.

"Almost, I just need to finish makeup and hair, and she'll be ready for the casket."

"Good, I'll relate that to the director." Rae's pert nose scrunched up. "I don't know how you can work in here. It smells."

"Part of the job." Lily shrugged her shoulder.

"So, how'd your date go with Mr. Bow Tie?"

"You just had to be nosy and introduce yourself."

"Of course, I did." Mischief danced in Rae's green eyes. In her late twenties like Lily, Rae lived in the same mobile home park and had conveniently strolled over when Lily's date had driven up.

"You should take a more active role in your own dating life and keep your nose out of mine." Lily's brows lowered. "You've had like what, one date since I've known you...and it's not due to the lack of men asking."

Six months ago Rae had moved to Vegas. Lily found it very odd that her friend never talked about family, never had visitors, and in the time it took to boil water, Rae's belongings could be packed up, and it would look like she'd never occupied her trailer.

Rae looked away and shrugged. Then she smirked, which appeared a bit forced. "It's more fun to hear about dates than experience them, so stop dodging the question. Spill it, and I want details."

"It was boring." Just thinking about dinner last night made Lily sleepy.

Rae laughed. "Well that's a shocker. Why did you turn down that hunky guy last week and agree to a date with a nerd who had the personality of cardboard? No offense, but after one minute, I figured out an evening with him would be a flatline."

"What's with all the questions? My date's looks were acceptable, and that hunky guy, as you called him, was just a flirt. He had a tan line where he'd taken off his wedding ring." A cheater just like her father. More than one stupid woman had shown up at Lily's childhood home unwilling to accept they had been dumped after falling for Father's charm. Mother had never gotten mad, just patted the sobbing lady on the shoulder and offered her hot tea. Lily's mouth tightened as she rolled a squeaking metal cart next to Ms. Viv. She inventoried the makeup and grooming items.

"Hmmm. Good catch. Didn't even look for a tan line," Rae said. "So, I'm on grandmother duty tomorrow, right?"

"Yes, and thanks again." Lily wouldn't have even considered going on vacation if she wasn't convinced her grandmother, who'd helped raise her, would be looked after. Not only did Lily resemble her grandmother in her youth, with the same fair skin, high cheekbones, and almond shaped eyes, but she'd become her caregiver of sorts. Lily missed her plush condo, but G-ma refused to leave her friends at the park and for some odd reason wasn't bothered by the rattling trailer as airplanes landed at the neighboring airport. Maybe after her vacation to Belize, Lily would stop clenching her teeth.

"Don't mention it." Rae straightened the sleeve of her blouse to cover more of her sun-kissed skin. "I still can't believe your friend called off her wedding and is taking you on the honeymoon."

Lily shrugged. "Frankie still insists Wes doesn't want to marry her. People in love act dumb. It's obvious Wes is crazy about Frankie." *He did save her from a ruthless loan shark — or was it Frankie who saved Wes?* Lily had heard so many versions of the event she couldn't remember.

"You think she'll really carry out her threat?"

"She already refunded Wes's ticket, and I purchased mine. I don't know what's up with those two, but that's their problem. Right now, I just want to get a tan and down some cheap umbrella drinks." Lily lifted her hand in the air. "And do whatever else you do in Belize." Maybe the fresh air would chase away the smell of formaldehyde that seemed to follow her like an aura.

"Don't blame you one bit, but be careful. I watched a documentary about how Belize isn't just paradise for tourists, but also for drug dealers."

"Well, I guess they need a vacation, too." Lily brushed a layer of foundation onto Ms. Viv's discolored skin.

"That's not what I mean." Rae lowered her voice as if the corpses might overhear. "It has a dark side. The police can't adequately patrol all those jungles, and the drug cartels are moving in."

"I'm not going there to buy crack. I'm going to relax,

hopefully on a beach."

"Were the final words of the American tourist."

Lily paused from applying makeup and peered over. "Would you like to be my next client?"

Rae laughed and planted a hand on her curvy hip, making Lily's straight figure seem almost boyish. "You hate working overtime. Well, be sure to keep your cell phone handy, because your grandmother doesn't like me. Do you know the last time I came over, she hit me with a broom?"

"Your crow tattoo is bad luck. It would be just as bad if you'd strolled into her living room arm in arm with the Grim Reaper." All G-ma's quirks took some getting used to.

"That's weird. It's just ink on my skin."

"Weird or not, you can't win over G-ma if you've been added to her evil list." Lily flipped a dismissive hand in the air. But the good news was that G-ma would be so busy trying to keep the *bad* **out of the house,** she wouldn't have time to miss Lily.

"My favorite band's The Black Crowes." Rae's brows furrowed. "Can't you just tell her that?"

"Won't make a difference." Lily studied the photo of Ms. Viv. With gentle strokes, she styled her client's wispy, gray hair. "Just let her whack you with the broom. It makes her feel better."

"I'm not letting her hit me, and I'm not getting the tattoo taken off. If I'm supposed to keep an eye on her for the next two weeks, what should I do about her carrying a broom?"

Lily stared at Rae. Sometimes people were clueless. "Simple. Duck."

The low ring from the wall phone diverted their attention. Lily removed her gloves and tossed them in the trash.

With a few short strides, she snatched up the handset and gave her token greeting. "Embalming, Lily."

Rae waved and walked back out the doors.

"Hey, it's Frankie," a familiar feminine voice announced.

"Your ears must have been ringing. I was just talking about you."

Silence stretched over the line before Frankie said, "Wes and I made up."

"I knew you would." A smile lifted the corners of Lily's mouth only to drop as she envisioned her vacation slipping away. "So the wedding's back on?"

"Err…not exactly. You know Wes, he's still nervous about marrying again, so we decided to wait six more months. I guess I pushed too hard about the marriage thing."

Lily shifted the phone. "So what's the plan? Want me to bow out so you two can go together?"

A long pause followed. "No, it would cost too much now to buy his ticket. Um, I feel really bad about this, but I can't go without him…so, Lily, you'll have to go on my honeymoon solo."

• • •

MOUNTAIN PINE RIDGE, BELIZE

Cooper Deforest shifted in his cushioned chair and tried his best to pretend he wasn't having iced tea on the balcony of a drug lord's two-story mansion. Birds chattered amongst the palm fronds as moisture from the May humidity made Cooper's dirt-streaked clothes stick to him, which was a complete contrast to Maximo, who looked like an aristocrat in a crisp, white suit. Neither man had touched the two plates of fruit that rested on the tempered glass of the patio table.

"Belize is paradise, wouldn't you say?" Maximo rested against the chair and scanned his vast empire guarded by a dozen armed militia and a high-voltage fence.

Cooper had heard the rumors circulating about how Maximo had assassinated his rival and fed his remains to the jaguars at the local reserve. Now at age thirty, just five years younger than Cooper, he'd become the youngest and most feared drug lord in the country. And what was astonishing, at least in Cooper's mind, was that Maximo had graduated from a university in Spain only to return to his native country to build a criminal empire.

Before Cooper could speak, Maximo continued. "Belize is a land for the people, without all the brainwashing you get from governments like your own."

Cooper seriously doubted Maximo had sent two armed men to the village for the suggested meeting to get his opinion on government. "I agree. Belize is a beautiful country."

Standing off to the side, Maximo's head of security known as the Samoan crossed his meaty arms, his expression: impassive. The scar slashed down the man's bronze cheek, along with his shaved head, added to his intimidation factor.

Maximo's scrutinizing gaze raked over Cooper. "If I had to make a guess, I'd say you're from California."

"I am." Cooper wasn't too impressed, given he had tan skin, blond hair to his shoulders, and more often than not people thought he should be brandishing a surfboard rather than a doctorate.

"Doctor, do you know why you're my guest this afternoon?"

"Can't say I do."

"We have a problem. Your research is getting too close

to my land holdings."

Cooper adjusted his wire-rimmed glasses and tried his best to ignore the rapid pounding of his pulse. Without a doubt his research was important, lifesaving even, but he was wise enough to know not to taunt death. "Well, I think we can find an easy solution."

"You Americans do consider yourselves the solvers of the world's problems. Please. Enlighten me." Maximo propped an elbow on the table and rested the three remaining fingers on his left hand against the temple of his close-cut brown hair.

Although Maximo spoke calmly, his posture had tensed. Cooper fought to keep his nerves from showing. He'd lived most of his life in third world countries, and although he'd been in stickier situations than this—with a gun pointed to his head and an ultimatum to leave the country or die, or as a teenager barely escaping his house that had intentionally been burned to the ground—that didn't stop a trickle of sweat from sliding a serpentine path down his back. "I could really use your advice on the best places to conduct my research. If an area is dangerous, maybe steep terrain or predators, I won't go there." Cooper held his breath.

A smirk spread across Maximo's clean-shaven jaw. "You are correct. There are lots of dangerous places, and I wouldn't want you or one of those villagers you trained to get hurt."

Cooper's hands flexed at the thought of one of the villagers being injured. This man held too much power. People shouldn't have to live in fear, but from experience he knew it happened all the time. Cooper listed off seven areas where he'd planned to conduct research. He gained approval on three.

Maximo gestured toward the acres of jungle that rose and fell with the curves of the hilly terrain. "Doctor, I didn't gain my empire by showing kindness, and I don't give second chances."

Cooper decided then and there that he would stop using the villagers to assist with his research. Too risky.

Maximo removed an orange slice from the plate closest to Cooper and placed it near a spider monkey perched on the railing. It snatched the food, flipped its furry tail in the air, and turned away. "The only reason you weren't just shot and left for the jaguars is because I am aware of who your father is…but don't test my kindness."

"I'm just here to do my research, and then I'll be on my way."

The monkey on the rail staggered, capturing Cooper's attention. A strange guttural sound emitted from its furry body, and it pitched forward over the balcony. A piece of the orange rind *plopped* on the slate floor. Cooper slid his gaze to the remaining fruit on his plate and then to Maximo's bland stare.

A tense moment stretched out. Cooper kept his expression neutral, not wanting his real reactions of fear and anger to fuel a power trip for this sick-ass who'd killed a helpless animal and could have killed him as well.

"Fate was on your side, Doctor. How easily you could have been tempted by the decadent fruit and died a painful death."

Cooper couldn't respond. He hadn't been tempted by the fruit, but with the high humidity, he'd almost taken a drink of the iced tea.

"You're cool under pressure. I could use a man like you to get things out of the country."

Great, a job offer from a drug dealer. The cascading water from the sculpted fountain now sounded as loud as a roaring waterfall. "My research leaves time for nothing else," Cooper said.

Maximo lowered his thick slash of brows and Cooper tensed, waiting for a knife to plunge into his chest or a bullet to plow into him. The Samoan widened his stance. With a snap of Maximo's fingers, Cooper would be dead and everyone knew it. Maximo stood, the chair scraping across the floor. "Do you think you have a choice?"

Maximo walked through the French doors, opened for him before he broke stride. Cooper stood. The Samoan approached and tossed a white envelope.

It bounced off Cooper's chest and hit the table. "I'm not interested."

In a fluid motion, the Samoan unsheathed a hunting knife from the waistband of his trousers. The razor-sharp blade glinted from the rays of the morning sun. "Exactly what I was hoping you'd say. Either take the envelope, and get in the vehicle, or I'll gut you, keeping you on the verge of consciousness, and then bury you alive."

Shit. Not in the mood to die today, Cooper snatched the envelope and strode toward the outside staircase in the direction he'd come. The envelope seared like a hot coal into his hand. He needed to finish his research and get out. Once in the vehicle with the two bodyguards who'd brought him, Cooper bounced around in the backseat as they drove down a dirt road etched through the jungle. Overhead, the canopy blocked out most of the sunlight. Cooper knew one thing for sure: after what he'd just endured, he needed a strong drink and sure could use the distraction of female company. Sometimes a man just had to celebrate life.

· · ·

After a grueling twelve-hour flight with two stops and another ninety minutes traveling from Belize City inland to Mountain Pine Ridge on an unpaved road, Lily reached the resort in the dead of night. Flanked by palm trees, the spotlighted HIDDEN PARADISE LODGE sign greeted her. This place was a lot smaller than she'd expected and very quiet for close to midnight on a Saturday. She stepped out of the rear door of the taxi. Inhaling a deep breath of the muggy air, she peeled her moist shirt off her back.

The gap-toothed driver with a heavy Spanish accent set down her luggage. "Here, pretty lady."

After handing him money, she marched down the stone walkway past a pair of hammocks swaying in the warm breeze. She veered onto an inclined plank walkway toward the tucked-away office. Animal sounds emitted from the jungle. A high-pitched screech followed a guttural snarl. *Is a wild cat enjoying a monkey dinner?* Lily shot a nervous glance to her left into the darkness of vine-infested trees and picked up her pace. She was not getting eaten by some creature before she even had a cheap umbrella drink. Even in the darkness, the lodge, elevated on stilts about five feet off the jungle floor, was charming, with its little silhouetted cabanas and lush vegetation, but she couldn't care less. She smelled, and her stiff body ached. A cold shower. Sleep. That's all she wanted.

She swatted away a mosquito and stepped into a bamboo-framed office exposed to the elements.

"Ah, our last guests. I'm Xavier. I was afraid you had gotten lost," announced a flat-faced older man with coffee-colored skin, a white mustache, and a big smile.

Behind the counter, a rifle hung on the wall above a painting of a woman weaving a basket. He followed her gaze. "Not to worry." His accent sounded like a blend of Spanish and Jamaican. "I keep my grandfather's—God rest his soul—rifle handy for the rare occasion a jaguar roams onto the grounds. Just the sound of a gunshot, and it runs away."

"Wonderful." Leave it to Frankie to book a vacation where you could tangle with a jaguar.

"Only one of you?" Xavier asked, a puzzled expression on his face.

She gave the man a leveled gaze from her five-foot-three frame. "Yes, Frankie Delenski couldn't make it. I'm Lily Sanborn. It's been a long trip, and I'm ready to drop."

The man looked alarmed for a moment and then laughed. "No, no that will not do. Best get you to your room. You can have a cabana with one big bed."

He snagged a key and took her bag. She followed, every step heavier than the last. After taking a maze of walkways, Xavier veered down a long, planked ramp to a private patio and stopped at a cabana with a tall, mahogany door and a hammock under the large, slatted window. A space of about twenty feet, jam-packed with palm and banana trees, separated her from the neighboring units. Lily noted if someone wanted to get to a neighboring cabana they had to walk to the main walkway and head down another ramp. *At least I'll have some privacy.*

"My wife, Yesenia, prepares all the meals," Xavier said. "She is the best cook. You will see. Breakfast starts at six a.m."

Lily nodded and then frowned. "Six a.m.? And when does breakfast end?"

He pushed open the door and placed her suitcase inside. "For the late sleepers we keep it going 'til eight thirty."

"I'll be a late sleeper. Does this place have AC?" She walked inside.

He laughed. "Oh, no. The cold air would just escape out of the thatched roof."

She forced a smile. If this place felt like a sauna at night, what would the day be like? After mumbling good-night, she closed and locked the door. Suspended from a thick beam above, the ceiling fan's wide palm blades rotated in a lazy cycle. She passed the bamboo-frame bed with its pastel bedspread. The place looked cute and tropical. Nothing fancy but kept up and clean. No TV, not that it mattered. She planned to explore the ruins and go on hikes. After removing her clothes, she squeezed into the miniature shower. She sighed in relief once the cold spray hit her sticky flesh. In no time, she climbed into bed, not bothering with PJs, and let sleep take her.

It felt as if her head had just hit the pillow when an annoying chirping sound started.

"Shush," she grumbled and turned over. The chirps grew louder.

"Quiet!" She covered her head with the pillow, inhaling the freshly laundered scent.

Finally, she gave up and rolled out of bed, surprised to see rays of sunshine slanting across the floor through the wooden blinds. She rubbed her eyes and listened to the chatter of birds outside. Where had Frankie booked their room? An aviary? In no time, Lily slipped on worn jean shorts and an ivory eyelet tank top. After scooping her hair into a ponytail, brushing her teeth, and washing her face, she decided to hunt down the owner. Did they warn their potential customers about all this racket? How could she last thirteen more days listening to these stupid birds? She stalked past groundskeepers pruning ferns and stepped into the open-air office.

The growl started to roll off her tongue as Xavier approached, his face splitting into a wide grin. "Miss Sanborn, did you sleep well?"

"No, actually—"

"I am so glad." He gripped her elbow and escorted her around the corner to an older woman with a round face and heavy lines of fatigue under her eyes. "Yesenia will give you breakfast."

"Yes, of course." The woman dished up items from food warmers perched on the wooden table behind her.

Lily blinked at the plate thrust into her hands, hoping it held a cooked bird. No such luck. The plate was stacked high with pineapple, mangos, and an omelet garnished with slices of avocado and a yellow flower blossom.

Xavier released her elbow. "You will never want to leave, for she is the best cook in Belize."

"Just in Belize?" Yesenia smiled and planted a hand on her hip.

"Oh, my dear wife, of course also the best in Guatemala." Xavier cupped his hand near his mouth and said in a whisper, "We have to go across the border a few times a year. Her cousin's food tastes like burned cat fur."

Yesenia giggled.

These old people are too cute to yell at. "Um. Thanks for breakfast." Lily plastered on a smile and strolled outside. The dining balcony consisted of eight tables overlooking the jungle. A mass of birds ate from feeders hanging from tree limbs. Wonderful, now she was front and center for the bird orchestra. Her eye started to twitch. She stopped at the breakfast bar to get a napkin and silverware. A man and child, sitting on stools at the bar eating breakfast, glanced her way.

Lily smiled down at the little Hispanic boy in a Mickey Mouse T-shirt as he sucked on a chunk of pineapple. "Hi," she said.

The boy, about four years old with unruly, brown curls, pointed into the jungle, worry riddling his expression. "Bird." His golden eyes settled on Lily.

As if struck, she staggered back. *Those eyes.* Pain stabbed into her chest. In her mind another little boy materialized. *Philip.* His golden eyes filled with mischief as he planted slobbery kisses on her face. Philip had trusted her unconditionally—trust she hadn't deserved.

"Bird."

She blinked back the moisture and pushed the haunting image out of her head. She focused on the child before her and smiled. "Yes. Lots of them."

A toucan landed on the rail. The boy jerked back, dropping his pineapple. The bird swooped down and devoured the fruit.

"He eat me?"

"Yes, Jaime." The father laughed. "It eats little toes."

Jaime lifted his thin legs and huddled in the chair. Lily glared at the scrawny man with the same unruly hair as his son but with eyes the color of swamp mud. She shifted her gaze back to the boy, who stared in horror at the bird.

"No, sweetie," she reassured. "The bird won't eat you." She stepped closer to the bird, and it flew away. "See? It's harmless. Do you like Froot Loops cereal?"

The boy nodded.

"It's like the bird on the commercials, and it definitely likes kids."

"It sings and flies like this." A smile lit up his face as he lifted both hands in the air.

Just watching him made her heart hurt. *Just leave! Stop doing this to yourself.* "Yes. That's right. So remember, you're bigger, and when you move, the birds will fly away." Lily tore her gaze off the little boy and drilled the father with a look daring him to contradict her, which he didn't, since he appeared too absorbed in staring at her bare legs. Creep. Balancing the plate in one hand, she spoke to the boy. "See you later." She grabbed utensils, pivoted on a heel, and debated which of the three empty tables to occupy.

Jaime announced, "I have to pee."

She started walking away as the father replied, "Hurry, and you'd better not wet yourself." Then came the sound of little retreating footsteps.

A hand grabbed her arm, halting her progress. Shifting her plate to the other hand, she shook her arm loose. She faced the father, who now stood before her.

"Don't touch me again," she said, through tightened lips.

"Come on, honey. I just wanted to ask how you doin'?" The father grinned, revealing crooked teeth.

"If you must know, I'm tired. You see I'm an embalmer. You know, I prepare dead bodies. Before the flight, I had a long day draining the blood from a corpse and replacing it with embalming fluid. It took forever to get the eyelids pried open to place the plastic covers in."

The man stopped grinning and took a sideways step. "My son is callin' me."

Never fails. Lily eyed him as he retreated, hating the tension stiffening her shoulders. After she made it to a table next to the rail, she picked at her lukewarm omelet. A zing from spices met her tongue. Xavier was right; Yesenia was one fine cook. Lily inhaled the heavy scent of flora warmed by the sunshine and allowed herself to enjoy the view. Bland-looking, brown birds chirped away. Hummingbirds hovered above clusters of pollen-covered flowers while a monkey scaled the tree branches.

She started to relax just as a pair of parrots began to squabble. Green and red feathers flew, and their high-pitched screeches caught everyone's and everything's attention. *Why couldn't Frankie have booked a lodge on a quiet, white, sandy beach?* With a huff, Lily snatched a palm-sized piece of pineapple from her plate and pitched it at the obnoxious birds. All the birds scattered.

"You know," a deep voice—unmistakably American—said from behind her. "The clay-colored robins will stay and sing you a pretty song if you *feed* them the fruit rather than pelting them on the head." A devilishly handsome man, skin tanned from the sun and clad in a white-linen shirt and khaki shorts, approached.

"I was aiming for the parrots. Anyway, who said I wanted them to sing?" She kept her expression blank as she peered up into his hooded, blue eyes. Instantly attraction sizzled through her. Without a doubt, her body betrayed her effort to be indifferent as her breathing grew rapid and her traitorous tongue moistened her lips.

"I take it you're not a birder." Amusement laced his words.

She struggled to focus on the conversation, growing more annoyed with herself by each passing second. "No. The only bird I like is one roasted on my dinner plate."

He unleashed a million-dollar smile.

Inwardly, Lily groaned—he even had perfectly straight, white teeth and dimples. This guy oozed sexy and had "flirt" stamped on his tan, wide forehead. Then and there she decided he was probably a little more than she wanted to deal with. It would be like going fishing and catching a marlin. You're going to want to keep it, polish it with oil, stare at it constantly, unable to believe your good luck, and place it on the trailer wall to show off to all your friends, but in retrospect, you're going to realize you really just needed a Red Snapper: something less time consuming and pretty good in the fish tacos department.

A stooped woman with the waist of her shorts pulled almost to her armpits ambled by with binoculars and a camera dangling from her neck.

"You better watch out," he said, in a mock whisper. "These people might throw down if they hear talk like that. Bird lovers travel from great distances to see the six hundred eighteen species of resident and migratory birds."

Lily shrugged, feigning disinterest. "And people drive from all over the U.S. to see the largest ball of yarn. You can't account for people's tastes."

He laughed and shook his head. "Wow, your tongue is razor sharp." A gentle breeze ruffled his sun-streaked, dark blond hair, which he wore shoved back from his forehead. With hair long enough to rest against his shoulders and a casual demeanor, he looked like he should be carrying a surfboard. "May I join you?"

She blinked at him. "Suit yourself."

"Not the warmest invite, but I'll take it." He sat across from her. As he rolled up the sleeves of his shirt, she couldn't help but appreciate the play of the corded muscles on his arms.

Of their own accord, her eyes glanced down at his left index finger. No ring, or tan line for that matter. *Still not interested.* With more force than necessary, she speared a piece of fruit. Lily studied his face as she bit into a juicy piece of mango. There was something familiar about him. Then it dawned on her. "Matthew McConaughey."

His brows lifted skyward, and he extended a hand. "No, actually I'm Cooper."

She rolled her eyes and shook his hand. "I know you aren't Matthew McConaughey, but you look like him."

"If you say so." He winked at her. "You have a thing for the actor? I'd be happy to make your fantasies come true."

Oh, I'll just bet you would. "Well, my husband, Bull, should be back from our cabana any moment. Why don't you ask him if he's interested?"

Mr. Dimple Man threw back his head and laughed "Bull, huh?"

"Yes."

"Sounds like a basketball player or a bouncer."

"Both."

Apparently he didn't believe her, because he kept grinning. "Nice try." He leaned closer. "But you came here solo. I got that information from a good source."

She scowled and glanced over her shoulder. With his usual wide grin, Xavier waved from near the doorway of the office. Did the older man understand the word *privacy*?

"Brilliant. Nothing like pinning a target on me as a single woman."

"Nah. It's not like that." Cooper gestured with his head. "Xavier and I go way back. He just mentioned it on the down low."

"And why, may I ask, did he do that?"

Cooper, aka too-sexy-for-his-own-good, with his first two buttons undone showing off his smooth chest, reclined in the bistro chair far enough it balanced on two legs. "You're a lovely lady. I have a weakness for petite Asian gals who don't think twice about ripping a man to—"

Oh brother. "Please." Lily held up a hand. "You could probably talk a monkey right out of its fur, but your words are useless on me...so save them."

He burst out laughing and settled the bistro chair back on the ground. "Well, heck, the last thing I want is a bunch of naked monkeys climbing around."

The corners of Lily's mouth twitched. "Okay, you're charming, I'll give you that. But I am not sleeping with you."

Chapter Two

Cooper's brows lifted skyward. "Sleeping with me? What, do you think I'm easy?" Without a doubt, this lady was a firecracker. He found her feisty nature and lack of coyness intriguing and completely opposite from most of the women he met. Earlier, when he'd seen her sitting by herself eating breakfast with the sunlight shimmering off her silky, midnight hair, he'd stopped dead in his tracks. After speaking with Xavier and learning she was on a solo trip, Cooper did an about-face and introduced himself.

"Hmmm. That thought did cross my mind." Her exotic eyes, the ends pointing slightly upward like a cat, lowered to his chest.

He swore he could feel the heat from her gaze. He shook his head, fighting against the grin threatening to surface. "Hey." He pointed at his face. "My eyes are up here."

A hint of pinkness appeared on the ivory skin along her high cheekbones. On closer inspection he noted the lightest spattering of freckles on the bridge of her nose.

"If you don't want me to look, then stop showing off your chest…wait that sounded wrong." A crease marred her brow. "How did I turn into the boy in this conversation?"

She looked adorable all flustered with her face scrunched up. If his partially unbuttoned shirt caused her to be so animated, so be it. Not that he was trying to be sexy, mind you, but it was humid as hell and he required a little ventilation. "And what's your name, if you don't mind me asking? I'd like to know what to call the temptress who considers me eye candy."

Her mouth pinched together as if to stifle a laugh, then she stood. "You're very dramatic. You should try out for a soap opera."

Cooper gained his feet and peered down at her; she sure was a little thing, only reaching to his chin. "I did, but I didn't last long. Too much staring at each other with repetitive music in the background. That's just not normal."

"You say the funniest things." She aimed a beautiful smile right at him.

His heartbeat kicked up, and he attempted to play it cool as they fell into step together and headed toward the walkway.

"My name's Lily."

Ah, finally he'd gotten through her first layer of armor. "Lily is the perfect name for you. You're regal and graceful like the flower."

He earned a *humph* for his flowery words. *Okay, tone it down. You're not Casanova.* They strolled past the open-air office, and the raised walkway forked. Lily was exactly the type of distraction he needed after the encounter with the drug lord. Last night Cooper had rented a cabana, shared a few glasses of rum with Xavier, and stayed up most of the night with an overactive mind that refused to sleep. In the wee hours he'd come to a decision: he wouldn't draw attention to himself. He'd stay out of Maximo's path and wouldn't do anything to cause the Belizean government to cancel his permit. He'd conduct his research and return to the U.S. His focus shifted to Lily as they strolled down the walkway, and he racked his brain for the best way to see her again. Finally an idea struck.

He snapped his fingers and stopped walking. "Have you had a chance to hike to the Macal River? A river I might add that's legend says it was named after a beautiful young girl. I'm headed there myself. I know the area well, and I'd be happy to show you around."

She pivoted and stared at him, blinking several times. Her lips pursed before she said, "Let me think about this. Go alone with a stranger into a jungle…I think I saw a PBS special on this when I was five. You tell me you lost your baby jaguar, and I get to have my face on a milk carton."

Okay. Maybe offering to take her to a secluded place had been a bad idea. "You don't know me. Understandable." He pondered if he should make another attempt and ask her to dinner when he caught movement in his peripheral vision. His college research assistant, William, with his brown ponytail poking out from under a ball cap, stood on the breakfast deck, and with the wave of his pale arm, he beckoned Cooper.

Cooper's hand shifted against the envelope in the pocket of his cargo shorts. He might be one hundred percent interested in getting to know Lily better, but the wad of cash burning a hole in his pocket took precedence. "I'll be seeing you around, my regal Lily."

She frowned at him, and he strolled away.

• • •

Later that afternoon, Lily doused herself in bug spray and decided to take a short hike. She adjusted the backpack, which held water, an energy bar, a bikini, a towel, cash, and a few other items, higher on her back. A handful of trails started near the office only to be swallowed up ten feet away by the encroaching jungle. With safety in mind, she headed down the one that appeared most traveled. Slivers of sunlight escaped through gaps in the canopy and slanted across the smashed abundant grass. It had sprinkled earlier, and she dodged a few puddles. The jungle seemed to be a life within itself, emitting animal noises with diverse flora dancing in a rapid rhythm in the warm breeze. She rolled her shoulders, ignoring the sweat trickling down her back. She might not have picked this place, but this was the first vacation she'd had in years, and she needed to relax and enjoy it.

The path forked, and without much thought, she veered left. After a few twists and turns, she came to a painted, wooden sign that read MACAL RIVER. Lily's steps faltered as a set of blue eyes slammed into her mind. If she ran into Mr. Dimples, he'd most likely think that she'd been playing hard to get earlier, and now she was following him. *Which I am definitely not.* She thought about heading back and going down another trail for all of about five seconds. She was hot and sweaty and just wanted to dive into the cool, tranquil water. At least it had better be tranquil and not green with floating debris.

She continued onward through the diverse jungle, exchanging greetings with the occasional passersby. On the plane ride she'd read that Mountain Pine Ridge was a subtropical pine forest. But viewing it up close, something felt wrong about seeing palm and banana trees hanging out with pines. It screamed identity crisis. She continued at a steady pace, pine needles and twigs crunching under her sneakers.

Finally after fifteen minutes had passed, she heard the unmistakable rush of water before she caught a glimpse of the steady, flowing river through a slender gap in the foliage. She'd just stopped at the bank, ready to make the decline to the river, when she heard whistling. Lily paused and listened. Someone was whistling "The Dock of the Bay." With both hands, she parted the branches of a broadleaf bush, and to her surprise, not twelve feet below stood a Caucasian man without a shirt; the muscles of his tan back flexed as he cast a fishing line overhead. Khaki cargo shorts, sun-streaked, dark blond hair. *No, it can't be.* The combination made Lily groan. Apparently out loud because he tossed a glance over his shoulder in her direction. With a jerk, she made a move to duck behind a nearby knobby tree only to lose her footing on a patch of mud. A scream ripped out of her as she fell, bounced off a tree trunk, and continued down the slick path through a throng of banana shoots before careening into a startled Cooper.

With a splash, shallow water lapped around her as she fought to stop her momentum from carrying her past the water's edge. A strong arm wrapped around her waist. Up ahead, the long span of murky water flowed with white caps appearing in the middle. Panting, she realized Cooper's body lay pinned beneath her. She pushed her fingers into the mushy riverbed, relieved they'd only fallen into the shallow water, and attempted to lift herself off of him. She peered down, and her eyes widened. With an inch of water surrounding his head, Cooper's face was literally smashed into her breasts, and their legs were tangled in a way-too-intimate manner. His breath warmed her skin through her moist tank top. She shivered either from the coolness of the water or from the feel of his hard body under hers.

"Oh, God." Lily scrambled back only to fall onto her backside into the sand. He held himself up, water sloshing at his forearms and dripping from the ends of his hair. Sand covered him, and moisture shone from his smooth chest. He shook his head rapidly, flinging water droplets before he settled his gaze on her. Confusion and amusement flashed across his face.

"Are you okay?" She shoved away her embarrassment and looked at him straight on.

"Never been better. How about you?"

"Fine."

He pushed to his feet, and streaks of mud slid down his wet, clingy shorts. "I'm glad to see you changed your mind."

She ignored his offered hand and stood on her own. "Changed my mind?" She rinsed her muddy hands in the water, knowing darn well what he meant but not about to admit it.

"About joining me." He leaned down and rinsed his hands as well and then straightened.

Of course he'd think that. She gave him her best bored expression. "Oh, I didn't change my mind. Actually, until you just mentioned it, I'd completely forgotten about the invite."

The lie slipped off her tongue before she could stop it, and she ignored the guilt knocking on her conscience.

Lifting a brow, he smirked. "All righty, if you say so." He reached out a hand toward her face and slowly withdrew something from her hair. He dropped a leaf, and it swirled before settling onto the sand.

She inhaled a deep breath, annoyed that her pulse raced and her fingers wanted to reach out and pet him. Why did her body react so strongly to his nearness? Okay, stupid question; he was hot.

She planted her fist on her hip. "You don't believe me? I fell—"

"I noticed." He had the nerve to laugh only for his expression to turn serious. "I was thoroughly enjoying our position...but we have a problem."

"We do?"

"Yep, when you knocked me off my feet, you made me lose my favorite fishing rod."

"I'm sorry, but it was an accident. I'll pay you, and you can replace it."

"That's kind of you, but still, it was a special rod. It's not like there's a sporting goods store up the street. How am I supposed to eat dinner?"

"Hmmm. Let me think. Oh, yeah the restaurant at the lodge." Did this guy really expect her to believe he survived on hunting and gathering?

"Deal. What time should we meet?"

"Huh?"

"I'd be happy to take you up on your offer to join you for dinner." He shrugged a glistening, muscular shoulder. "After making me lose my prized fishing rod, it's the least you can do."

"I didn't —"

"Seven thirty works best for me."

It was on the tip of her tongue to decline when a thought struck her. *Why not? It's a vacation. I'm all alone. He's entertaining, that's for sure.* It wasn't like she had to keep him. She could just pretend he was a Red Snapper not a marlin. "Fine. Seven thirty."

"Hey, Cooper, you ready?" A man's voice came from above on the bank.

Her head whipped around, and through the break in the foliage, she caught a glimpse of a pale man. She noted he was young, and his long, brown hair was pulled back in a ponytail.

"Be right there." Cooper grabbed his backpack off the sand and shot her a wink. "Lily, as before, I enjoyed talking with you. See you at seven thirty."

Her gaze raked over him as he climbed up the bank. Heat instantly swirled low in her belly. *Get a grip. It's just dinner.*

. . .

By the time Lily arrived back at the lodge from the river, humidity clung to her body. She returned to her cabana, took a cold shower, and changed into a pale-blue sundress. After turning the ceiling fan full blast, she fell asleep on the unmade bed. A faint thumping woke her. Her eyes fluttered open to a gray room. The thumping sound came again, and she peered toward the darkened window. Drums. Her stomach growled. Maybe it was the dinner music. Her eyes widened as she jerked her gaze to the clock: seven forty p.m. She was late!

Lily bolted to her feet, quickly smoothed out the wrinkles of her sundress, and washed her face in the bathroom. After running a comb through her long strands, brushing her teeth, applying lip gloss, and dousing herself in bug spray, she slipped on a pair of sandals and headed out the door. In rapid steps she made her way along the maze of walkways following the rhythmic sounds of the beat. The dense trees only allowed a glimpse of the vibrant pink-streaked sunset. She strolled onto the deck where breakfast had been served. Tiki torches flickered over the group of about twenty people, all socializing and eating. Lily searched among the throng of people but didn't find Cooper. She sighed and made herself a plate from the buffet-style dining of rice, beans, corn tortillas, and something that looked like chicken. The delicious smells made her stomach growl again.

"Miss Sanborn," Xavier greeted with his usual grin. He pointed to a tray of umbrella drinks in his other hand. "Would you like one of my piña coladas?"

She accepted the tiki-style glass. "Thanks, I've been wanting one of these all day."

"It is my special recipe. Enjoy." He strolled off, passing out drinks as he went.

Lily peered around again but still didn't see Cooper, so she sat at a table in the corner. As she ate, she watched couples speaking intimately and laughing. The awkwardness of being alone settled over her. *Well, if I hadn't overslept, I'd be with Cooper.* He probably thought she was a complete flake. She pulled the umbrella out of her glass and took a sip through the straw. Although refreshing, the volume of alcohol in the cool drink made her grimace. She took another swallow, deciding she liked the sweet combination of the pineapple and coconut.

Two older women started dancing together as the four-member band picked up the beat with the next song. A guitar, accordion, conga drum, and some kind of tinny-sounding instrument were played. Lily swatted a mosquito that landed on her forearm. Blasted bloodsuckers.

She'd just finished her dinner and ordered another drink from a passing server when a masculine voice came from behind her. "There you are. I thought you'd stood me up."

"Oh, hey." She gestured for Cooper to take the seat across from her.

He slid into the chair, looking all sexy in the flickering glow from the torches. He'd changed into a fresh navy-colored T-shirt and beige cargo shorts. "I just started to double back to see if you'd shown up when I caught Yesenia carrying a heavy tray into the kitchen, had to practically wrestle it from her, and then we started talking."

"Sorry. I took a nap and overslept."

"It's your vacation. You should relax. I see you've eaten, and so have I. Maybe we can just have drinks together and enjoy the entertainment."

"That works."

"Where do you call home?" he asked.

"Las Vegas."

"So you're used to the heat?"

"Heat, yes, humidity, not so much."

Her second drink arrived at the table, and she took a long, cool gulp.

Cooper ordered a rum and Coke from the female server

who batted her eyelashes like a ninny before strutting off, then he turned to Lily. "Better slow down. Those drinks are potent, especially how Xavier makes them."

She took another sip and gave him her best bland look. "Really? Is this girly drink too much for you?"

He smirked and pointed at the empty glass from her first drink. "Not me. But I weigh a lot more than you. Those concoctions aren't called 'panty rippers' for nothing."

Lily almost spit her mouthful of drink at him but closed her lips in the nick of time. She coughed, and he leaned over and patted her on the back. A few people looked their way before returning to their dinners and conversations. The server brought Cooper's drink and moved on.

"Panty rippers? You just made that up. He called it a piña colada," she rasped. Somehow her focus had zeroed in on his firm mouth. Just the word panty forming from his lips made her feel tingly.

"Well, he couldn't use the real name, but believe me panty rippers can take grown men down." He took a slow sip of his drink.

She straightened, shaking off the funny feeling swirling low in her belly. Lily eyed the half-finished beverage in her hand. She doubted this thing would take her down. Cooper was full of it.

"Don't worry. I won't be ripping off my underwear." She smiled and swallowed the rest of her drink. She set the glass on the table and rested back against the seat. Closing her eyes, she tapped her toes to the beat.

"Ah, tempting fate. That coconut rum mixed with pineapple juice has fooled many people."

"If you say so," she said without opening her eyes. The

band changed to a slow song. The sound of the smooth male voice and strum of the guitar floated over the still night. Time drifted away as she lost herself to the passionate lyrics of a man in love, and for the first time on her vacation, she found herself actually relaxing.

A warm hand engulfed hers, and her attention settled on Cooper. "Dance with me, Lily, before you pass out."

He stood and pulled her to her feet. With a firm hold on her hand, she had little choice but to follow. *I don't dance!* Her mouth refused to push out the words as her eyes explored the width of his shoulders. He led her away from the group, past a few couples dancing, to a more secluded spot, riddled with shadows, on the walkway. He spun her, and before she knew it, he held her in his arms. *Just one minute, then I'm sitting back down.* They swayed to the rhythm of the music with the inky jungle to his back and, after a slow rotation, to hers.

She burrowed her face against his upper chest, enjoying the feel and masculine scent of him. He pressed her closer, and his nearness made her knees weak. *I'm tipsy, and I'm dancing with a flirty, handsome stranger. Push him away!* Lily knew the moment she licked her lips and ran her hand over his pec that she had lost all reason. The song ended only to flow into another ballad.

"You're exquisite. I love the shape of your exotic eyes," he whispered into her ear. His warm breath lit a path along the sensitive flesh of her neck.

"Hmmm. That feels nice." *Did I just say that out loud?*

"Good to know." Before she realized his intentions, Cooper leaned down and kissed her. He tasted hot, sugary, and a bit like the rum he'd consumed. Her eyelids slid closed, and her breathing grew fast and shallow. A shiver of pure lust danced over her flesh. Her hands eagerly reached out to touch him, splaying over the contours of his muscular chest and looping around his neck to bring their kiss closer. His body felt solid, powerful, and she knew this was getting way too hot and delicious for a first kiss. She needed to slow things down, but she didn't because his closeness felt too wonderful. Cooper's tongue brushed against hers in smooth, slow strokes that sent desire surging through her. His long fingers wrapped around her waist, and without breaking the kiss, he lifted her only to gradually lower her partially down the length of his body. Sparks ricocheted behind her eyelids.

Lily jerked back, and their mouths separated. She gulped in a lung full of air and laughed. "I think you caught my shoes on fire." She leaned back and lifted her arms skyward.

"Whoa!" he said and grabbed onto her.

"Tonight's so beautiful. Look at all these stars." She reached for them.

He shifted her in his arms, returning her upright.

"Are you going to kiss me again? I liked it." Lily felt so alive and free. She touched his mouth with her fingertips. Desire flared inside her.

"I think you're drunk." He took her hand and held it in his. The faint light revealed the lopsided grin on his face.

"Maybe." The world started to spin, and she latched on to him tighter. "We're floating."

"Nope. Just your head. You'd best go to your cabana and sleep it off."

"You don't want me to sleep. You want the panty ripper to work its magic." Her free hand slipped under the bottom of his shirt and caressed his flat stomach, and she reveled in her power as his body quivered and his breath hitched.

"Well, I won't lie. The thought of removing your panties has entered my mind." He removed her hand from under his shirt. "And I know when you're sober, this opportunity probably won't present itself again, but as much as I hate to admit it, I'm a gentleman."

Lily scrunched up her nose and stared at his shadowed face. "Says who?"

His body shook with laughter. "My mother."

By the time they were halfway to her cabana, Cooper was carrying her. She snuggled deeper against his shoulder. "You smell good. Like a man: spicy and clean."

"Hmmm. Good to know."

She couldn't help herself; she captured his earlobe and nibbled.

"Lord have mercy, stop that; you're killing me." He sounded in pain and moved his head to the side.

She settled back against his shoulder and half listened to friendly banter from a passing man.

"Do you have a key?" Cooper asked in a low tone.

"Not locked."

He shifted her and pushed open the door. When he lowered her, Lily didn't release him. Instead she pulled him down with her. The bed bounced and settled as his body halfway covered hers. Somewhere in the middle of the swirling darkness their lips met, hot and hungry. Deep in his chest he made a moaning sound. A rush of longing swept through her, and instinctively she moved against his hard body.

"You feel so good…so soft and beautiful," he said, his voice raspy as he gently bit her throat.

Her pulse quickened, and she arched her neck to savor

the heat of his mouth on her flesh.

He tore his mouth away, his breathing heavy. "You're a temptation, Lily, but you're drunk. This has to stop, or I won't be able to look into my own bloodshot eyes tomorrow morning."

The bed shifted, and his weight left her. He stood, and she blinked up trying to make out his silhouette in the thick darkness.

Her eyelids grew heavy, and she struggled to keep them open. "Stay with me."

"No way. I said I was a gentleman, not a monk."

"Hmmm." She smiled. "Too bad."

"Pleasant dreams, sweetheart."

She snuggled against her pillow as drowsiness engulfed her like a fuzzy blanket, and she drifted to sleep.

· · ·

Lily woke up slowly, her mouth feeling as if it were stuffed with cotton. She squinted at the clock. "Ten?" she rasped. Somehow she'd managed to sleep right through all the bird racket and breakfast. She staggered to her feet, a light pounding in her head. Ugh! After sipping some bottled water, she fished out a package of saltine crackers that had been on the bottom of her purse for weeks. She ate them before swallowing two ibuprofen tablets to fight off the threatening headache. She strode into the bathroom, hoping a shower would make her feel human again. She stepped into the cool spray and lathered up, all while heat burned her cheeks at the thought of how she acted the previous night. After that delicious kiss from Cooper, she'd dragged him into her bed like some tramp. She rinsed and turned off the water. *Stay with me.* She groaned loudly, remembering her words, how she practically begged him. What had gotten into her? Her mouth pressed into a thin line as she dried off with a fluffy towel.

"It was the panty ripper. Xavier has some explaining to do. Telling innocent people it's a piña colada."

Cooper warned me. She ignored the voice that floated in her head. Lily slipped on cotton undergarments then jean shorts and a green tank top. After combing through her wet strands, she let them fall loose down her back to dry and went to the door. She opened it an inch and peeked out. All seemed quiet except for the birds. She opened it farther and stepped out. Dark patchy clouds circled overhead, and light drizzle floated through the air. She braced her hands on the patio rail and scanned through the gaps in the trees. The planked walkways lay empty.

Lily squared her shoulders and shook off the uneasiness as she walked the stretch to the office. If she did run into Cooper, she would just pretend she hadn't acted like a fool. The drizzle felt warm against her skin. She made it to the eating area to find no Xavier or Cooper. Breakfast had ended almost two hours ago, so she snagged a banana from a bowl of assorted fruits. After eating it, she deposited the peel, took a bottle of water, and headed back the way she'd come.

What if Cooper checked out of the lodge? The thought made her stomach knot before she shook off the feeling. She frowned as she continued to stroll back to her room. No, he would have mentioned it. A housekeeper passed, and it took all her willpower not to ask if a certain guest had departed.

Lily gave a polite nod and kept a forward pace. The drizzle ceased, and she decided to lie in the hammock and read a book. If Cooper happened to walk by, she was just doing her own thing. He would stop to chat, and she'd ask him if he wanted to go to the ruins. That was on her to-do list after all.

On the front patio, she'd just set down her novel and water bottle, preparing to climb into the hammock, when a childish giggle came from behind her. She turned around to see the little boy standing before her, wearing the same Mickey Mouse T-shirt as the previous day. She glanced around, surprised he was alone.

"Hey, Jaime." She ruffled his curly hair.

He gave her a chubby-cheeked grin and held up the sucker in his hand. "Candy."

"I see that. Looks yummy."

"Want some?" He held the sucker out to her.

"Thanks, but you can keep it." She cleared her throat and forced herself to look into those golden eyes. *He's not Philip.* Her baby brother was long dead. *And it's my fault.* She released a haggard breath. "Where's your dad?"

"Daddy's there." He pointed a sticky finger in the direction of the next cabana.

She peered through a break in the vine-infested jungle at the neighboring patio. Empty. Was his father taking a nap or too busy picking up women to notice his son had wandered off? Was there a mom in the picture? For Jaime's sake, she sure hoped so.

"Caddapiller." He dropped to his scraped knees and lowered his face to a plank. His sucker rested on the ground, forgotten.

She crouched next to him, and they watched an orange

and black caterpillar inch along.

"Do you know what that caterpillar will turn into, Jaime?"

He nodded his head, sending his wild locks flying. "A budderfly and then a worm again."

"It won't change into a worm, but you're right, it will become a butterfly."

The caterpillar crawled safely through the planks, and Lily returned to her feet. "All right, little man, time to get you back to your father."

"I wanna stay here. Will you play with me?"

Out of nowhere a bittersweet memory materialized. Pressure spread in Lily's chest, and suddenly she was seven again.

"Play with me." Philip said as he climbed onto the mint-green kitchen chair and leaned over the artist tablet she drew on. The smell from homemade egg rolls permeated the room.

She moved the tablet away from his grubby fingers and glared at her brother. "You made me mess up."

"Whatcha drawin'?"

She rolled her eyes. "It's the bride of Frankenstein."

Philip scrunched up his face, making his cheeks even chubbier. "What's a bride?"

Boys were clueless. "A girl in a white dress." Lily spoke as she drew the stitches across the oblong face.

"Can I draw, too?" Hope filled his eyes.

"No. You're too little; you just know how to scribble."

"Will you play with me?" A hand patted her leg, forcing her to focus on the child before her. *Not my brother.* Months later she would have given anything to have her pesky brother following her around. He could have even taken her prized art tablet and scribbled on every single page, and she wouldn't have cared. She sighed and looked at Jaime.

"I have dinosaurs in my packpack."

This kid was turning her heart into mush. Lily pictured herself on the floor with a plastic pterodactyl as his father sent her inviting looks. "I love dinosaurs, but maybe next time."

His little lip stuck out in a pout.

She sighed and knelt. "Okay, one thumb war and you have to go back."

"What's a hum war?"

"Thumb." She wiggled her digit back and forth then took his sticky hand. "It's like wrestling. You try to pin my thumb first without using your other hand and without letting go." She demonstrated and easily pinned his smaller thumb against his fingers. "See? Now you try."

They clasped hands again, and after a few seconds, he pressed her thumb down. She gasped. "Hey, how'd you win so fast?"

He giggled, excitement on his face. "Again! Again!"

"One more time, but give me a chance." Thirty seconds later he pinned her thumb. "You won again. Okay, time to get you back to your father." Lily pushed to her feet, recaptured his hand, and walked back down the ramp.

"But I don't wanna. Let me stay, *pleeease*."

"You need to go back to your cabana. Your dad must be worried." At least he should be.

Jaime's mope lasted about five seconds before he was chattering again. As they headed down the main walkway, he bounced like a rubber ball beside her.

"You sure have a lot of energy. Did you eat a bowl of sugar for breakfast?"

"No, silly. I eat fruit and eggs."

"Hmmm. I missed breakfast, so I'll have to take your word on that."

They made it to a long planked ramp. Through the window of the cabana, Lily could see the father talking on a cell phone. The sound of his laugh escaped from the open door.

Her mouth tightened. *Loser.* "Better go tell your dad you're back."

"Will you play with me later?"

"Maybe. Why don't you decide which dinosaur is your favorite? Mine's the T. rex. " She battled against the guilt of getting the little guy's hopes up.

"Okay!" Jaime grinned, waved, and raced inside.

She returned to her patio and zeroed in on the sucker on the ground. After peeling it off the plank, she tossed it into the trash. She rolled her sweat-dampened shoulders and grabbed her novel. *This is a vacation! Remember?* She eyed the hammock before cautiously climbing on. As the hammock rocked back and forth, she stiffened and grasped the bleached netting. After the swaying ceased, she scooted up, resting her head on the built-in pillow. The surrounding air held a heavy, floral fragrance, and she found herself starting to relax.

A few minutes ticked by, and she realized she was thirsty. She huffed and stared at the water bottle perched on the rail. "Wonderful."

Deciding against getting up again, she reached out her hand in an attempt to snatch her drink. She missed. After shifting her body, she rocked the hammock a bit but still couldn't get close enough. Using her fingers to push off the floor, she swung the hammock. In a swoop, she caught air, flipped out of the netting, and slammed facedown onto the floor. The oxygen expelled out of her lungs. White, fuzzy spots danced before her eyes. Shouting in the next cabana filtered through her dazed mind. She shook her head, inhaled an unsteady breath, and propped up on her elbows.

A crash sounded from next door and then another holler. Lily leaned forward and separated a cluster of banana leaves. Inside the other cabana she caught a glimpse through the window of a giant man of Islander descent with a nasty scar across his cheek. Loud voices filled the air. If Jaime and his dad had company, they didn't appear on good terms. Her stomach soured. The father had the parental concern of a gnat. Would it even occur to him to get his son out of harm's way? She craned her neck but couldn't locate the Islander again or anyone else for that matter. She frowned and listened. A man said something about the Che Chem Ha Cave.

Then a deeper voice commanded, "Maximo wants the kid."

Jaime! Lily hopped to her feet and sprinted down the ramp and the planked walkway. She slowed her steps once she reached the ramp to their cabana. She approached with care, her eyes scanning, her body alert. Since the Islander obviously wasn't a friendly tourist, he most likely would pose a threat if she encountered him. Best aim for the crotch if she had to take him down, because she wasn't certain she was tall enough to reach his throat.

The patio was eerily silent. She swallowed hard and stepped past the hammock. She paused at the closed mahogany door. *Squeak, squeak.* She had a bad feeling about this. With a turn of the knob, she shoved open the door.

Creeeeak.

Clothes and a toppled table littered the floor. Then Lily's

eyes widened, and she staggered back, grabbing on to the rail. *Oh, God.* With a leather strap wrapped around his neck, Jaime's father hung from the ceiling fan, the motor squeaking as it wobbled its rotation. Her breathing increased, disbelief spreading like icicles through her veins.

Frantically, she glanced around, fearful the murderers might still be near. No one seemed about. Lily peered into the room and approached the suspended body. Saliva trailed out of his blue lips. From the pale skin to the bulging blank eyes, he was beyond saving. After a quick search under the bed and in the bathroom, Lily's heart sank. *They have Jaime!*

Chapter Three

Lily paced back and forth on the outside dining area as officers carted off the covered body of Jaime's father. A few gasps could be heard from onlookers. *If only I hadn't sent Jaime back, he'd be safe.* She struggled to swallow the lump in her throat. She'd learned from eavesdropping on the police conversation that the father—Mr. Flores—had been at the lodge for the past ten days and was a citizen of Panama. Apparently his son had been dropped off two days ago by a woman of unknown identity. She didn't believe for a second he was a tourist. Her mind played out every scenario he could have been involved in. None of them legal. At least not in the U.S.

A small crowd had gathered along the lifted walkways. Amongst them, Xavier stared at her with an odd expression. He was probably concerned that a murder would cause his guests to leave. Xavier turned and spoke to a tall, lanky young man with a ponytail, who she instantly recognized as

Cooper's friend. If his friend was still here, then maybe Cooper hadn't checked out after all. He wasn't going to believe everything that had happened since she'd seen him last.

Lily focused on Superintendent Castillo and Inspector Reimer from the Cristo Rey Police Department, who'd been questioning her for the last ten minutes.

"Did you know Mr. Flores?" Superintendent Castillo asked. His double chin and the buttons threatening to pop off his snug, khaki uniform were evidence he didn't get away from his desk much. He reminded her of a walrus.

"No. We'd met for the first time yesterday morning. Only exchanged a couple of words." She waved a hand in the air. "I didn't pay much attention to him, but today his son, Jaime, had wandered off, and I'd returned him to his cabana not even fifteen minutes before the...the murder." She closed her eyes and attempted to shake off the gnawing guilt. "Did you write down the name Maximo? I mentioned someone said that name?"

"That is not an uncommon name...and you don't need to tell me how to do my job, Miss Sanborn," Castillo said.

The shuffle of footsteps diverted Lily's attention.

Xavier shooed the looky-loos away and neared with a somber expression. "I am sorry, Superintendent, I tell my guests to go inside, but they keep coming back."

Castillo pointed a thick finger at an officer striding along the walkway. "We have it covered. Thanks."

"Oh, okay. Does anyone want some ice water? Very warm today."

All three declined.

She fought against the frustration that surfaced. How could they be talking about ice water when a child was missing? "Are you guys even searching for Jaime?"

Inspector Reimer leaned against the wall with his hands tucked into the pockets of his blue uniform trousers. He had a shock of thick, white hair, and his skin coloring was a few shades darker brown than Castillo's. "We have men scouring the jungle for the child and also heading to the Che Chem Ha Cave. This cave is set in a remote area inland from the Macal River, and it is going to take some time to reach it."

"You have to get Jaime back!"

Xavier patted her shoulder. "Miss Sanborn, just give the police time."

Lily nodded and sat in a patio chair.

A phone rang from inside the lodge, and Xavier excused himself.

"You are sure you saw a man of Islander ethnicity with a scar on his cheek?" Castillo questioned.

"Yes." She pursed her lips in thought and added, "He is huge, has to be close to six-five with a broad nose. Trust me, this man would stand out."

"Your view was obstructed. How could you see into that other cabana?" Suspicion etched across Castillo's face. The man clearly had a chip on his shoulder. Or maybe he didn't want to bother with actually doing police work.

She sent Castillo a searing look. "I managed to see him just fine. Why are you acting like I'm making this up?"

That comment seemed to bother Castillo. He started pacing, swiping at the beaded sweat on his forehead and exposing a moist ring under his armpit. "Everyone knows you Americans think you are important—always calling attention to yourselves. You could have seen this man anywhere."

She tamped down the anger churning in her gut. *How*

dare he call me a liar! She wished she could shake some sense into the superintendent—but she refrained—barely. Then the reality of the situation dawned on her. "You know the Islander with the scar, don't you?"

"Miss Sanborn," Reimer said. The heavy bags gathered under his kind eyes most likely were a testament of how hard this inspector worked. "I am going to bring a printed statement for you to sign in a few hours. For your safety, please do not leave the lodge."

She frowned. This was her vacation. "For how long?"

The inspector sighed and glanced at Castillo.

"Until we tell you otherwise." The superintendent turned away with a dismissive wave.

• • •

After taking another swim in the Macal River, Lily trudged back toward the lodge carrying the backpack with a few necessities. A mosaic of lush trees covered the shady bank and gathered along the trail toward the lodge. The late afternoon mugginess set in, making it difficult to breathe. The birds still chattered away, but the racket didn't grate on her nerves as much. She veered left on the trail and batted away a swarm of mosquitos buzzing around her head.

She'd waited an hour and a half before deciding it was too hot to just sit around. If the police didn't like that she'd taken a half-mile hike, they could go hang. Lily cringed at the image that slammed into her mind: Mr. Flores's dead body dangling from the fan. Her flesh broke out into goose bumps. Sure she'd seen hundreds of dead bodies, but stumbling onto a murder scene was a completely different matter.

Worry gnawed at her stomach. Jaime. He must be so scared. She wouldn't even entertain the idea the boy was dead. Knowing the murderers could have killed Jaime along with his father gave her hope that for some reason they wanted him alive — or at least had a conscience about harming a child.

The thatched roofs of the cabanas came into view through a break in the jungle. She stopped dead in her tracks. Covered with leathery-looking scales, one of the longest iguanas she'd ever seen rested across a flat rock. She stepped a little closer only to see its eyelid creep open.

"Do not get too close," a man said.

Lily whipped around to see Inspector Reimer approaching her.

"You know in the fall during breeding season, male iguanas change to a shade of orange and can be very aggressive. More than one tourist has gone to the hospital for stitches. Very sharp teeth."

She flipped a hand in the air. "It's summer, and I wasn't going to pet it."

He stopped before her, his smile uneven. "I hope not. I have the statement for you to sign."

They fell in step together and walked up the trail toward the lodge.

"Okay." She sent him a sideways glance. "Aren't you upset that I left the lodge?"

"Would being mad make a difference?" He shrugged a shoulder. "I have four adult daughters. They do not listen either."

She laughed but quickly sobered and stopped walking. "Jaime?"

Reimer shook his head and faced her. "We have not found him. But we are still looking."

"You know, something's bothering me." She reached back and tightened the rubber band that started slipping from her ponytail. "Why didn't Superintendent Castillo believe me about the Islander with the scar I saw in Mr. Flores's room? And then when I asked if Castillo knew the murderer, you cut me off."

He sighed and rubbed the back of his neck. "You need to stop asking so many questions, and leave the police work to me."

"You don't like the superintendent." She stated it as a fact.

He lowered his voice. "Please listen closely. This is a small town, and everyone is practically related to everyone else. The man you saw is the head of security for a drug lord named Maximo, a powerful man who happens to be the superintendent's cousin."

Dread jabbed into her stomach. "So Castillo knows exactly who killed Flores?"

"Based solely on your account that would be our suspect."

"So the police pretended not to know this Islander who took Jaime?"

"The man you speak of calls himself the Samoan and is very dangerous. We, the police, must first build a solid case against him."

Lily crossed her arms. "You mean the corrupt police?"

"Some are, some aren't. It is common knowledge the criminals and police around here often eat Sunday brunch together after Mass."

"You know the department's corrupt, your boss for that

matter, and you're doing nothing about it?"

"Not the department, but of course, individuals within. Miss Sanborn, it is a fact that our police force is poorly funded and underpaid, some seek extra funds elsewhere for their own reasons, or they value their lives more than their jobs and look the other way. We may live in paradise, but we have our battles so close to the border of Guatemala. The drug runners and paramilitaries who illegally cross and our own drug cartels are all better armed than we are."

"Wonderful. So this drug lord actually runs things. The police are just for show?"

"No. It's a constant power struggle. Maximo isn't the only drug lord in the Mountain Pine Ridge area, but many people are in his pocket, including the locals…I don't say this lightly: watch your back, Miss Sanborn, and trust no one except me."

A chill shimmied up her spine before she shook it off. "So let's cut to the chase. Obviously, the kidnapping of a four-year-old boy is just going to be ignored." Lily's hands tightened into fists. She had to do something—but what?

"That is not true. And I warn you." He wagged a finger at her. "Do not get involved in my investigation. Maximo is not a member of my family. And even if he was, I would have no qualms about arresting him."

"Let me guess. You're not corrupt?" Like Reimer would admit otherwise. Her head started to throb.

"No." He looked her dead in the eye. "I come from old money. I do the job because I believe in protecting my people."

She held his gaze. He could be lying, but for whatever reason, she believed him. "Well, that's nice to know. So, you're going to be a one-man army then?"

"Never. I'm too old for that, but I have called an old friend, who happens to be the senior superintendent in Belmopan. He has agreed to discuss the issue with the assistant commissioner and try to get jurisdiction of this case."

Hope surfaced. Maybe Reimer was a good cop after all. "And what if he doesn't get jurisdiction?"

"You, Miss Sanborn, are a pessimist."

She shrugged a shoulder. "Think of it more as a realist. If things can go wrong they usually do."

Lily noticed how quiet the jungle had become. Reimer appeared to have sensed it as well; he scanned the trees, his hand edging toward the holstered gun on the belt at his hip. Only seconds passed when he grasped her arm. "We had best get back to the lodge."

Did he think they were in danger? The fine hairs on her arms stood. She looked up at him, about to voice that very question, when his body jerked back and the echo of a gunshot cut through the air. She shrieked. Blood splattered across her cheek from the bullet hole in his chest. She attempted to grab his collapsing body. They hit the ground— hard. *Bang, bang!* Lily flinched as bullets whizzed by, hammering into the dirt near their heads. She flattened herself against the ground. Fear caused her breathing to cease.

Next to her Reimer shifted, his pain-filled eyes locked on to hers. His hand held his chest, blood oozing between his fingers. He opened and closed his mouth before he whispered, "Run."

He needed medical care. "I'll get a doctor."

"Do not go to…lodge…won't make it."

Her stomach pitched at his warning. The shooter would

kill her before she reached it. But she couldn't just leave him. He'd die. "I need—"

"Run...now," he wheezed as he staggered to his feet.

She hesitated a second before doing as instructed. She rolled to her feet in a swift motion and bolted into the jungle the opposite direction of the lodge. If she got away, she could double back and get some help. She flinched as two more shots rang out. She glanced over her shoulder long enough to see Reimer's body fly backward. She stifled a scream. *Oh, God, no!*

A surge of adrenaline pumped into her veins as she sprinted for all she was worth. Lily vaulted over a downed palm tree and slipped through a gap in an outcrop of boulders. With no other choice, she burst into the solid wall of the jungle, only for vines to capture her legs. She crashed to the ground, pain splintering into her right arm. The world rotated out of control as she rolled down a hill; rocks and branches jabbed into her body before she plunged into the cool water of the river.

Lily sputtered and coughed as the current carried her downstream. She went under, the gloominess of the river swirling before her eyes and the rushing sound of water filling her ears. After shoving a drifting branch out of her way, she kicked hard with her legs. Once she surfaced and took a mouthful of air, she swam in overhead strokes. Could the shooter see her? She twisted, needing to know if he stood on the bank watching her. For a moment she floated on her back while the current kept her moving farther away. The backpack weighed her down, but when she attempted to remove the wet straps, she sank. She kicked back to the surface, inhaling a haggard breath and shoving her wet hair out of her eyes. She doggy paddled while she scanned the heavy tree line. So dense. So many shadowed areas the sun couldn't reach. The shooter could be anywhere. She felt like an easy target. She had to get out of the water. With shaky arms she swam again, and all the while, her heart pounded in her head.

Finally she reached the opposite bank and collapsed into the mud. She didn't know if she should cry or scream in rage. Her mind struggled to grasp that Inspector Reimer had been killed right in front of her. Someone had been watching them. Had it been the Samoan or maybe the superintendent? If the superintendent learned Reimer had gone over his head, would he have silenced Reimer to protect the criminals of his family? She needed a plan. Reimer's warning rang through her head. If she went back to the lodge, it would be her death. Between the shooter and the corrupt police, she didn't stand a chance.

She struggled to pull off her saturated backpack then rolled onto her back. Her lungs heaved in gulps of air as fluffy white clouds paraded above her head. She should keep running, but she couldn't seem to make her exhausted body move. A few moments passed before she retrieved a bottle of water from her backpack. She took a swig, glad to rid her mouth of the bitter taste of the river water.

She winced in pain as she returned the bottle. Blood trailed from a deep cut on her upper right arm about an inch long. Had she gotten it falling down the hill? *That cut will be the least of my worries if I stay out in the open like this.* Lily crawled a few feet behind a jagged limestone boulder and contemplated her options. No way could she make it to Belmopan to find this senior superintendent of police. By car it took fifty minutes.

She swiped the tears that trickled out of the corners of her eyes. *Enough! Emotion will get me nowhere.* She had to think and quick—just in case the shooter was tailing her. *The map.* She'd stuck a trail map in her backpack along with some other necessities: cash, bug spray, room key, swimsuit, towel, an energy bar, and a bottle of water. Blowing out a breath, she glanced behind her to verify the shooter wasn't in pursuit and withdrew the soggy map of the Mountain Pine Ridge area and her red-white-and-blue-striped bikini top.

Lily cringed as she struggled to tie the bikini top around the cut on her upper arm to slow the bleeding. The ends slipped several times until she finally secured the knot. She released a shaky breath and opened the map, tearing the moist paper in a few places. Using her index finger, she pointed to what she believed was her current location. If she went north about ten miles, she should reach another lodge. But then what? The owners would call the police and…

In frustration, she tugged at her long, wet hair. She was in a foreign country with no place to turn. *Wait!* The U.S. Embassy was east of here in the city of Belmopan. She could call them. The weight on her shoulders lightened. She still had a chance of finding a way out of this situation. Then as if the jungle whispered to her, Jaime's name sailed across the heavy air. In her mind, the look in his golden eyes pleaded for her to save him. Once she contacted the U.S. Embassy, would it be too late for him? It could take days for a representative to come to assist her. It was as if she was eight years old again and seeing her little brother floating face down in the pool, knowing no matter what, she couldn't rewind her mistake. Helplessness and self-loathing washed over her.

Staring back at the map, she trailed her shaking finger north until it stopped at the Che Chem Ha Cave. She was closer to the cave than the other lodge. It had been so dark when the taxi had taken her to the Hidden Paradise Lodge there was a good chance she'd passed the sign for the cave. The police probably weren't even searching for Jaime. Thoughts raged war inside her head. Her shoulders straightened as self-preservation lost. No matter what, she couldn't abandon that child.

Folding the map and slipping it into her backpack, Lily decided it would be best to keep close to the river until she found the cutoff to the cave. She didn't know exactly how she'd rescue Jaime, but she had a lengthy hike to decide her plan of action. Maybe she could blend into the shadows of the cave and just smother the Samoan with her American-flag bikini bottoms. Her mouth tightened as she gained her feet. With determined strides, she headed north.

Fatigue crept up on Lily even before the sun set. Between the immense height of the jungle and the dark gray clouds that had rolled in, she found it difficult to determine the time. She ignored the aching blister forming on the back of her heel and kept placing one sneakered foot in front of the other. The narrow trail that cut through the jungle appeared well traveled, with the red soil visible through the mat of grass. Could there be a house, a town? The river roared as it flowed nearby. As she continued onward, the terrain turned rockier, steeper. She licked her dry lips, tasting the salt from the perspiration drenching her skin.

Maybe two hours had passed since she'd crawled out of the river. She had about an hour to find shelter before she had to face the threat of night. From the heavy scent of rain, it would most likely be a wet one. On autopilot, she kept a steady pace, oddly comforted that the annoying birds kept her company. She slapped at a mosquito buzzing around her thigh.

Hoot, hoot. Her steps faltered. Perched on a broadleaf bush, a mere handful of a bird with a flashy turquoise crown gave another *hoot*.

"You have an identity crisis, and by the way, you're not fooling anyone," she mumbled and forced herself to start moving again. Then out of nowhere a wave of lightheadedness hit her. She staggered, grabbing on to a pine tree draped in moss for support. Blood had soaked through her bikini-top make-shift bandage. Dull pain pulsated in her arm. She blinked back the blur that coated her vision. *I can't stop now.* She had to keep moving until she found shelter or she'd just be a convenient dinner for a jaguar.

Inhaling and exhaling even breaths, she observed a parade of ants holding tear-shaped leaves as they marched across the jungle floor. She decided she needed food and pulled out the energy bar and took a bite. It tasted like honey coated gravel. She struggled to swallow the lump in her throat. After the second bite, she started hiking again, contemplating the wisdom of her decision to head north. Twigs snapped under her weight as she struggled to maintain her footing on the steeper terrain.

On the downward slope she stumbled upon a sandy beach, her sneakers sinking ever so slightly in the sand. Approaching a small wooden dock, Lily stopped to examine the battered motorboat locked to a secured, thick post. A chain clanked from the constant movement of the current. There had to be a house or village somewhere. She sighed in relief.

"About time. I was starting to wonder if people actually *lived* in this country," she grumbled and strode past a massive outcrop of bamboo.

Squeal!

She paused mid-step. The fine hairs lifted off the back of her neck. *Squeal!* In a flash two scrawny gray pigs bolted across her path. She jumped, her half-eaten energy bar flying out of her hand. The pigs noticed her, changed direction, and crashed back into the tall brush. A couple of seconds ticked by, then she laughed and shook her head. She'd be so pissed if she'd made it this far only to be taken out by a couple of sausage patties.

Lily had only gone a short distance when a root with a rope tied around it caught her eye. She'd just taken another step when a buzzing sound registered. A net ejected from the earth, ripping Lily's feet out from under her. Screaming, she protected her face with her arms. Her stomach somersaulted as she was propelled upward. Now captured inside mesh netting, she swayed back and forth, staring in disbelief at the ground five feet below.

"This isn't happening!" she groaned. "What moron places an animal trap on a trail to the river?" All forest chatter ceased, the silence broken only by the rustling of the leaves from the warm breeze.

"Hello?" she hollered. She couldn't afford delays. Jaime. Just thinking about the child—scared and possibly hurt—brought on a burst of energy. "Hello, someone help!"

She thrashed around in an attempt to break the rope. No such luck. The momentum of her movements just made her sway like the pendulum of an overwound clock. Her stomach rebelled from all the motion, and she swallowed the bitter-tasting bile coating her throat. She stilled until the swaying stopped. Slipping her fingers through the holes, she attempted to rip the netting. The threads cut painfully into her tender flesh.

"Wáng bā!" she blurted out the Chinese curse word and then sucked on her sore finger. She thought back to another time she'd used that word. She had been ten and her sister eight. They'd just spent time with their maternal grandfather. Upon returning home they'd found that their father had moved back in—again—after it hadn't worked out with his newest girlfriend. Mom always took him back. Some would say Chinese women tended to be submissive, and in this instance they would be correct. He'd been absent for two months, but instead of hugs, Lily had gotten a spanking for cussing, and her sister Jasmine had been sent to her room as Mom unpacked his bags.

The sound of male voices tore Lily from her musings. She tensed and swallowed hard. One word came to mind: defenseless. She couldn't even throw a punch. Maybe a jab with her fingers, but that didn't sound too promising. She held her breath, waiting. Two squatty men with glossy, black skin and straw hats approached. One clutched a machete at his side and wore a misspelled Capp'n Crunch T-shirt with cut-off jeans. The other, the older of the pair, rambled on in a foreign language while pointing a crooked finger her way.

After a closer inspection of her opposition, Lily exhaled. She could take 'em. Capp'n Crunch with the machete had a white eye—blind on the right side. If necessary she could use that to her advantage. The men stopped short of the suspended net. Her gaze bounced from one glaring eye to a matching set. The old man blabbed away again, his tone agitated.

What? Were they mad because she wasn't a pig dinner? She scowled back. They could be mad all they wanted. If they didn't like it, then they needed to be better hunters.

"Well, are you going to cut me down or stand there talking all day?"

Old Man stopped his chattering, and the other one grunted. Then they disappeared behind her and into the bushes.

"Hey, get back here!" She squirmed, trying to change positions to get a better view. "You can't just leave me h—"

The word ended in a scream as she dropped like a bag of stones. She hit the ground with a *thud*. Before she could gain her bearings, the net was tugged out from under her. The momentum caused Lily to flip face first in the dirt. "Enough!"

The men folded up the net, giving her a level-eye view of their callused, bare feet. As she wobbled to a standing position, the men started to walk away.

These two have the manners of goats. "Hey! Wait just one minute." She planted a hand on her hip.

Old Man stopped and cocked his head. Capp'n Crunch scratched his arm with the apparently dull blade of the machete, his mouth downturned.

"You can't just capture a girl in a net, drop her in the dirt, and leave. Your mothers would be ashamed." *If these two even have mothers. Probably just mutated from sludge off the jungle floor.*

They didn't appear moved by her speech. As pathetic as these two male specimens were, she needed their assistance. New tactic.

"I need water and food." She gestured toward her mouth. "I can pay."

The men looked at each other. With obvious reluctance Old Man motioned her to come their way, then both men disappeared into the jungle.

She scoffed and threw her hands into the air. "Do you guys have somewhere important to be or what?" Apparently in this culture women walked behind the men—*way* behind. Given little choice, she sprinted after the would-be hunters and prayed she hadn't just volunteered for a mugging.

Only ten minutes had passed when Lily popped out of the jungle into a clearing. She wiped the perspiration from her forehead and hurried to keep up with her two unhappy guides. Before her stood a dozen weathered shelters lifted several feet off the ground by stilts. Some were constructed using metal siding and others made of wood painted in vibrant colors. Rickety stairs without rails and storm shutters adorned each dwelling. Clotheslines hung between the buildings, many with drying garments. A scattering of wires connected the modest homes to a tall, wooden pole. It could be electricity or telephones. Maybe she could call the U.S. Embassy from the village and in the morning head onward to the cave.

Lily wrapped her arms around herself as she continued to follow the men deeper into the village down the wide, dirt path. A baby with dark, chubby legs waddled around in a cloth diaper, while nearby, several men and women worked in a communal garden. There wasn't a single car in the village, and she wondered if the secluded place even had a road so they could get to town. Maybe they just used the river. But shouldn't they have more boats? The guides, with Lily following, shuffled by a dwelling similar to the others with a wooden sign nailed above the door. She couldn't translate the foreign word scrawled in purple but figured from the painted fork and knife that it was a diner. Beside the structure, chickens pecked away inside a coop, and a goat tied to a pole bleated. In the distance dogs barked. The eatery door opened, capturing Lily's attention. A woman in her twenties with caramel-colored skin and a brown braid sent the trio a quizzical look.

Old Man spoke to the pretty woman who now climbed down the stairs, her worn, yellow dress swaying with her movements. A few other locals stared their way. Lily widened her stance, trying to keep an eye on everyone's positions. Then the woman gasped and rushed toward them.

Lily balled her fists prepared to ward off an attack.

Instead of the anger Lily expected, the woman's eyes widened and she gasped. "Oh, no, you are hurt. I am Mary. Come with me," she said with a heavy accent and took Lily's hand.

"You speak English. Thank God."

"Oh, yes. God is good." Mary led her between two dwellings. The foul smell of sewage polluted the air as they passed the community outhouses. Lily held her breath until her lungs demanded she inhale. A teenaged boy eyed them as he burned a pile of garbage.

"Where are we going?" Lily licked her dry lips, fatigue making her steps falter.

"To Dr. Deforest. He will fix you. He is very good."

"May I have some water, some food? I told those men I could pay."

"Yes. Yes. I will see to it." Mary nodded.

They headed away from the village in the direction of two canvas tents, both a little larger than the dwellings. Mary lifted the flap of the closest one and entered. Lily followed and, once inside, blinked repeatedly, her eyes adjusting to the darker interior. A curtain blocked the view of the back part of the tent from the twelve-by-twelve space in which they stood. A cot and a stack of plastic tubs lay on one side and on the other stood a man, partially obscured by shadows, with a broad back and tanned skin, exposed by his rolled-up, white-linen sleeves.

He bent his head over whatever he worked on. He flipped a page of one of the notebooks scattered across the workspace and leaned forward to type on a laptop. Lily stared at his well-formed backside clad in cargo shorts. Her gaze traveled down and stopped. She narrowed her eyes, unsure if the shadows of the room played tricks on her. Then he shifted. Nope. The man wore mud-coated rubber boots and shorts. Lily laughed, covering her mouth with her hand. *Not exactly GQ.*

"Is that you, Sweet Mary?"

"Yes."

"Perfect timing. My shoulders could really use your magic fingers right now," he said in a deep, smooth voice. He flipped another page, his attention never diverting from the notebook.

Lily frowned, unsure of why this guy seemed familiar. She peered closer trying to get a better view.

Mary cleared her throat. "I'd be happy to give you a

massage…later. We have company?"

Did the doc and Mary have a little love in the jungle going on?

The doctor turned around, and Lily's jaw almost hit the floor. Cooper! Hooded blue eyes peered at her through wire-rimmed glasses. A tense silence stretched out before he said, "Well, well, well, if it isn't my favorite birder. Did you wander a little too far away from the lodge?"

Chapter Four

Lily narrowed her eyes, confusion swimming in her brain. "You're a doctor…living here? I thought you were a tourist."

Dr. Cooper Deforest flashed a killer smile. "Nah, I live here temporarily, and when work is slow, I like to go play cards and drink a little rum with Xavier."

The mention of rum made her cheeks burn. "And do you do that often?"

"'Bout every few weeks."

"Is this some kind of game?" Lily growled, planting her hands on her hip. Did he get a kick out of messing with the tourists? The knowledge that he'd left the lodge without bothering to say good-bye spoke volumes. It left little doubt that if they had slept together, she would have woken up alone. The humiliation ran deeper.

He frowned. "Game? Not sure what you mean. Sometimes I'll rent a cabana and sleep in a real bed for the night." He pulled off his rubber boots and slipped his feet into flip-flops.

And not alone. She'd almost said the words aloud but glanced at the other woman and decided to hold her tongue.

Mary's gaze bounced from Lily to Cooper. "You know each other?"

"Met her a couple of days ago. She was feeding birds her fresh fruit at breakfast." He winked.

"Oh." Mary handed Lily bottled water. "Here is something to drink."

Lily accepted it and thanked her. Why hadn't Cooper said they'd gone on a dinner date? Dread bubbled inside her. If Cooper hadn't bothered to say he was a doctor at the local village and led her to believe he was a tourist, then he most likely hadn't planned on her ever setting foot here. Her stomach soured. Was Mary his girlfriend? He didn't seem fazed at all about having his "girl" in the same room with a lady he'd recently kissed. Lily clamped her eyes shut and counted to ten. Maybe she was reading too much into this. But then why all the games? Well, whatever. She'd just met Cooper, and she had bigger issues to deal with than a little kiss and being played a fool. She needed to help Jamie. Lily gripped the cap to the water and, when it didn't budge, applied more force before it opened. Cooper switched on another lamp. As he closed the space between them, his expression grew serious. She took a swig from the bottle, the cool water stuck in her throat, and she choked.

"Easy there." He gently patted Lily on the back.

She wiped off the dribble from her mouth with her hand and took another—slower—drink.

"What happened?" He pointed to her injured arm.

"Umm." *Two people have been murdered, a child*

kidnapped, and I want to apply a swift chop to your throat. Oh, and by the way, would you mind taking me to this cave, so we can both get killed by a giant Samoan with a scar on his face? Lily started to blurt out the whole story but paused. She didn't trust Cooper. Who knew what else he was hiding? It was possible he'd been at the lodge when the father had been killed. Could he also be working for this drug lord, Maximo?

Cooper's brows furrowed, mirth dancing in his eyes. "Did I ask too hard of a question?"

She lifted her chin. "Maybe it's none of your business, nosy man."

"What is with you? Stop acting so defensive. Come on. I'm *dying* from the suspense."

Lily sighed. She couldn't deal with another dead body on her day off, so she gave in. "I went on a hike and fell down the bank, hit a rock, and landed in the river." Not quite the truth, but close enough.

"Really? So why didn't you go back to the lodge? It's a heck of a lot closer than here."

She blinked at him. "I got lost."

He shifted his stance, a strand of his dark blond hair falling over his forehead. "All righty, if you say so." He withdrew an orange First Responder medical bag from the top plastic tub. After placing it on the ground, he withdrew a sterile gauze pad and slipped on latex gloves.

"Not to worry," Mary said. "The doctor will make you better. I will get you some food, and then you must rest."

Cooper smirked. "Sweet Mary here is a born mother."

"Thanks, I appreciate your help." Lily noted the blush coloring the woman's cheeks as she left the tent. If Mary was indeed Cooper's girl, the poor thing was doomed. Doctor Love had *heartbreaker* written all over every I-think-I'm-sexy inch of him.

Lily winced as he peeled the last part of the bikini top from the gash.

"Sorry 'bout that. It stuck." He clasped her elbow. "Why don't you sit down? I need better light."

She studied the gash in her arm, relieved it had stopped bleeding. After she sat on the cot, he examined the wound. It took all her willpower not to command him to back off. His closeness made her flesh tingle, like all of her nerve endings had stood all at once. She inhaled his scent, like fresh earth mixed with something minty—possibly toothpaste, or maybe he'd been rolling in a spearmint plant like a dog. Lily frowned. Why was she thinking about how Cooper smelled? She must have lost more blood than she'd realized.

He flashed her a sideways glance, his face mere inches away. "You okay?"

She nodded and peered toward the slit in the door. Dusk had settled, lengthening the shadows inside the tent. A light rain danced across the canvas roof.

"You sure? You mumbled something about a dog."

She made a *humph* sound. "Who's Mary?"

"A villager. Did you have a headache this morning?"

She tensed, not liking how quickly he changed the subject. "No."

"You're lucky."

"Yeah, I'll always remember this as my lucky day." Lily forced her expression to void of emotion as she added, "Thanks, by the way, for taking me to my room. Those drinks hit me hard—as you warned. I just remember leaving the table, and the rest of it is a blank." He wanted to play games, she could play them, too.

"Really, nothing else? Not even when we—"

"I said nothing else."

He finished his inspection and leaned back. "You need some stitches to close this up. With the humid environment, not to mention the river water, it's bound to get infected if it's left open."

Briefly she closed her eyes and then schooled her expression. Not exactly her first choice of a place to be doctored. "I take it you know how to stitch people up?"

"I've done it a time or two."

Of course he had. He *was* a doctor.

He adjusted the glasses higher on the bridge of his straight nose. "Are you allergic to any anesthetics or antibiotics?"

"No."

"Lie down. I'm going to irrigate the wound with saline."

Lily lay back, her long, black hair fanning out above her head. "Is there a phone in the village?"

"No. Just electricity. Sometimes."

Calling the U.S. Embassy was out. She needed to figure out her exact location. The cave couldn't be too much farther.

He positioned a small trash can under her shoulder and knelt beside her. "This will just catch the dripping saline."

"I was wondering if you know where the Che Chem—" She gasped from the intense sting as the liquid met her open wound. She clenched her teeth, the air suspending in her lungs.

"Doing well," he soothed.

She wanted to snap at him not to talk to her as if she were a child, but her teeth wouldn't unclench.

"Lily, you're holding your breath. Come on, give me slow, even breaths."

If given a choice, the next twenty minutes of her life she would happily forget. Except for her pledge to tie up Dr. Deforest and beat him with a stick until he begged for forgiveness. After he had injected her with a local anesthetic, he used sutures from a sterile package to stitch the wound. Then he coated the wound with antibacterial ointment, covered it with a clean bandage, and told her to eat some stew and sleep.

Okay, he'd done a decent job of stitching her up, but hell it hurt, and he'd seen her cry. Exhaustion settled over her. Now surrounded by darkness, alone in a tent with the nocturnal animals chanting outside, she allowed herself to succumb to sleep.

· · ·

A repetitive thumping sound resonated from the darkness causing Lily to stir. Just too comfortable, her limp body refused to move. She heard it again and realized it was the beat of drums. Was there a dinner band at the lodge again? A guitar strummed. Her eyes flickered open, and she stared up at the darkened angles of a canvas tent's ceiling. For a moment she froze, and panic made her pulse quicken as her mind struggled to identify her location. Not home, not the cabana. Then she remembered being stitched up and falling asleep in Cooper's tent.

Something from outside cast a dancing, orange glow on one of the walls. She peered around and noted she was still alone. Curiosity got the best of her, and she decided she had to investigate the source of the tribal music. She staggered to her feet and ran her fingers through her tangled, waist-length hair. Lily slipped out of the tent flap into the sultry darkness. A soft, beautiful voice, wafted through the air. She followed the glow, stepping across the dirt and grass pathway, and passed the tent beside Cooper's, only to stop short to stay in the shadows.

Some fifty feet away, flames from a bonfire licked toward the starry sky. Thirty or so villagers gathered in the open space, some standing and others perched on lengthy logs. The soft voice belonged to Mary, and in the background an older man strummed a guitar while another tapped a slow conga beat. Mary's hands lifted toward Heaven then gestured to the men reclined on a log near her left.

Lily's mouth tightened at the sight of Cooper, his gaze fixated on Mary. Next to him was his pale friend and a younger native man, and like Cooper, they hung on every soft, foreign, word that slipped from Mary's lips. Mary could have been singing about lost love or how to weave a basket for all Lily knew. But whatever it was had the audience mesmerized.

Part of Lily wanted to make herself known to Cooper, but the other part wanted to forget about him and go back to sleep. Her indecisiveness left her immobile. *If I don't leave, he's going to see me watching him.* And that was the last thing she wanted. The song ended, and the conga beat picked up, a youth rattled maracas, and a man she hadn't noticed before tapped on drums that looked like tortoise shells strung from his neck.

The villagers, apparently knowing the tune, sang in unison and danced to the rapid beat. Children maneuvered quick steps, and young adult couples swayed against one another in provocative movements. A white-furred mutt joined the party and bounced around yipping and wagging its tail. A dry branch was thrown on the fire, causing the flames to leap up. Lily squinted against the sudden brightness.

Mary grabbed Cooper's hand and his pale friend's and with the sway of her hips started dancing with the men. *How many guys does the lady need?* The firelight flickered over her caramel-colored skin and her loose, wavy, brown hair. Lily's jaw clenched. Cooper stepped closer to Mary, and his laughter could be heard over the boisterous singers. Whatever. He could do what he wanted as long as he left Lily alone. Just as she decided to return to the tent, Lily locked gazes with Cooper. His swaying hips didn't miss a beat as his mouth curled into a slow, sexy grin. A wave of heat tingled over her flesh.

Suddenly she morphed back to when they danced at the lodge: the warmth of his hands on her waist, and the heat that had swirled low in her belly when he'd brushed his muscular body against her. Just then the music paused, and a rapid drum beat followed. Lily blinked, realizing she stood there like a ninny, staring dreamy-eyed at Cooper.

As if he had read her thoughts, Cooper shot her a wink while his hand rested on one of Mary's swaying hips. Lily glared and stomped toward the tent. Inside, she plopped onto the cot. *How dare he flirt with me while he's practically feeling up Mary!* Time passed, and the music faded. Still fuming, she stared into the darkness.

Feet shuffled outside and then came whispered voices. "Come on. I won't take no for an answer. My bed has a soft mattress. You know you want to," a woman said, and immediately Lily recognized Mary's voice.

"So tempting," Cooper said.

Lily stiffened and narrowed her eyes. Mary's and Cooper's voices drifted away, and the rest of the conversation was lost.

Lily clenched her fists. That untrustworthy, mongrel dog! Obviously Mary and Cooper were together. Lily had hoped she'd been mistaken, but she wasn't blind—or deaf. Cooper was a player like her father, and she'd been dumb enough to fall for his games.

• • •

Slivers of morning light and the suffocating heat woke Lily. She lay quietly as the powdery glow illuminated dust motes that floated about. Footsteps sounded outside followed by the voices of a man and woman conversing in a foreign tongue. A dog barked, and the voices faded. Glancing at her bandaged arm, she was pleased to see it hadn't started bleeding again. The strong earthy fragrance from plants engulfed the tent and made her nose twitch.

Lily sat up and attempted to work the kinks out of her neck. Shouldn't Cooper have returned by now? This was his tent after all. *Mary.* The name slammed into her like a punch to the head. Apparently Cooper had enjoyed her "soft mattress" so much he hadn't bothered to return to his quarters. How many girls did he flirt with, kiss, when he already had a girlfriend? Probably one in every lodge and village. Her teeth ground together knowing she'd almost become one of his conquests. She was quickly becoming unfond of alcohol. The panty ripper more specifically. She shook her head, hating how much Cooper consumed her thoughts. What did she care where he slept? The answer was simple. She didn't.

She gained her feet, running her fingers through her long strands in a futile attempt to comb her hair. Near the door, she approached a make-shift sink: a five-gallon water jug and a bowl. Next to it stood a small mirror, toothpaste, razor, and a towel. She eyed the items before temptation won. After finger-brushing her teeth and washing her face, she felt better.

While Dr. Love was still out on his booty call, Lily looked over his quarters. Maybe she'd luck out and find a map and pinpoint the location of the village. She needed Cooper's help. But if he were in the pocket of the drug lord, she'd do Jaime no good dead. She sighed in frustration as she pushed aside the curtain and entered the other room. A folding table stretched the length of the wall, and in front of it, a woven rug covered the floor. She skidded to a halt and frowned. Hundreds of insects and plant samples were stuck and labeled on boards. One board contained rows and rows of various species of beetles.

Strange. Her mind searched for an explanation. This was a bit extensive for a hobby. Where were his medical supplies? A stethoscope? Something other than a well-stocked first aid kit? Wasn't he the doctor for the entire village?

A large-scale map tacked on the wall caught her eye, and she rushed toward it. Groups of different-colored tacks decorated the map of the Mountain Pine Ridge area. She brushed her finger down the Macal River but couldn't pinpoint the village. She squinted, trying to find the Che Chem Ha Cave. Nothing. This map just had the bigger town of Cristo Rey, rivers, mountain ranges, and elevations.

"Useless. Absolutely useless," Lily mumbled, tempted to rip the stupid map down and stomp on it. She shoved away one of the plant specimens sealed in a Ziploc bag to snatch up a GPS device. When she pressed the "on" button, it beeped, and the black and white display lit up. She studied the screen: coordinates, elevation, date, and time. After pressing the menu button, she still couldn't make sense out of the information. Fighting back frustration, she shut off the device and set it down. *Stop and think.*

Okay, I'll have to ask Cooper about the cave on the sly. I'll pretend to be a cave junkie. The idea of exploring a dank hole filled with bat crap and murderers made her squirm. *No time to dwell on the unknown.* She had to stay focused—to remember Jaime.

The heat of the tent became stifling. Perspiration beaded along her forehead and trickled down her back. Paper littered the tabletop. She edged closer. A survey and inventory chart had a zillion handwritten numbers on it. Possibly coordinates. Next to it was a permit from the Belize government that allowed limited access for research and collection. Lily swiped the sweat from her brow. Why would a doctor be here collecting insects and plants? She glanced behind her before fanning out a stack of disheveled papers. A motorboat rental. Must be the boat on the dock. A leather portfolio caught her eyes and she studied the gold lettering stylishly engraved across the front.

Cooper Deforest Ph.D.

Professor of Entomology and Applied Ecology

University of California, Berkeley

Her eyes widened in disbelief. Explanation after explanation swirled inside her head. Her gaze flickered to the stuck bugs and then the word entomology. "You can't be serious."

"About what, my regal Lily?" The sound of a deep voice came from behind.

She whirled around. Cooper stood near the curtain separating the two rooms, his mouth tilting up in a smile. His tan, muscular chest peeked out through his half-buttoned, white-linen shirt. He set down a change of clothes.

"You!" Fury coated her tongue, causing the words to stick in her mouth. "You fraud! You aren't a doctor!"

"Now, sweetheart, that's not true. I have a doctorate—"

"You don't have a medical degree! You're a professor of entomology," she spat, her hands clenching at her sides. Amusement twinkled in his eyes, sending her blood rolling to a full boil.

He rubbed his hand across his clean-shaven jaw and moved closer. "Now, I never said I was a medical doctor."

She was sick of his games! "Well, you led me to believe you were. Oh, God, I had a doctor of bugs stitch me up. I'm probably going to get an infection and lose my arm!"

His expression sobered. "Now, wait a minute. I have medical training. I've been conducting field research for years in remoter places than this. I have almost as much training as a paramedic. I didn't lie to you. I have stitched people up several times."

"And I bet none of them lived!"

He had the nerve to laugh, the sound deep and rich. "Lily, you're priceless."

She saw red. "That's it! I'm tired of you making a fool of me!"

• • •

Holding up both hands, Cooper tried to stop laughing. "Don't you think you're being a tad dramatic?" He studied the fine, ivory planes of Lily's face and didn't miss that her little nostrils flared like a baby bull. She'd been ticked at him ever since she'd shown up at the village. Okay, he hadn't mentioned he lived temporarily in a local village, but the subject hadn't come up. And even though he really liked her, he didn't pour out his life story to a woman he'd just met. In all honesty, there had been a good chance he wouldn't have seen her again, so he'd kept things light. People popped in and out of paradise like it had a revolving door.

"You think this is funny, *Doctor*?" Her almond-shaped eyes narrowed to slits.

Lord above, she looked even more beautiful all full of fire and sass. He couldn't help it—he grinned like an idiot. "Oh, yeah, this is hilarious. And I never claimed to be a doctor of medicine. You just assumed, and that's hardly my fault."

His gaze traveled the length of her slender body that held enough curves to tempt any man. He envisioned getting wrapped up like a cocoon in her long silky hair and exchanging hungry kisses. He tasted her before, and every inch of him wanted her again. No doubt he'd get a black eye for his effort, given her dark mood. But, hey, he was a risk taker. Uncomfortable, he shifted his stance, his blood pumping south.

Lily advanced on him, her finger jabbing into the air, but before the retort could escape her lips, she tripped on the rug.

"Watch—" His words cut off as she stumbled into him, and he lost his balance. He secured her against him seconds before he slammed into the floor. The air *whooshed* out of his lungs. Now flat on his back, he stared up at the ceiling, waiting for it to stop spinning. Lily wiggled on top of him, and her small, firm breasts pressed against his chest. He drew in a breath and tightened his hold, not quite ready to end the sensations her movements created.

She gasped. "Get your hand off my butt!"

"Huh?" It took a second for the words to register. Cooper flexed his hand and realized he indeed had a firm grip of her backside.

Before he could move his hand, she knocked it away.

"Now, I didn't do that on purpose," he said. "Well, not the first time anyway."

"How dare you!" In a sudden movement, she straddled him, and her hair fell in waves over her shoulders and around him.

Hell's fire! What a woman! His fantasies took center stage, imagining what she would do to him next. Her glare and pinched expression made him smile.

She whipped back her hand, and he caught her wrist in mid-air before it connected with his cheek. "Now don't get all worked up. I just grabbed you so you didn't hit the floor. I apologize for giving your backside a squeeze."

"Let go of my arm."

"Promise to be nice."

"Yes," she said through her straight, white teeth.

He'd been thinking about Lily in this position since he'd first seen her at the lodge, but she needed to get off her high horse. Cooper released her arm and threw his weight to the side. He had at least seventy pounds on her and, in a tangle of arms and legs, flipped her onto her back. Keeping his weight on his elbows, he nestled his torso between her legs. He inhaled a slow breath through his nose. She smelled tangy—like insect repellent.

He gave her a wink, his face inches from hers. "Now, this is much better."

"What do you think you're doing?"

This was just too good to pass up. He lowered his head and captured her warm pink mouth. She responded immediately and parted her lips, her tongue brushing in tentative strokes against his. The warmth of her hands trailing up his torso seeped through the fabric of his shirt to his skin. He deepened the kiss, and she met him with the same urgency. Her fingernails burrowed in his hair, and a moan formed deep in his chest from the jolt of arousal. His blood pressure soared. Then her fingers caught a fist full of his hair and jerked his head back.

He stared at her and tried to smooth out his erratic breathing. Cooper could still taste her minty sweetness.

"Don't kiss me again." She released the hold of his hair. Her gaze lowered to his mouth as she moistened her lips.

He propped higher onto his elbows. "I thought you liked kissing me. Something about it being so hot your toes caught fire."

Her brows snapped together. "Shoes, and I was drunk. It doesn't count."

"Hah! You do remember." He hadn't bought her lapse in memory for a second. Their kisses packed too much of a wallop for even alcohol to erase.

A throat cleared.

Cooper's and Lily's gazes jerked in that direction.

"Um. Am I interrupting something? I thought we were heading out to region four."

Cooper shifted his weight off Lily and glared at his twenty-two-year-old Canadian research assistant, William. Sunscreen coated the younger man's extremely pale skin, and his brown ponytail poked out from under a ball cap adorned with a beer mug. William was a good assistant—an asset, really, since he'd conducted research in Belize before—but right now Cooper wanted to chain him to a tree at the jaguar reserve.

"I've seen you before." Lily sat up.

Reluctantly, Cooper sat up as well. He was definitely feeding William to the jaguars. A man didn't interrupt a bud when he was having a little wrestling match with a hot number like Lily.

"You were at the Hidden Paradise Lodge." She gained her feet, continuing to speak to William.

Frowning, Cooper also got to his feet. *Why is she so curious about William?*

William's Adam's apple bobbed up and down as unflattering splotches of red appeared over his pale flesh.

Cooper almost laughed. *This kid clearly needs more experience with women.* This reminded him of when they had gone into a bar at Cristo Rey last week, and a local girl had taken a liking to William. His friend had been reduced to a mute puddle on the floor.

"Um. I-I guess you might have seen me. I went to the lodge with him…with Cooper."

"I saw you when the police carted off Mr. Flores's body.

Did you know him?" Lily asked.

"What?" Cooper's frown deepened.

The younger man's gaze ping-ponged between Cooper and Lily. "Um. Some guy hanged himself. Cooper, it was after you left for the village."

"No," she corrected. "He didn't hang himself. Someone killed him."

Cooper straightened. He didn't like this one bit. *Why is Lily really at the village?* He hoped she wasn't caught up in something she couldn't get herself out of. He grabbed her shoulder and turned her to face him. "What are you talking about? Who got killed?" He didn't want to know by whom. Around here ignorance was survival.

"Breakfast." The sound of Mary's soft voice floated into the tent.

"Well?" Cooper didn't take his gaze off Lily.

Lily stepped back, and his hand dropped, breaking their contact. Her eyebrows lowered as she eyed him and then William. "Go find a newspaper if you want the inside scoop. I'm just a tourist." And with that useless information, the conversation ended.

Chapter Five

Lily sat on a barstool for breakfast at the only restaurant in the village, savoring the brief attention from the oscillating fan. She tapped her toe to the rapid beat of the music and tried to guess what the foreign writing on the wall just above the low ceiling could mean. "*Yu kyaahn travl pahn emti stomak*." Something about traveling on an empty stomach, and given this was an eatery, it probably cautioned against it. The place had room to seat ten between the clean yet worn, mismatched barstools and dinette sets. It was cooler outside, but Mary owned the diner and Lily needed to speak to her. Lily sighed and straightened the strap of her green tank top, feeling like a tramp for wanting a favor from Mary after she'd just locked lips with Cooper. *This isn't your fault. Cooper kissed you. But it's your fault you kissed him back—that you enjoyed it.* He'd turned her into someone she swore she'd never be: the other woman. Was this how the women her father had seduced felt? Angry at themselves for wanting an unavailable man, but too weak to resist his kiss, his touch? "Ugh!" Lily felt disgusted with herself. An older man eating at a table shoved against one of the bright-yellow walls glanced her way before returning to his meal.

Okay, she was done with Cooper. She locked in her mindset. Nothing romantic would be happening with him. He was off-limits—end of story. She stiffened her spine. She had to stay focused on her plan to save Jaime. She couldn't let him down. Earlier it had been on the tip of her tongue to tell Cooper everything and plead for his help. But with his assistant, William, listening, she'd thought better of it. Reimer's warning echoed in her head: *watch your back, Miss Sanborn, and trust no one except me.* Trusting the wrong person could leave her dead. After careful consideration, she decided Mary was her best bet to approach for help. She was local, and Cooper had placed her up there with the saints. Lily just prayed Mary wasn't Maximo's cousin, too.

Lily swatted away a fly, and then she took a bite of her breakfast. Greasy sugar coated her lips as she swallowed the fry jack, which was nothing more than a deep-fried flour tortilla. Glancing around, she failed to locate a napkin so she brushed the sugar granules onto her legs exposed beneath her shorts. She slathered jelly over the next piece and took another bite, licking the fruity remnants off her fingers.

"Can I get you something else?" Mary asked with warmth in her brown eyes. In orderly rows behind her on two shelves sat spices, beans, rice, flour, and baskets of fresh fruits and vegetables.

Why is this lady always so blasted happy? Oh, yeah. She had Cooper as her bedmate last night. It was on the tip of her tongue to tell Mary that Cooper was a two-timing fleabag, but at the last second, she decided against it. She needed information, not for the conversation to get sidetracked by the emotional drama brought on by a man.

"No, thanks. Breakfast's very good. " Lily returned a tight smile and glanced at the older man still eating. She wished he'd leave, so she could question Mary. "With this being the only eatery around, I'm surprised it's not packed; food's good."

"Oh, it often is, but you missed the breakfast crowd. They get up with the sun, so they can work before the heat sets in."

The heat was always on, but the humidity did feel lower in the morning.

"I would advise you to get here about six if you wish to stay for dinner. *Dukunu* and *kow fut soop* will be served." Mary paused a moment and then added, "That means chicken tamales and cow foot soup."

Lily quirked a brow. "Foot soup, huh?"

"It is a local favorite. I boil the foot until it is sticky and chewy…lots of spices." She lifted her hand to her mouth and then flung open her fingers. "So good. Don't be afraid to try new food."

Lily stiffened. If Mary thought Lily would cower away from a eating her Belizean dish, she'd better think again. "My grandmother cooks chicken feet, so I have no problem eating a cow's." She frowned in thought. "I haven't seen any cows around."

"My uncle has a farm about three miles from here. He comes in to trade about once a month."

Lily perked up. "Is there a road then? Does someone in the village have a car?" Maybe it was just hidden by the dense jungle.

Mary grinned. "No road. No cars. He comes on his mule."

An image of herself being bucked off a stubborn mule surfaced in her mind. With a *humph*, Lily returned her attention to her remaining breakfast, and Mary disappeared into the rear room. The front door creaked as it opened, and the old man finally left. Lily finished off her boiled egg and milk. She unzipped her backpack and took out five American dollars to cover the bill and placed it on the counter. After a quick inventory of the contents, Lily realized her remaining twenty bucks, room key, hiking map, bug spray, and towel weren't going to get her much further. Her passport, credit cards, and remaining cash were in her room at the lodge—possibly in the hands of Castillo.

Mary strolled through the doorway, removed the empty plate, and set it behind her in the sink.

"What language is spoken in the village?" Lily asked, eager just to blurt out her real question but knowing she needed to tread lightly.

Mary pulled her thick braid over her shoulder. Her brown skin glistened from the heat inside the diner. "Kriol."

"Really? Belize appears very diverse. My taxi driver had a Spanish accent."

"Yes, we are." Mary beamed and collected the money on the counter. "We are truly colorful, with many different languages: Spanish, Kriol, Garifuna, German, Maya."

"Garifuna?"

"African based language."

"Ahh. How did you learn English?"

"Most Belizeans speak English. Just a few isolated villages, like this one, only speak other languages. English is taught in school and is important to know." Mary lifted her chin in a proud tilt. "I was allowed to take a class once at the university."

"That's great."

"Yes, Cooper, he took me. He says I am very smart and taught me to assist him…and to collect samples."

I'm sure he did. Lily realized she was scowling and forced her face to relax. She leaned her elbow on the chipped counter and rested her cheek in her open palm. "How long has he been here?" As soon as the question rolled off her tongue, she wanted to kick herself. She wasn't here to discuss Cooper.

"About three weeks this time."

"This time?"

"Yes, he spent several months at the village last year, too. That is when I went to the university. He says he also came to Belize with his father when he was a teenager."

Cooper did mention he and Xavier went way back. Mentally Lily filed away that information. *Bouncing country to country, scientists could be perfect to use as couriers for drug trafficking.* "Do you know where the Che Chem Ha Cave is?"

Mary inclined her head but didn't elaborate.

"Where?"

"In the mountains."

Brilliant. And this girl went to the university? This is going nowhere. "Could you show me on a map where this village is and the route to the cave?" Lily pulled out her torn hiking map.

"Why do you want to know how to get to the cave? It is not good for a woman to hike alone. Lots of danger."

Lily crossed her fingers behind her back. "I'll find someone to hike with me. I'll pay a guide."

Mary's mouth dipped downward. "You had best talk to Cooper. He will find a good guide. He's down that way. Past the garden. Near the river."

Just then a scrawny, teenaged boy in worn clothes entered and approached Mary. She handed him two baskets filled with flour, rice, and other goods. Mary said something in Kriol, and the boy responded with a big grin. The door clicked shut when he left.

Lily didn't miss that money hadn't been exchanged. "Do you run a food bank?"

"I just started one again. A large sum of money was donated to feeding our village. Many people go to bed hungry, so having enough food for the needy for half a year was an answer to my prayers."

That was truly amazing. Someone had a big heart, but she hadn't seen anyone who appeared wealthy. "Is the donor from outside the village?"

"Somewhat. It is Cooper."

Lily's eyes widened. "Is he rich?"

"No, not at all. He said he got a donation, but it wasn't allocated for research so he couldn't use it."

"Wow." Lily chewed on that. Knowing he was so generous to the villagers made her opinion of him yo-yo. Could a man be a cheater and still care about others? Her head started to throb, and she rubbed the pain between her eyes. "Thanks, I'd best be going."

The door opened, and a woman with a crying baby entered. Lily sighed and slipped her map into her backpack. She returned Mary's farewell wave and pushed out the door, almost tripping over a chicken. With the side of her foot, she nudged it out of her way. After stomping along the wide, dirt pathway, she veered down a trail cut through the overgrown trees. *Okay, go ask him about the cave and leave. I can do this.*

A toothless man with leathery skin sliced a papaya, feeding a piece to the monkey perched on a branch. Next to him, two men gutted the carcass of a gray pig. A bucket collected all the dripping innards. The men paid her little heed as they concentrated on the task.

Clouds cut in front of the sun, casting shadows as she passed villagers in worn clothes tending a garden. A bushel of barefoot children played outside of a leaning shack with a thatched roof. Lily followed the route to the river and stopped dead in her tracks. Punching something in a handheld electrical device, Cooper wore wraparound Ray Bans, blue-and-black-striped swim trunks, hiking boots, and no shirt. A fine sheen of sweat coated his skin as the sultry breeze ruffled his blond hair against his shoulders.

"Lily?"

She approached and glared at his tan, muscular arms as he slipped on a light-gray Berkeley T-shirt. Damned man!

He sidestepped to allow a short, older lady with laundry to pass from the direction of the river. He offered to carry it back for her, but she blushed, laughed, and shook her head. Even the senior women were under his spell. Water trailed behind the woman from the wet bundle as she continued on.

Cooper removed his sunglasses and tucked them and the device into his backpack. "Are you going back to the lodge? I know a couple of teenaged boys who could be your guides. They're heading to the closest town to trade with the merchants."

"What's that device you just put away? A cell phone?" Hope surfaced. She hadn't considered the possibility of a cell phone.

"Nah, they're worthless out here. No reception. That's a gadget I use to enter plant-location data."

She scratched her neck and glanced around to make sure they were still alone.

"Come on." Cooper shrugged on the backpack and walked toward the village while speaking over his shoulder. "Let's get Pedro and his brother to take you back to the lodge. Most of the time, you'll be in my boat. You'll be safe."

He sure wanted her out of here. Was attempting to sweet talk two girls in such close proximity becoming too much for him? Whatever. That was his problem, she had more pressing matters. With a few quick strides, she caught up to him. "No. Wait."

He stopped and turned.

"I'm not going to the lodge. I want to go see this cave I've heard so much about." She unfolded the map. "Could you show me where this village is located?"

"What cave?" He ignored the map.

"Che Chem Ha Cave. If you would just show me where we are now."

He crossed his arms over his chest. "You have no business hiking on your own. If you want to go explore the cave, then return to the lodge, and Xavier can set up a tourist excursion."

Lily pinched the bridge of her nose. Why wouldn't anyone tell her the location of the blasted village? *Did I wander into Area 51, or what?* This clearly wasn't working. She couldn't afford to be cautious anymore. Time was running out. She clasped his forearm and tugged him into a cluster of young palms.

"What are you doing? Talk about giving a man mixed signals. You're either flirting with me or glaring at me—"

She swatted his bicep. "Shh. I need your help."

"Okay." A crease marred his brow. "I'm afraid to ask, but here goes. How may I be of service?"

Lily inhaled a deep breath. "The man killed at the lodge has a young son, Jaime. The murderers took him and mentioned the cave. I heard it all, and I need your help to reach the cave before they hurt the boy."

"Huh?" Cooper's eyes widened, his eyebrows shooting skyward. "Are you insane? Call the police. They—"

She waved a dismissive hand. "I did, and the man who ordered the hit is the superintendent's cousin, and the police are going to just ignore the kidnapping. The only clean cop…" She inhaled a shaky breath, shoving away the image of the bullets plunging into Inspector Reimer's body. "Was shot right in front of me."

"Good Lord." Cooper ran a hand down his face and climbed out of the palms.

She trailed on his heels. "So you see, with the corrupt police, no one is going to save the little boy."

"And what are you going to do? You got an arsenal in that backpack of yours?"

She shook her head. "No. I was hoping you would loan me a gun."

"Sweet Jesus! Absolutely not. But what I will do is take you back to the lodge and speak with the police."

"Didn't you hear a word I said? Inspector Reimer was

the only one willing to go against the superintendent, and he's dead."

Cooper grabbed her arms and gave her a light shake. "Exactly Lily—dead. No coming back. Sayonara, sucker. Don't you get it? This isn't the U.S. Having parents as missionaries, I've lived half of my life in third world countries. You don't screw with bad cops or criminals." He dropped his hands and blew out a breath. "The best thing we can do is call the police in another town."

"Will they be corrupt?"

"Hard to say. But we won't know until we try."

Lily scoffed and shook her head. The dark clouds rumbled, and rain poured down from the sky.

Cooper tugged her with him under the palm tree, partially shielding them from the rain. "Listen. Be realistic. The police have resources and knowledge of the area that we don't."

"So you're just going to do nothing?" she yelled, shoving her wet hair from her face.

"Twist it how you like, but that isn't what I said. I'm going to pray that a respectable cop picks up the phone, and the boy is found. What I am not going to do is allow you to march across a wild jungle where you could get hurt or killed."

"Then you take me."

"I'm not a cop. I'm a scientist, not to mention a guest of the University of Belize. If I start doing the police's job, causing problems, the government will withdraw our permit faster than I can spit."

"You think collecting plants is more important than a child's life?"

"No. A human life is priceless, and I'm not just collecting plants. What I do saves lives."

Lily heaved in a deep breath and crossed her arms. Rain continued to pound down as they glared at each other. Mud rivulets flowed across their shoes. Any other time she would have enjoyed the reprieve from the heat, but right now she was beyond frustrated and scared—scared she would fail Jaime. She would rather die herself than feel responsible for the death of another child.

"You haven't listened to a thing I've said, have you? Your mind is set, and that's it. I must be missing something here." Cooper cocked his head. "Are you in law enforcement or possibly special forces in the military? Do you have a vast background in self-defense?"

She lifted her chin. "No, I'm an embalmer."

"Ahhh. Well, that will be useful." He laughed, his hands lifting into the air. "I can see the headlines now. 'Embalmer single-handedly rescues child from the evil kidnapper and then prepares the dead bodies of the bad guys, their deaths a mystery in itself, since she never had a weapon. Was it divine intervention? The Embalmer—soon to be turned into a made-for-TV movie."

I can't hurt him. Breathe in and out—in and out. Her calming exercise didn't work, because he was still looking at her like she was a dimwit. Lily swept her arm out toward the jungle. "Then at least tell me the direction of the cave."

"No way."

"Fine. Whatever. I'll find it myself. I'm taking your boat." She marched toward the dock.

He followed close behind. "Nice try. Not happening. If you haven't noticed, I'm saving your life here." Before she realized what he intended, he'd lifted her off the ground and tossed her over his shoulder.

The items in his backpack jabbed her in the chest. She propped her hands on his backside, lifting herself up. "Let me go!"

Behind them the river flowed in a steady current. The hum of a motor registered.

"Sorry, you leave me little choice. I'll take you to the nearest lodge and call the cops in Belmopan myself." He spun around and stalked toward the village. "Women can be such a pain in the—"

Gunshots rang out. A bullet slammed into the tree above their heads. Bark splintered. Cooper dove to the ground. The impact slammed the air straight out of her lungs. Her ability to think momentarily ceased as his body imprisoned hers beneath him. Lily shook the haze away and inhaled a weak breath.

Another shot hit lower on the tree—way too close to their heads. "We have to move!" she urged and attempted to squeeze out from under his weight.

He didn't respond or move.

Oh please don't let him be hit. Fear pooled in her stomach. Tossing a fleeting glance toward the river, she almost swallowed her tongue.

Three armed men in a metal motorboat bore down on the dock. Lily's gaze collided with a huge Samoan with a scar just before he took aim for another shot.

Chapter Six

A bullet whizzed by Cooper's head. He flinched and attempted to cover Lily with his body; that was if she'd stop trying to wiggle out from under him. His gaze searched the nearby foliage for an escape route. *Come on. Come on.* Time was running out. His gaze locked on to a path heading away from the gunmen—and away from the village. Now if the boat would just veer enough so they wouldn't be direct targets. He prayed the villagers had heard the shots and secured themselves in their homes. *Why the heck are these guys shooting at us anyway?*

"Cooper, are you hit?" Lily asked, her hands wrapped around his biceps giving him a little shake.

He gritted his teeth as realization dawned on him. *Lily! The gunmen are after Lily.* "No. I'm not hit."

"Then get off me." She shoved harder at his upper body. "What are you waiting for? Do you know how to panic?"

"I'm not going to jump up and get my head shot off."

Cooper peered back at the boat, unable to get a good view of the gunmen. The boat bounced from the current as it edged up to the dock. One of the men grabbed for the post and missed.

Now!

He wrapped his arms around Lily and, with a swift movement, sent them into a roll behind a boulder. The air swooshed out of her lungs. If someone wasn't trying to kill him, he would have smiled. It took smashing her to make her stop all that harping. Once behind the cover of the boulder, they simultaneously gained their feet. He snagged her hand, and after a yank, she raced with him through the vegetation. The jungle opposed Cooper's and Lily's every move. Time and time again, vines hooked their arms and exposed roots clipped their shoes. She fell, releasing a soft *oomph* on impact. Cooper backtracked, dragged her to her feet, and pulled her, limping and all, into a run. Again he took the lead, but her steady footfalls reassured him she followed.

The urgency of the moment kept shoving at the disbelief bouncing around the walls of his mind: gunmen were trying to kill them. Between the drug lord threatening him two days ago and now this, one thing was for sure: his latest stay in Belize was not going smoothly. A branch scratched his cheek as his booted feet pounded along the zigzagging trail. Not that this was the first time his life had been at risk, given he'd lived in third world countries throughout his childhood and to conduct research as an adult. But this *was* the first time the threat was because of a beautiful woman. He tossed a glance over his shoulder, past Lily's moving figure, and thankfully didn't see a pursuer.

Just as he focused forward, he burst into a marshy

clearing, causing a flock of egrets to scatter. *Great!* He shook his head in frustration. *Nothing like announcing our location.* His feet sank into the mud as he glanced around for the best place to take cover.

"What are you doing?" she asked breathlessly, stopping next to him.

"Shhh." Narrowing his eyes, he scanned for any signs of the gunmen. All clear. Which in the jungle meant a distance of about six feet. He inhaled through his nose, trying to slow his breathing so his heartbeat would stop the jam session in his ears. He waited, listening. Half of him hoped the gunmen hadn't figured out the direction they'd fled. The other half did. He didn't want the villagers hurt. "We can't run out across the clearing. Climbing up the side of the mountain isn't the smartest choice either. We'll have to risk swimming across the river."

"No, that's a bad idea. What if one of the gunmen took the boat?" Lily's chin jutted out. He didn't like the hard glint in her eyes. "We've gotta fight." She picked up a large rock with both hands.

"You're going to throw a rock at them?"

She rolled her eyes. "No, I'm going to climb up that Tarzan vine and take cover in the nook of the tree concealed by all of those leaves. You can hand me up the rock and hide in that tree over there. The one with the parrots. You'll have to carry the rock and climb. When one of them stops under us…" She slashed a hand across the air. "We'll drop a rock on his head."

"Oh, for Heaven's sake. And then the other one will shoot us." He lifted one foot up and then the other, the mud creating a suction sound. The trees had enough foliage to hide an overgrown gorilla. But he wasn't going to tell her that. A blind man could follow their footprints—a gift from the earlier downpour.

"Obviously if two men pass, and we both can't hit them, we don't move."

He cleared his throat. "Too many things could go wrong. The safest bet is the river."

"No. If we strike first, it'll take them by surprise."

He yanked her arm, and the rock dropped to the ground. "Enough of this nonsense. Let's go." With Lily in tow, Cooper skirted the edge of the jungle. Red soil crumbled under their shoes as they climbed down the bank. Once on flat ground, she bumped into him, and he held out a hand to steady her. He took a moment to search the river for the men. "Everything looks clear."

She scanned the area and gave a curt nod.

He shifted his backpack. "If you have anything heavy in your pack, I can stick it in mine."

"No. I'm fine."

"Come on." Threading his fingers through hers, he raised his voice over the roar of the river. "Start swimming to the other side, but don't tire yourself out. Let the current carry you. If we get separated, head north and stay near the river."

"Okay."

The cool water lapped up his ankles as he entered. A fish darted away. Lily slipped on the rocky bottom, and he tightened his grip on her hand. After righting herself, they waded into the widening band of the river. In the middle, light rapids rushed over a scattering of rocks. As long as the gunmen didn't get into the boat, allowing the current to carry Lily and him downstream—away from the village—would be to their advantage. When the water reached his waist, he released her hand and started swimming. He turned his wet head to the side to inhale another breath. The pungent taste of the water seeped into his mouth.

With his next stroke, he caught a glimpse of Lily over his shoulder. She swam a few feet away. He had little time to enjoy the feel of the cool water on his heated skin. Every few strokes he would pause and scan the passing scenery for the gunmen. Above them, gray clouds circled, the scent of rain heavy in the air. The current strengthened, whisking him downstream as if he weighed nothing. For a moment he allowed himself to float to determine their position. *Half-way across, the rest will be a piece of cake*. He added a few more powerful strokes and lifted his head in time to dodge a protruding granite boulder. *Hell!* He yelled out a warning to Lily, but her head was submerged, her arms cutting into the water with determined strokes.

"Lily!" His attempt to swim against the current was futile. A split second before the collision, she looked up and twisted to dodge the boulder. *Wham!* His stomach pitched as she bounced off the edge of the rock like a tennis ball. She disappeared under the rushing water. Adrenaline pumped into his blood. His overhead stroke sliced into the water with intensity. She struggled to come up for air as the current carried her downstream. Finally her body floated close enough for him to grab her wrist.

In a quick motion, he flipped her over to get her face out of the water. "I've gotcha."

She coughed and didn't fight him as he secured his arm around her and positioned her in front of him. He kicked his legs and flailed his remaining arm in a battle to get to the shore. He couldn't see most of her face through her clinging, wet hair, but he could feel her legs kicking along with his. When his hiking boots met the river bottom, he stood, lifting her into his arms.

He laid her on the bank. She coughed, and he rolled Lily partially onto her side facing him. She reached up and touched the scrape across the right side of her forehead and cringed. Blood trickled from her forehead into her wet strands. She pulled back a red-stained hand.

Please don't go into shock. "Head wounds bleed a lot. You're okay." Cooper shrugged out of his shirt and pressed the garment to her head. She groaned.

"Just relax and get your bearings," he said.

"God, my head hurts. I almost knocked my brains out," she said, her words coming out breathlessly.

"That you did." He tried to keep his tone light, although adrenaline had his heart galloping in his chest. How had his life spun so out of control? He kept a hand on her shoulder, halting her effort to rise. "Give yourself some time, just be still."

She closed her eyes and then opened them to stare up at him again. Water glistened across her smooth, ivory skin. "I think I'm fine."

He lowered his shirt and examined the scrape, relief spreading through him at the confirmation that it was just a flesh wound. No real swelling. "Thank God you dodged the rock in time, or you could have had a concussion." He continued to hold his shirt to her head and applied pressure. *Maybe all this drama will make her forget this ridiculous notion about not going to the cops.* Once satisfied the bleeding had stopped, he rinsed his shirt in the river, wrung it out, and shrugged it back on. "You think you can walk? We need to trek to the closest lodge. It's just a few miles." He assisted her into a sitting position.

"No," she said, her voice surprisingly strong. "We're going to the cave."

Cooper ran a hand down his face. *Dealing with this lovely woman is as easy as swallowing a brick.* "We seem to have a problem in communication. I told you I'm not taking you to the cave. This isn't a game."

Lily accepted his hand as she stood. Although he had several inches on her, somehow she managed to stand nose-to-nose with him. Her exotic eyes narrowed into threatening slits. "This is how it's going to play out. You're going to grow a pair, bugman, and take me to that cave, understood?"

He gave a short, mirthless laugh. "Oh, I have a pair, sweetheart, and just because you can stand on your tiptoes and scowl doesn't make you bulletproof." Anger simmered to the surface, and his jaw tightened. "Do you realize what you've done? Have you taken one damned second to recognize the damage you've caused?"

She stepped back, managing to appear baffled and angry at the same time. "Me? I've caused nothing."

He scoffed. "Lord forbid that you look beyond your problem before you waltz into the village and endanger the lives of those people, not to mention jeopardizing my team's research permit."

"I'm sorry about the villagers. I had no idea where I was going or that those men would follow with guns." She crossed her arms over her chest. "You act as if it's my fault the police are corrupt, and murderers kidnapped a child. That wasn't mentioned as entertainment in the brochure from the lodge."

Silence ticked away as he struggled to gain control of his frustration.

"And I'm sorry about possibly messing up your permit. If the government's a jerk about it, can't you just apply for another one somewhere else? Mexico maybe?"

Cooper blew out an audible breath. "No. It has to be here. We're talking about years of research, and this is our best chance to locate the necessary ingredient for the meningitis B vaccine."

"And this is a plant?"

"Not just any plant, but *ashwagandha.*"

She frowned and rubbed her fingertips in a circular motion at her temples. "Ashsh-*what*?"

He flung a hand in the air and started pacing. "It's an herb used in the successful trial vaccine. Grad students found that specific batch growing in the Mountain Pine Ridge area. Which is odd, since it needs a drier climate and is native to India."

A few seconds of silence passed before she said, "Grow the plant in a lab. It's safer."

He stopped pacing, tempted to shake her. But since she was still rubbing her temples, clearly fighting a headache, he refrained. *Doesn't she realize the uniqueness of this region?* "Geez, why didn't I think of that?"

The screech from a howler monkey caused them both to pause and scan the dense trees.

"Maybe it's because you're a doctor of bugs. They need to get—"

"I have a doctorate in ecology, and I am one of many scientists working on this."

She pulled her moist tank top from her slender body

only for it to cling back to her like a second skin. A surge of deep need thrummed through him, and he tore his gaze from the contours of her breasts. He reminded himself that Lily was tempting, yet toxic, and at this rate quite possibly the cause of his demise.

"Oh, then stop worrying." She waved a dismissive hand. "The other scientists will handle it. After you explain a boy was in danger, the vaccine company will understand. And if they don't, you're better off not working for them so…"

Cooper tuned out the rest of her advice and stared at the river. Tension knotted in his shoulders. He and William had two more weeks to locate all of the areas where the ashwagandha grew before the University of Belize sent over a research team for harvesting and replanting. Panic hovered at the fringes of Cooper's mind. If the government pulled the permit, the director of the private research lab who'd secured the grant would cancel the project. In a financial sense he didn't give a crap about losing this job; his cash flow came from the undergraduate classes he taught at Berkeley. Heck, he even paid half of William's plane ticket to get the kid here. All that mattered was, after all these years of hard work and putting his life on hold, he had the key to the vaccine in his hands. No more senseless suffering. No more deaths because the meningitis B strain was always one step ahead of the scientists.

"But I can't rewind the past so let's deal with the here and now. We can do something about Jaime," she said.

He realized she'd been talking away while he'd allowed his mind to drift. Tense seconds ticked by as he scanned the river. He leaned against the twisted trunk of a strangler fig and met Lily's gaze, reading the pleading look. Under all those ruffled feathers, she had a lot of compassion and courage, to the point of recklessness. Maybe if he went with Lily, he could make sure the boy was safe and keep her from harm. If he deemed it too dangerous, he would get her out—even if he had to bind and gag her—and contact the police. "Fine," he ground out, swiping a hand down his face. "We'll go to the cave. But on one condition."

"What?"

"You obey me."

She quirked a brow.

"Okay, obey is the wrong word to use with you, a man-eater."

"You talk nonsense."

Yeah, right. He'd bet all of her ex-boyfriends were sporting nubs in lieu of hands from all the theatrics she put them through. It dawned on him he knew next to nothing about her. "You expect me to believe I'm the only guy whose life you've turned upside down?"

She shrugged a shoulder, her expression bland. "You're the one who insisted on going to dinner."

Touché. He did seem to learn things the hard way. He blew out a breath and stared across the span of the river again. "Trust me, I'm regretting that. I'll bet I know the reason you became an embalmer. Most of the men you come in contact with are dead!"

"True. I never thought of that before. Dead men are less annoying, because they can't talk."

His eyes widened, and he jerked his gaze to her face only to encounter a genuine smile. He kept his expression serious, although as usual, a part of him thoroughly enjoyed their banter. "This is how you talk to the guy you want something from?"

"You started it."

He released a short laugh and shook his head. He should let her walk in circles for the next several hours and wear herself out, but he didn't like the thought that she might intercept the gunmen or a wild animal. Too many things could go wrong, and he couldn't just leave her fate to chance. "If we do this, you have to listen to me. I have more experience in third world countries. If I say it's too dangerous, we leave—no arguing."

She cocked her head. "Agreed."

All of a sudden she's reasonable? He narrowed his eyes. "Come on, we have to head inland and up the side of the mountain. It will take us a few hours by foot."

She fell into step with him.

"So why did you become an embalmer? That profession would make most people squirm."

She shoved away low-lying tree branches. "I like hanging out at cemeteries and watching zombie movies. So I—"

"Come on. Give me the real reason."

She made a growling sound in her throat. Would she make that sexy noise if they made love? Cooper rolled his eyes skyward and shook his head. After all this, she could turn his thoughts to hot sex with the littlest of effort.

After he waited for her, he slipped sideways between two protruding boulders. "Well?" he prompted. He thought she wasn't going to answer.

She finally spoke. "Fine. I went to a funeral when I was fourteen, and the person in the casket looked so peaceful I knew she was happy. Wherever she was, she was happy, and just like that…" She snapped her fingers. "I stopped crying, and I decided I wanted to make other kids feel better when all they had wanted to do before was cry over their loss."

Cooper stopped, not because she sounded emotional, but because of how monotone her voice had become. "Who died?"

Lily didn't break stride. "It doesn't matter."

He started walking again and after a few lengthy strides caught up with her. They hiked for several minutes before he said, "Tell me what you have in mind once we locate this kidnapper and the boy."

"When we find the cave, we scout it out, find a way in, and save Jaime."

His steps faltered. After listening to her asinine plan, a wise man would walk—correction—run from the impending disaster named Lily Sanborn. Instead he shook his head. "Great. It's nice to know you've given this a lot of consideration." He huffed and gave her sexy jeans-clad backside an extra boost, earning a screech in return. Why did he have the sickening feeling that this was going to be a decision he'd regret? Given he lived that long.

• • •

Lily took a refreshing drink from the canteen Cooper had removed from his backpack. Perspiration drenched her skin. For the past hour they'd scaled up the side of the mountain. Her muscles screamed from overuse.

"Your stitches are holding up." He studied her shoulder. "How's your head feeling?"

She swallowed another drink and waved him off. "Fine. Just a light pounding."

"I'm surprised the bruising is so minimal. You must have a hard head," he said.

She ignored his jab.

Cooper leaned against a slab of sandstone, accepting the canteen from her. Tilting his head back, he took a long drink. Sun rays glinted off the lighter blond streaks in his hair. A sheen of sweat glistened across the strong column of his neck. Something purely female awoke inside of her. Heat pooled in her lower body, her breathing growing shallow.

He wiped his mouth with his hand. Their gazes collided. *Snap out of it, you fool*, Lily scolded herself.

"You know, what's with all the glaring? You've had a chip on your shoulder since you showed up at the village."

"I don't know what you're talking about," she said.

"Yeah you do. If you've got something to say, just say it."

Lily ignored the question and gestured with her head to the backpack on the ground. "You have anything else useful in there—like a gun?"

Cooper stared at her for a moment. "No gun. I'm not a Belizean citizen, and my license application is in limbo."

"You go into the jungle unarmed?"

"I borrow Mary's gun when I plan to go deep into the jungle. She has a license."

"So what's in the backpack?"

"Um, let's see. I have the device for data collection, which has GPS. I have some beef jerky, a travel first-aid kit, insect repellent, flashlight, and a pocketknife." He placed the canteen inside and zipped up the top.

She sighed. "Why couldn't I have stumbled upon a mercenary with a bunker of ammo and a bunch of buddies who could be bought with the promise of cheap liquor?"

A laugh released from deep inside his chest. "Well, I could take you to the watering hole at the next village; you might have some luck there. I met an ornery group of men with scars and missing teeth, but their ripe smell will probably give you away during a sneak attack. You might have to give them a bubble bath."

"No time. You'll have to do."

"You know," he said, his tone thoughtful. "I could use a bubble bath. You could wash my back."

Before she could stop it, an image of Cooper snuck into her mind: his naked muscular torso glistening with water droplets, his long legs sprinkled with hair draped over the sides of the tub. Her hand almost started moving as she imagined rubbing a suds-filled cloth over his tan skin. Mentally she gave herself a shake. "Stop talking about baths."

"It was worth a shot."

She scanned the rolling green hills and grabbed for another subject. "It would be smart if we had easy access to the knife. I can hold on to it."

He shuddered. "No way."

She widened her stance, planting her hands on her hips. "Just because I'm a woman—"

"It has nothing to do with your gender; it's your temperament. You pounce first, ask questions later." He shook his head. "Come on, break's over."

"You're melodramatic." She started down the leveled path blanketed with soft pine needles. Insects and seedpods periodically dive-bombed them from the jungle canopy.

"Ah, that might be," he said. "But I'm still alive, sweetheart."

The endearment swept over her, making her skin tingle.

The rush she felt caused her jaw to tense. "I'll bet this is how you charmed Mary."

Falling in step with her, he scratched his head and frowned. "Mary?"

Really? Like he didn't know. She wasn't buying his confused, puppy-dog look. Bushes encroached on both sides of the trail. He lifted a branch, allowing her to precede him down the narrow path.

"I know you and Mary are a couple, and I resent the fact that you kissed me." She kept her eyes focused straight ahead.

After a lengthy pause he said from behind her, "Is this what has you all worked up?"

"I'm not worked up. No woman likes a two-timing man." An image of Mary and Cooper in a heated lip lock assaulted Lily's mind. Her hands clenched into fists.

"You've got to be kidding me," he scoffed. "I am not in a relationship with Mary. She's like a sister to me."

"A sister? Give me a break. One that rubs you with her magic fingers?"

"Huh?"

"When I first went to your tent, you were requesting some special attention."

"Are you talking about a neck rub? Oh, please. There's nothing sexual about that. She's damned good at it, and it's relaxing."

Lily rolled her eyes. "Then why did she invite you to sleep in her soft bed the night of the bonfire?"

"Heard that did you? Try because you were in my hard bed, and Mary offered to stay at her mother's place, said she needed to clean up anyway since her mother has arthritis."

Silence stretched out.

"It's true. Think about it, Lily. Have you seen Mary and me kiss? Hold hands? Anything a couple would do?"

"No." Hope bobbed in her heart before she sank it. *How can I be so gullible?* "I'm sure if I ask Mary, she'll have a different story."

"No, she won't. We have nothing romantic going on. What is it with you anyway? Hey, you're jealous."

An ant as plump as a red grape landed on her arm. She paused to flick it off then continued walking. "Dream on, bugman."

Cooper sidled up to her with a stupid smirk on his face. "A little jealousy is healthy. I'm flattered."

Lily stiffened. "I am not jealous!"

"Okay, fine. What is it then?"

"I don't like cheaters."

"Cheaters?" He had the nerve to sound offended. "What's that supposed to mean? Just because you're delusional doesn't make me a cheater. You sure are a piece of work."

Their words ceased. A constant stream of animal chatter surrounded them. Could Cooper and Mary really just be friends? Lily frowned as she marched onward.

"So… this is where you say, 'Cooper, I'm sorry I assumed you were an untrustworthy, womanizing rat, and I projected my insecurities onto you.'"

She winced, trying to replay all the facts in her head. Was he being honest, and she'd completely misunderstood? "My insecurities? I don't know what you're talking about."

A moment later he said, "I think I've got your defensiveness figured out."

"Good for you."

"When was the last time you had a boyfriend?"

She shook off the knot forming in her stomach, but her emotions went every which way.

"Come on, answer the question."

"A while ago." She met a fork in the path and glanced questioningly at him, veering right when he pointed. *Great! More uphill.*

He held back a sage bush spilling onto the path. "What was the length of your longest relationship?"

"Is this the Spanish Inquisition?" She skirted the bush, the potent scent making her fight back a sneeze.

Screech! Lily stopped at the deafening sound.

Cooper collided with her from behind and grabbed her to keep her from falling. "It's okay. Just a howler monkey."

"Oh, that was loud." She shrugged out of his hold and started moving again. The monkey had sounded like a banshee from some horror flick.

"You haven't answered my question," he persisted.

She sighed. A smart man would have gotten the hint and changed the subject. She shoved away her annoyance. Cooper was taking her to the cave. Answering a few of his dumb questions wouldn't hurt. "My longest relationship lasted six months."

"Hah! See? My point exactly. You won't let men get too close because of your distrust."

Toucans socialized in the nearby trees. Lily quickened her pace, eager to get away from him, but with his longer legs, it didn't make a difference.

"We have some time on our hands, and I'm past due for some community service," he said. "I've been told I'm a good listener. Why don't you start with your first memory involving a man, unless…Lily, a man never mistreated you, did he? There are perverts out there and—"

She hated the direction his Neanderthal mind was headed. "No." She scowled and stepped over a protruding root. He grunted and stumbled. A faint smile touched her lips as she kept a forward pace.

"You could have warned me about the root," he scolded.

She needed to steer this conversation in another direction before he had her on a couch reliving her childhood and sucking her thumb. "And you, Doctor, have you ever been married or in a long-term relationship?"

"I haven't been married, but I was in a relationship for three years."

Lily tied her long hair into a loose bun without breaking stride. The coolness that met her neck was a welcomed reprieve. "What happened?"

"Well, we both worked in field research on different continents and only saw each other a few months out of the year. It was destined for failure."

Then why had they stayed together so long? Could it have been friends with benefits? "And how many times did you stray?"

"None," he said, his tone hard. "I'll have you know there are men, me included, who have things to focus on besides sex."

Her step faltered, and she turned to face him. "Like what?"

His mouth pressed together, and a line creased his forehead. He stopped and gestured with a hand. "Finding a cure for a terrible disease."

"Why? Why is it so important to you?"

"People shouldn't have to die like that."

She waited, but he just stared blankly into the foliage above her head. Then she caught a glimpse of something in his eyes, something like pain.

Before she realized it, she'd touched his forearm. "What happened?"

He shrugged. "When we lived as missionaries in Guatemala, a friend of mine died. Francisco was my age, fifteen. He was malnourished; most of them were. But he was always such a happy kid, so he seemed okay to me. Then wham!" Cooper slammed his fist into his palm, and his lips tightened. "He had a rash, raging fever, severe body pain, and constantly vomited. Within a week, after his second seizure, he died. Meningitis B caused inflammation in his brain. His youngest brother also died from the disease."

Her heart twisted into knots at the storm of emotion in his eyes. "I'm sorry." Those two words seemed so worthless, but what else could she say?

He blew out a long breath. "I grew up around poverty and death. Usually my friends were other missionary kids, not the villagers. Francisco was one of those people who made life dynamic. Nothing was out of reach. I took him up on all of his challenges: cliff diving into the river, insect eating. The kid was dirt poor but exuded happiness." He looked skyward, appearing lost in thought. A steady patter of raindrops sounded, but the abundant jungle canopy kept them mostly dry.

"So you decided to find a cure?"

"After I stopped being angry, I knew God had put Francisco in my life for a reason. As soon as I graduated high school, I locked on to my quest, and I'm still on it." He cleared his throat, his expression grim. "Then I blink, and I'm thirty-five years old, single, and I missed a lot of family events, because I was doing research. But I don't care, I'll find a cure."

"Your sacrifice is noble." She paused. Besides her maternal grandfather, she'd never thought highly of a man. She gave a curt nod. "Yes, you're noble."

"Why, Lily, I'm blushing to the tips of my ears. You just complimented me." Cooper took another step and glanced down at his shoe. "Well, shit!"

She jerked in response. She'd never heard him curse before. "What?"

"Pardon my language. I stepped in…poop."

She couldn't help but smile as he rubbed his shoe on a rock.

"Looks to be from a peccary," he grumbled.

She cocked her head. "The pig creature?"

He nodded, still focusing on his task.

"Well, in the Chinese culture this is good."

"Stepping in poop?" His brows rose.

"Yes, you should expect some good luck in return."

"Well, shoot." He tossed his hands into the air. "Why didn't you say this earlier? I would have started stepping in big piles of it sooner."

Chapter Seven

Lily stopped at the top of the rise, exhaustion wearing her down. The late afternoon sun emitted a powdery glow over broad treetops sprinkled with white orchids. A citrusy fragrance clung to the air. After taking another bite, she swallowed the leathery beef jerky Cooper had given her. He sidled up next to her. Like hers, perspiration soaked his shirt.

Okay just say it. "I'm sorry I accused you of being a two-timing dog," Lily said, relieved to finally be rid of the guilt that had been chewing on her.

Cooper swiped the moisture from his forehead and peered down at her. Heavy silence lingered between them for a moment before he said, "Apology accepted...I replayed that conversation about the bed, and I can see how you could have misunderstood."

It frustrated her that she'd been in the wrong and had snapped at him. "It did sound suspicious, but no matter," Lily said. "I should have asked instead of jumping to conclusions."

"Agreed. It's best to give someone the benefit of the doubt… Come on. We're almost there." He clasped her hand and led her several feet before he assisted her down a steep incline.

"The cave's over there, about a hundred yards." He pointed down the path crisscrossed with gold and green oblong leaves. "Keep an eye out for anyone around, and try to make as little noise as possible."

"Okay." Her stomach tensed into a tight ball. *What am I doing?* She was going to get herself and Cooper killed. No! Cooper could take care of himself. He had survived this long in third world countries after all.

He descended the gradual slope first. The grade sharpened, the rocky floor turning slippery from the humidity. Upon the final descent, he scanned the area and, apparently satisfied no one was about, swung down from a narrow tree trunk growing at an odd angle from the mountainside.

His hands gripped Lily's waist as she also dropped down. "You doing okay?"

"Yes." She followed in his wake.

The trees thinned, allowing the hazy, gray sky to peek through. Finally the trail leveled out, and they approached a trio of long, wooden benches.

Cooper announced, "We're here."

"We are?" She glanced around and, through the encroaching branches, saw a dark opening carved into the side of the mountain, only wide enough for a large adult to crawl through. An iron gate with a cross and two rising suns stood ajar. She swallowed hard. She'd expected a vast cave, one you could stand and maneuver through. How could she sneak up on someone crawling on her hands and knees?

"Either someone's inside, or they forgot to lock the gate."

"This can't be right. That is the size of a worm hole." She didn't consider herself claustrophobic, but envisioning entering that dark space surrounded by crumbling earth made raw nerves claw down her spine.

"Don't worry, I explored this cave last year when I scouted this area. It widens once you enter, although the cave has several chambers, and we'll have to crawl at times."

"Won't the kidnappers see our flashlight?"

"Possibly. But if we go inside without light, we can save them the trouble of killing us, because we'll break our necks."

Lily pursed her lips, not liking this one bit. *I have to do this. Jaime's in danger. He's scared, maybe hurt.*

"Anyway, this cave is occasionally visited by tourists. If these guys killed people who entered, I would've heard of their deaths or at least that they'd gone missing. Wherever these men are, it must be deeper than where usual cave explorers venture."

She shuddered. *I can do this. I'm just crawling into the belly of the earth to hunt for the devil.*

Cooper withdrew his flashlight and the pocketknife. She snatched the knife from his grasp. "I'll hold that. You have the flashlight after all."

She slipped the knife into the pocket of her jean shorts. He grunted and crawled into the opening first. Over his form, she saw a few feet of earth, and then it dropped off into inky blackness.

Upon entering, the cave floor descended, and her eyes struggled to adjust to the meager daylight seeping from the opening. The chamber could house twenty standing people, and the damp, musty air was refreshingly cool.

"We have to climb down a rope ladder," he whispered.

He reached the bottom, and she followed suit. She rolled her tense shoulders, her senses on high alert. The bottom of the cave crunched under their feet, echoing as loud as a bass drum. Lily cringed and kept after a slow-going Cooper. They rounded a bend and entered another cavern where fragments of ceramic pots lined a high niche along a carved wall.

The next cavern was also large, but soon the path narrowed, and the cave walls closed in on them. The thin beam of the flashlight etched into the looming, black surroundings. They squeezed through the opening, avoiding stalactites, which reached down from the ceiling like crooked fingers.

He stopped and whispered into her ear. "I'm going to turn off the flashlight now and listen. We're deep enough we should hear something if someone's near." Then the beam of light vanished.

Her hand clutched his bicep as the darkness closed in around her. Lily's breathing increased, panic surfacing. Faraway drips of water and squeaks from either a rodent or a bat sounded inside the limestone walls. They waited and listened. Time dragged past, and soon she felt something she hadn't since she'd come to Belize: chilled to the bone. The light switched on, and she jumped.

She swatted his shoulder and whispered, "You mongrel dog, you could have warned me."

The glow was bright enough she could see the amusement in his eyes. He slipped by her, headed the way they'd come.

She grabbed his arm, halting his progress. "What are you doing? We need to go deeper."

He shook his head. "No. No one's in here."

"But we've only gone part way."

He pried her fingers from his arm. "We'll talk outside. It's near dusk, and I'm not going to risk getting locked in here." He strode toward the opening.

Lily was forced to follow or lose the light. Blasted man! Emotion built up inside her as they retreated out of the cave. She blinked against the onset of light and inhaled a breath of fresh air. He took ahold of her arm while he led her farther down the side of the mountain abundant with lush ferns. Frustration compounded with every passing minute. After distancing themselves from the cave, Cooper stopped at the bottom of a waterfall cascading off a sheer cliff. A cloud of constant mist floated across the pool.

She tugged Cooper to face her. "We can't quit! He's still in there! Give me the flashlight, and I'll keep looking for Philip myself. I don't understand you—"

"Listen, you have to calm down and think," he said, the tone of his voice softening. "Face it. Nobody's in that cave. I even walked through a spider web going into the last chamber. Are you sure it was the Che Chem Ha Cave?"

She swiped moisture off her face. *Oh, wonderful, I'm crying like a fool.* She looked away, not wanting him to see her weakness, and tried to calm herself. *Think Lily.* She replayed the bits of conversation she'd overheard while on the patio before she'd discovered the father's body. "Yes, that cave was mentioned. But other things were said, just too low for me to understand."

Cooper ran a hand down his face then stared at the waterfall's spray as the powerful water pounded onto flattened stones. Behind him, glimpses of the vibrant hues of an orange-and-yellow sunset peeked through the tree line. "It could have just been mentioned as a reference point for another cave. You have to understand Belize has the most extensive cave system in Central America." He quickly lifted his hand in the air before dropping it by his side. "Heck, in the world. There are like three hundred identified caves and a lot more unexplored."

More than three hundred caves? Lily wanted to scream. No way could she search that many places. She'd failed. If only she'd heard the entire conversation, they wouldn't be on this wild-goose chase. Why did she think she could out-maneuver a drug lord on his own turf?

"It'll be dark soon, so we can't search the area for nearby caves."

"But we have a flashlight."

He shook his head, his expression serious. "We're not roaming around here at night. But if there is activity nearby, we should see lights."

Lily's head lolled back, and she clamped her eyes shut.

"Lil, it's been a long day, and we need rest. We'll be fresh tomorrow, and we'll find this cave."

She focused back on him. "Okay. You're right. I just…"

"I know. Want to find him. " He glanced around. "Let's find a place to camp but not next to the water. Too many critters will stop by for a drink."

They both made a bathroom stop, and she was grateful for the cover of the overgrown foliage. After they washed their hands and faces in the stream, he refilled the canteen. Then they climbed up to a granite ledge about eight feet from the ground and a safe distance from the water.

Lily withdrew the towel from her backpack and spread

it on the ground. They both doused themselves in bug spray to ward off the mosquitos, and then she waited while he grabbed something to lessen the hunger. Soon she found herself munching on another piece of jerky and grape-sized fruit from a Pokenoboy tree.

Cooper sat down next to her, popped a piece of fruit into his mouth, and chewed. "Lil?"

"Hmmm?" She swallowed her own fruit, the taste in her mouth an odd combination of sweet and sour.

"Who's Philip?"

She whipped her gaze to his, the lump forming in her throat threatening to choke her. "How do you know about Philip?"

"You said his name, not Jaime's."

She recalled the name mix-up but had hoped he hadn't noticed. Her shoulders sagged. Other than that fateful day, she hadn't talked about what had happened with Philip with anyone.

Cooper stretched out and rested his head on his back-pack. "You're emotionally involved in this kidnapping, which doesn't make sense. You hardly know this kid."

Tension tightened her shoulder muscles, and the sound of her own rapid breathing pounded in her ears.

"I have a right to know everything. When you decided to involve me, you gave me that right. What's really going on, and how is Philip involved?"

She leaned her head against the wall of earth as the painful images of Philip's death assaulted her mind. "He's my brother. He died when he was three."

"What happened?"

A heavy silence filled the space between them.

She rubbed her hands over her eyes as years of pain and guilt churned in her gut. "I killed him."

Cooper rose to a sitting position, a crease marring his brow. "I can't believe that. I'm sure it was an accident."

He would hate her just as much as she hated herself. She'd killed her brother and ruined her family. She bit down hard on her lip, welcoming the pain. "It doesn't matter. He's dead because of me!"

He touched her shoulder, and although she didn't deserve comfort, she couldn't make herself move away.

"Tell me…tell me what happened," he said in a hushed tone.

Suddenly, she felt a hundred years old and bone weary. "I was eight." She swallowed hard, her vision blurry. "I went swimming with my friend, and we were in such a hurry to go ask Mom for ice cream that I didn't latch the gate." She remembered the sweetness from licking the hot fudge off her fingers, the excitement when Mom stuck two cherries on top. She cleared her throat and choked out the words. "My parents had told me many times 'you must hear the click.' I didn't pay attention, and the gate didn't shut all the way. Mom was busy scooping out ice cream, and then we couldn't find him. I can still hear my mom's screams when she found him floating in the pool, still see the paramedics rushing his little body off."

Cooper's warm embrace surrounded her, and she clung to him. "Your parents must have told you it was an accident."

She buried her face in his shoulder. "My father yelled at me. I'd never seen him cry before or since. He said I'd killed my brother, and he was right."

"Good grief. You were eight. It wasn't your fault. You

shouldn't have been swimming without an adult in the first place."

She longed to believe Cooper, tempted to grasp on to his words and make them the truth. But she knew better. If not for her, Philip would be alive, fresh out of college, and ready to take on the world.

"Killing yourself to save Jaime won't bring your brother back."

"I know it won't. But Jaime would be safe right now if I'd played with him like he'd wanted and not returned him to his cabana."

"You had no control over what happened."

Absently her finger traced a letter of his Berkeley T-shirt. The sounds from an off-key frog symphony grew louder.

"Your parents still alive?" he asked.

Lily lifted her long hair and draped it across her exposed shoulder. Something about Cooper made her want to share her misery when she'd always shut everyone else out. "My father is, but we haven't spoken in seven years." She sighed. "He's a freelance investigative journalist, and sometimes I find myself looking him up online just to see if he's still alive."

"Nothing's wrong with that." His fingers rubbed the back of her neck and her muscles loosened. "What happened? Why'd you stop speaking?"

"At my sister's high school graduation he had the nerve to show up and act like a proud father. He had no right. He left us for my grandparents to raise. I yelled at him. Told him to leave and that I hated him."

"What about your mother?"

The question sent a jab of pain knifing into her chest.

"After my brother's death, my dad began flaunting his constant stream of girlfriends." Emotions choked her, and she took a moment to collect herself.

Cooper just held her, his fingers working their magic as he rubbed the muscles across her shoulders.

Finally she said, "Mother became depressed. When my father would wander back home, she'd start cooking again and humming, but that never lasted. His affairs were like a revolving door until my mother killed herself after Father had filed for divorce. I was fourteen. After that my sister, Jasmine, and I went to live with my maternal grandparents."

"Good Lord." Cooper pressed a kiss to her forehead. "I'm sorry you had to go through that."

She shrugged, comforted by his closeness more than she could have ever imagined. Lily had worked so hard to be an independent person, only to count on herself for what she needed. But always being on guard was so tiring and lonely. As an adult, her sister sought out dysfunctional relationships, and Lily couldn't stand to witness Jasmine cower to cheating and abusive men. That just left Lily and G-ma. A family of two.

"That's why you decided to become an embalmer? The woman who looked so peaceful in death was your mother?"

Lily nodded, remembering her mother in the casket: flawless skin and the slight tilt of her lips in a smile she had rarely used in life.

Cooper shifted her in his arms and whispered against her hair, "You had a lot to deal with at such a young age. I wish I could take that pain away from you, but I can't. We're shaped by everything that happens to us. Lil, you have to stop dwelling on the past and keep moving forward."

"You must have taken a psych class."

"A couple. But my dad's a preacher. I listened as he advised others. He's the wisest man I know. When my friend died, he told me to pray. I did, and I had peace with it, and then I realized what I had to do with my life."

He made it sound so easy. But there was a difference between their situations: he hadn't been responsible for his friend's death. Wrestling with her turbulent thoughts, she took comfort in Cooper's strength, a strength she desperately needed right now. His heart beat in a steady rhythm beneath her palm, and she couldn't remember feeling so content being held in a man's arms. Time slipped by as the light weakened, and she listened to the powerful waterfall. She'd just snuggled deeper in his arms when she felt Cooper tense. He whispered against her ear. "Lil, don't move."

Confusion spun in her head. Was someone nearby?

"Slowly turn your head toward the waterfall."

In gradual movements Lily peered over her shoulder and swallowed her gasp. About sixty feet away, a jaguar drank from the pool below. She held her breath, her mind in fast-forward on the best way to react if the feline attacked.

"It hasn't seen us. Just don't move."

She froze.

The spotted carnivore's sleek muscles flexed as it scanned the area and lowered its head to drink. Then just as she started to get a cramp in her neck, the jaguar slunk away and disappeared into the jungle.

"You okay?" he asked.

Her pulse ticked away in her ears. "Not really...I almost got eaten by a wild animal. Maybe we should sleep someplace else."

"No, this is a good spot. We're off the floor with a cliff to our backs. I'll keep guard for a while; you'd better hand over that pocketknife."

Lily glanced around the vegetation, cast in shades of gray and black, and withdrew the knife from her pocket and handed it to him. "What would you have done if the jaguar had seen us?"

He gently pressed her back to rest on his shoulder. "I wasn't worried. I had a fifty percent chance the jaguar wouldn't try to eat me first."

"That's an awful thing to say!" She poked him in the stomach.

He grinned and looped his strong arm around her. "Oh, you know I'm just playing. I would throw my body into the mouth of that ferocious beast to save your life."

· · ·

Something startled Cooper, and he tensed. Night pooled before his eyes, and the feel of Lily's body warmed his side. He waited, wondering why he had awakened. His fingers touched the pocketknife on the ground. A choir of cicadas chirped, and in the distance came the constant roar of the waterfall.

Lily whimpered and mumbled something. She sighed and then said in a clear voice, "G-ma, stop choppin' chicken." She shifted as if to burrow between him and the hard, granite ledge.

His body shook with laughter as he drew her closer to him. The movement must have woken her, because she gasped and sat up.

"It's Cooper. It's okay."

She lay back against him. Her breath warmed him through the material of his T-shirt, and her heart pattered a rapid rhythm against his chest.

"You were dreaming."

"Oh. Was I talking in my sleep?"

"Yeah." A smile spread across his face. "Who's G-ma, and why is she choppin' chicken?"

"Oh, God. I can't believe I said that. The curse of being a sleep talker."

"You sounded very annoyed."

"You would be, too, if your grandmother was your room-mate, and when she can't sleep, she gets out a hatchet and starts hacking up a chicken carcass."

Cooper's brows lowered as he rubbed his hand down her sleek hair. "Sounds scary."

"Not really. She likes to cook, but between her, the land-ing planes rattling the trailer windows, and the half-deaf neighbors blaring their game shows, it can make me moody."

"You moody? I can't see it."

"Real funny." She poked him in the ribs.

"Be nice." His fingers touched the smooth skin of her jaw as he pressed a kiss to her lips.

She responded by inching closer and released a little moan. Their lips glided in measured, unhurried movements. Spending this time with Lily was special. Just talking. Kiss-ing. Contentment settled over him. He broke the kiss, and she returned to her place on his shoulder.

A comfortable silence lingered before he recalled some-thing she said. "Did you say you live next to an airport?"

"Unfortunately. I live in a trailer park and have nosy

neighbors, but the upside is people watch your back."

Didn't embalmers make better money? He didn't want to insult her by asking the question on the tip of his tongue, so instead he said, "Did you grow up in a trailer park?"

"Just in high school when I moved to Vegas to live with my grandparents. A year and a half ago G-ma broke her hip, and Grandfather had passed away a few months before that." In the darkness he felt Lily shrug a shoulder. "I was worried about her living all alone. She wouldn't move into my condo, so I went back to the park."

"She's lucky to have you." His admiration for Lily went up a couple of notches. Not only was she beautiful but loyal. There was something intriguing about her that made him want to figure out what made her tick. Gradually Cooper was peeling through the layers of armor she'd placed around herself.

An owl hooted, and Lily stiffened. "It's so dark. It's creepy," she whispered.

"This coming from an embalmer."

"I work with the dead. They can't hurt you. It would be like being afraid of Barbie."

A warm breeze played across his skin, followed by a rustling sound.

"What was that?" she whispered.

She always came across so tough. He liked this vulnerable side of her.

"Leaves." He rested his chin on the top of her head and inhaled her sweet scent.

Lily jerked, and a slapping sound followed. "Stupid bloodsuckers."

His chest shook with silent laughter.

"Are you laughing at me?"

"Only in a good way...I sleep outside sometimes, so the dark doesn't bother me, although I use netting to keep the mosquitos away." Just then something buzzed by his ear, and he whipped his hand that direction.

"Shouldn't you cover yourself in fly paper so you can capture the pests and study them?"

"I'm not that interested in mosquitoes. Now Coleoptera, a.k.a. beetles, on the other hand, are completely fascinating."

"Have you always been interested in insects?"

Cooper was taken aback by the question. At this point in the conversation, women usually changed the subject. Something that his father once said surfaced in Cooper's mind: sometimes it's worth getting poked by the thorns in order to have your rose. "As far back as I can remember. As a kid, my bedroom looked like a lab with rows of jars with the insects I studied."

"And your mom was cool with all those bugs in her house?"

"Not really. I think she thought it was strange when my lab expanded in high school, but she felt guilty because we moved so much, so she let me keep it."

"Well, I got you beat with the strange. I became obsessed with the dead in high school, and my G-ma was convinced I was possessed with the devil."

"She take you to counseling?"

Lily scoffed. "She's old school. She followed me around most of my senior year trying to get rid of the bad mojo, burning protective herbs, and making figure eights with the smoke."

Cooper smirked. Like himself, Lily had a very interesting

childhood. "Why an eight?"

"Eight is considered the luckiest number in the Chinese culture."

"Ah. Well I guess it didn't work since you became an embalmer. Does that cause a problem between you two?" He blinked in the darkness, his eyes growing leaden.

"No, she's said my mojo's fine now, because I have a college degree."

Cooper frowned, struggling to connect the reasoning. "Your grandmother sounds interesting. I think I'd like to meet her." Fatigue relaxed his body. He kissed her forehead and allowed his eyes to close.

Lily yawned and nestled against him. "Be careful what you wish for."

Chapter Eight

Cooper felt as if he'd just drifted to sleep when the faint stirring of daylight seeped into the jungle. Lazily he lay on the hard ground, holding Lily. Golden rays already warmed the morning air, the scent strong like moist soil. A break in the branches revealed mist shrouding a mountaintop. About an hour passed, and his thoughts remained on Lily and how much she had opened herself up to him, something he believed she didn't allow herself to do. Birds chattered away as the sun crept higher and the humidity grew heavier.

Lily moaned and stirred in his arms. He peered down at the scrape on her forehead then focused on her face, softened by sleep. Her dark lashes rested against the ivory planes of her cheeks. Her pretty pink lips parted. Even the slight moisture from her drool on his shoulder was a turn on.

There was something about this petite, fierce, exotic woman that drove him wild and crazy at the same time. Half the time he wanted to shake her for being such a pain, and the other half he hoped she would wrestle him to the ground and kiss him until he couldn't even name the elements of the periodic table.

Her hand shifted downward and relaxed on his abdomen. Her splayed fingers moved dangerously low, touching his waistband. He sucked in a breath. A man already had enough trouble with his anatomy in the morning without having a beautiful woman rubbing against him like a frisky cat with its favorite scratching post.

Okay, focus on something else. He listed the elements in his head: hydrogen, helium, lithium, beryllium—

"No, Cooper. Hmmm. Okay, that's nice." She moaned, arching against his side.

Oh, Lordy. He swallowed hard, battling against his desire. Lily was dreaming about him. What was he doing to her? He'd happily volunteer to reenact whatever it was that made her sound so breathless.

He shook his head. Where was he? Hydrogen, helium, lithium, beryllium, boron, carbon—

Over the soft flow of the waterfall, the sharp sound of snapping twigs ripped him out of his mental ramblings. Someone or something was coming. He scanned the floor near the stream and glanced higher at the trail that cut down the side of the mountain. He tensed but stayed lying flat. A figure dressed in camouflage, wearing a ball cap, hiked down toward the waterfall.

Covering Lily's mouth with his hand, he whispered against her ear. "Someone's nearby. Wake up."

She stiffened in his arms and peeled his hand off her mouth. He glanced her way and noted her eyes were alert. His gaze returned to the trail. A breeze caused the branches to sway and white flower petals and seedpods to helicopter down from the canopy. In gradual movements Cooper eased onto his belly. He studied the slender man hiking down the trail. He couldn't make out his ethnicity, because he wore long pants and a long-sleeved shirt. Although still a good two hundred feet away, Cooper noted there was something familiar about the man.

The knife? He looked back and frowned. The pocket-knife was gone from where he'd left it on the ground after he'd fallen asleep during guard duty. *Great! I'm just armed with my wit and Lily's claws.* He waited, anticipation humming through his body. Next to him, she hadn't moved a muscle. When the man reached the bottom, he took off his hat and scratched his brown hair secured in a ponytail. Cooper's posture relaxed, and he laughed. Lily flinched next to him and grabbed at his leg as he stood.

William jerked his head in their direction. "Damn it, Cooper. You scared the life right out of me."

"William?" Lily stood and slugged Cooper lightly in the shoulder. "You could have said something before you stood up like a big dope. Blasted man!"

Cooper peered at her other hand, and his eyes widened. She closed the blade of the pocketknife and stuck it into her back pocket. After Cooper hopped down, he reached up to assist her, but she shooed him away with the wave of her hand.

He approached William. "Fancy meeting you here."

William stuck his beer-mug-emblazoned cap back on his head. "Everything okay? Yesterday there were gunshots, and you disappeared." William's gaze bounced to Lily and back to Cooper. An invasion of red splotches spread over his stark-white neck.

"Are the villagers safe? Are the men gone?" Cooper asked, his humming nerves making his hands shake.

"No one was hurt. The gunmen searched for a while but then left the village."

"Thank God for that." The tension eased from Cooper's shoulders.

Lily joined them. "Good morning, William." Her eyes narrowed. The sun gleamed off her black hair that hung loosely down her back. Damn, even battered and tousled from sleep she was lovely.

"Um. Morning." William's gaze darted about. He seemed to find the surrounding jungle fascinating.

"So…how did you know where to find us?" She crossed her arms over her chest.

Cooper scratched the stubble on his chin. *Yeah, how in the heck did he find us?* Cooper widened his stance and scanned the vegetation. Had what he dismissed as embarrassment really been William looking for someone?

"Mary was worried. She told me about the cave Lily wanted to see. When you didn't return, I headed this way."

"That was nice of you to search for Cooper." Lily patted his arm, which made William brighten like a freshly changed bulb in the red-light district, and then Lily looked at Cooper, sincerity reflecting in her eyes. "And for Mary to be concerned about her friend."

Her statement made a smile tilt up on one corner of Cooper's mouth.

"Um, thanks," William said.

"Cooper's fine," Lily said. "Best you head back and go find that plant he's all worked up about."

Cooper rolled his eyes skyward. "*Ashwagandha.*"

"Yeah that one."

"Oh." William licked his chapped lips. "Well, I—"

Cooper crossed his arms "You're not his mommy. Why are you bossing him around?"

"I um, I—" William sputtered.

Cooper almost burst out laughing. The poor kid fidgeted with both pockets on his cargo pants.

"I was hardly being his mother. We have something to do this morning, and I know how much you want your work to keep moving forward—"

Ping! A bullet ricocheted off the granite ledge, sending chunks of rock flying. Pain slashed across Cooper's cheek as he dove for cover, shielding Lily the best he could. More shots rang out. Seeming to appear out of thin air, men materialized out of the jungle. With the cliff to their backs and surrounded, Cooper didn't bother to attempt to get away. Panic ran wild through him. "Just be quiet, let me do the talking, and don't make any sudden movements," he whispered to Lily and William.

Half a dozen armed men approached. The air suspended in Cooper's lungs, and his gaze traveled up a pair of camouflage cargo pants, past a bulging chest that strained against a threadbare T-shirt, and into the scarred face of the Samoan. A chill crept into Cooper's bones. This situation had just gotten worse. Way worse.

"Get up!" the Samoan barked, his mouth tight and his finger positioned on a pistol's trigger.

Cooper pushed to his feet, his heart pounding in double time, and stood in front of Lily. William also staggered to his feet.

"Dr. Cooper Deforest, we meet again so soon." The Samoan glared at him.

"It appears so." The hair stood up on the back of Cooper's neck. Was the Samoan after Lily, or had they wandered into Maximo's land holdings? This location hadn't been one of the areas he'd mentioned to Maximo.

The Samoan gestured with his head. "Who's he?"

"My assistant."

With lightning speed the Samoan lifted his gun to William's forehead and fired at point blank range. Cooper lunged in an attempt to shove William out of the way, but it was too late. William's body collapsed onto the ground.

"Noooo!" Cooper yelled and swung, connecting with the Samoan's jaw. Pain splintered into the back of Cooper's head, and he staggered. Next to him, he caught a glimpse of a dark-skinned man with dreadlocks lifting the butt of a semi-automatic rifle, ready to strike him again. He blinked the blur away that coated his vision. The warmth of blood trickled down his neck.

"Stop! Please, stop," Lily screamed, grabbing on to him. Nausea swam in Cooper's stomach. He heaved in deep breaths as he stared at William's unseeing eyes and the blood pooling around his friend's head and shoulders. Disbelief clung to his slow-moving mind. *What the hell just happened?*

The Samoan spat on the ground. "You will pay for that."

Cooper lifted his gaze to the murderer, and he wanted nothing more than to throw another punch. "You didn't have to kill him! You could have just said that I'd wandered into the wrong area!"

"Keep up. This isn't about you," the Samoan said. "It's about her."

Cooper hollered, "Then why did you kill him?"

"To get your attention. Would you have preferred I shot you?"

Cooper flexed his hands. His mind struggled to find a way out.

"Cooper, please," Lily whispered, still gripping his arm.

The Samoan smiled, revealing blood smeared across the front of his teeth. "You're lucky I have orders to capture you both alive. But as soon as Maximo gives the word, you're a dead man." The giant's black gaze shifted to Lily. "And Maximo especially wants to meet you, the little bitch who got the police sniffing around and cost him money. I look forward to making you beg for your death."

Cooper stepped in front of Lily, earning a laugh from the Samoan. Disbelief clogged his throat. Had the Samoan murdered the man at the lodge and kidnapped the boy? Cooper wanted to holler. Never in a million years would he have allowed Lily to look for the boy if he'd an inkling of whom she actually pursued.

"Are you her champion, too, Doctor?"

"Let him go. He has nothing to do with this. It's me Maximo wants," she blurted out, attempting to move in front of Cooper, but he held her back. "Cooper won't say anything; he just wants to go back to do his research."

"Lily, shut up!" Hadn't she just seen them shoot William? For whatever reason, Maximo wanted them alive. Unless she talked them out of it.

"He's an important doctor from a prominent university. You'd best let him go, or this will be all over the media—all over the American news—"

"You talk too much." The Samoan lifted his gun.

Cooper's heart stopped mid-beat. Thank God Lily wasn't stupid. She shut up. The gun lowered, and Cooper's knees almost buckled in relief.

"Bury the body," the Samoan said to one of his men and withdrew a walkie-talkie from his belt and spoke into it. "We have the Americans." The Samoan stepped away, and all Cooper heard was static and mumbled words.

He glanced down at Lily's pale face as tears trailed down her cheeks. Fear clogged his throat, making it difficult to breathe. Maximo was quite clear that he didn't give second chances. Technically this was a completely different issue, but if he were a betting man, he doubted Maximo would agree. How were they going to get out of this alive? He didn't like the answer that filtered into his brain: *we're not.*

"Get them to the cave," the Samoan ordered his men and hooked the walkie-talkie to his belt.

In no time Lily's and Cooper's wrists were bound in front of them, and gags cut into their mouths. A man shoved Cooper from behind, and with the others, he started hiking up the side of the mountain. The trail grew steeper, and in front of him, Lily slipped. A gunman with a shaved head yanked her up and pushed her, causing her to stumble before righting herself. Cooper glared at the gunman, who just smirked in return.

God help us. He started praying a mile a minute. The ground leveled out, and the path forked. Instead of heading toward Che Chem Ha Cave, they veered east on the trail. He peered down to the waterfall and had a perfect view of the granite ledge where they'd slept. Their discarded backpacks and her rumpled towel were the only evidence of their stay. His gaze strayed to the gunmen carrying William's body off.

Pain sliced into his chest. *Why?* The word echoed in his head.

At the top of the trail they came upon two men, and Cooper's step faltered. Next to a gunman stood an older man with coffee-colored skin and a white mustache.

"Xavier?" Cooper said, his words muffled by the gag. They'd captured Xavier, too. Anger tempted Cooper to strike the nearest gunman. *No, your hands are bound, and you have to think of Lily.*

"I'm sorry," Xavier said, in a hushed tone, his eyes lowered.

Sorry? Cooper stared at his friend. *Why is he sorry?*

"Move it!"

Cooper was shoved from behind.

Then the Samoan's deep voice came from farther back. "You were right, old man. She headed to the cave for the boy. Take this and go."

Cooper whipped his head around in time to see the Samoan toss an envelope at Xavier.

The older man's sad gaze met Cooper's. "I am sorry. I did not know you and William would be here. My Yesenia is very ill. The doctor says her heart is bad. I need the money, but I did not mean it to be like this."

Cooper's blood ran ice cold and seconds later boiling hot. The betrayal felt like a sucker punch to the gut. Rage clogged his throat. He hadn't realized he rushed Xavier until a guard swept his feet out from under him, and he slammed hard against the ground. Then a boot connected with his head, and Lily's scream penetrated through his wall of pain before everything faded into blackness.

• • •

The gunman with the shaved head released a low-hanging branch, and it slapped Lily in the face. The sting barely registered. After witnessing William's execution, numbness had settled throughout her body. She risked a glance back at Cooper. Blood dripped down his face. His limp form sagged between two men dragging him, and the tips of his hiking boots bounced against the ground.

Panic caused her thoughts to scatter in a million directions. She hadn't missed that the Samoan and Cooper seemed to know each other. Cooper said something about wandering into the wrong area. Regardless, this was her fault. Her throat constricted. *Come on, Cooper, wake up. What if he dies?* That waste of human flesh had kicked Cooper hard. Tears pricked the backs of her eyes. *Man up, girl! Think!* On autopilot, she stepped over an exposed root. Oblong leaves and pine needles crunched under her shoes. For the past fifteen minutes they'd headed away from the river on trails that zigzagged along the mountainside.

She had to find a way out of this, but what could she do? Without a doubt the Samoan would kill Cooper for spitting in his face. He'd killed poor William just for breathing. Lily swallowed hard and tried to squeeze her hands out of the rope bindings. She winced. All her twisting and pulling had managed to do was peel a layer of skin from her wrists.

The fools had bound her hands in front of her, which she could use to her advantage. Not that she could strangle anyone, because she was too short. The gunman in front of her wasn't too big, and he held his gun with a loose grip. Could she snatch it? How many of these knuckle-dragging apes could she shoot before her head met with a bullet? She released a frustrated sigh and followed the gunmen. With

Cooper unconscious, escape was impossible. And on top of that, her rash actions would get him killed.

The foliage grew denser with every step. The sunlight dimmed, and only sporadic patches escaped through the canopy. The walls of the path were so close the jungle touched both of her shoulders like reaching fingers attempting to halt her forward movement, trying to warn her of the impending doom. Dread lay heavily on her chest, making it difficult to breathe. They marched single file for a stretch of time as Lily battled with her thoughts. Perspiration trickled from her forehead and coated her skin. So hot, the air seemed to have stopped circulating inside the canopy. She glanced back. The men had changed their hold and now carried Cooper by his arms and legs like freshly caught game.

The gunman with dreadlocks, now behind her, gave her a nudge between the shoulders. "Eyes forward, girly."

She gritted her teeth and focused straight ahead. The walls of foliage widened to a well-traveled path, and her sneakers sank into the dense sand as she trudged onward. Periodically tire tread marks lay stamped into the white granules. It had to be from a quad or motorcycle. Someone had missed a few spots in their attempt the sweep away the evidence.

The path made an abrupt curve at a moss-covered boulder bordered by spiky ferns. From opposite sides, the jungle spit out two men armed to the hilt. Lily frowned and slowed her steps, only to receive another push. The camo-sporting men didn't look their way but shoved against the left side of the boulder. It slid away from the mountainside, ferns and all, and revealed the gaping mouth of a cave.

Lily shook her head and flexed her tingling fingers.

Although they were not too far from Che Chem Ha Cave, she and Cooper never would have found this location. She approached the crevice and examined the odd-looking boulder. It was fake. Possibly fiberglass. Roots and moss dangled from the stones above. She stepped across a flush metal track and followed the gunmen inside.

Initially, darkness hindered her vision, but once Lily's eyes adjusted, the natural skylights bathed the carved limestone walls enough to see without a flashlight. Magnificent chandelier-like stalactites draped from the ballroom-sized ceiling. A shallow stream flowed just inside the entrance. The gunman in front of her trekked through ankle-deep water the color of rust. Lily inhaled the faint scent of iron as she also crossed.

The cave forked. Without breaking stride, they headed right. Lights with yellow, glowing bulbs adorned the walls of the six-foot-wide tunnel. *This is insane. The lights must be run from a generator.* A musty smell like wet grass teased her senses. She pressed her face against her shoulder to stifle a sneeze.

The tunnel opened on one side to a beer-belly-shaped cavern filled with at least a dozen men and women who worked at tables under bright lamps. Some type of machinery hummed. On either side of them, crates stood stacked almost up to the ceiling. A couple of quads sat parked against the wall, and Lily caught a glimpse of a horizontal slash of light at the bottom of the cave wall. *Another false opening?* Oddly enough, several bunk beds bordered the farthest corner.

"Eyes forward!"

When she received a push to the side of her head

from the jerk with dreadlocks, Lily realized she'd stopped walking. She continued on but risked a backward glance. She squinted, attempting to find Cooper amongst the shadowed bodies of the gunmen. Panic caused her pulse to quicken. He wasn't there.

"Where's Cooper?" She whipped around.

Mr. Dreadlocks dug his fingers into her shoulder. "This is ya last warning, girly, before me not so nice."

She scowled and kept moving. Pain twisted in her stomach. They'd brought Cooper inside the cave. The gunmen must have taken him into the large cavern with the workers.

The tunnel branched off, and a stocky Hispanic man stood guard next to the narrow archway to another cavern. Past him, fans circulated the warm, floral-laden air. Lily caught a glimpse of workers between rows of plants that hung upside down from wires strung wall to wall. Marijuana? Cocaine? They both came from a plant. She knew little about the production of drugs, so she couldn't say for certain.

After walking past an empty chamber, they climbed down a ladder. Lily's heart sank with every step. They'd lost most of the entourage, and now she was being guarded by only two armed men. Would they shoot her and leave her body to rot? G-ma would never know what happened to her. She choked back a sob. What a mess she'd made. *Who will take care of G-ma?* The idea of helping someone else would never cross her sister's mind. Rae would at first, but they weren't even related.

Lily prayed. *God, find someone to take care of G-ma, and send in an army of kick-ass U.S. soldiers to wipe the floor with these maggots. Rescue Jaime and Cooper and, if I'm not pushing it, me.* The air grew cooler, heavier, and the light dimmer. Then in the distance came another tunnel entrance, not much taller than her and crisscrossed with iron bars. Her stomach plummeted. A cell, way down here? She eyed the man to her left then her right. Could she take them? Just kick Mr. Dreadlocks in the nuts and then elbow Baldy in the solar plexus. If the mangy dogs were rolling on the ground long enough, she could rush up the ladder and take out the other men.

Okay, the plan didn't leave her odds for survival very high, but neither did getting locked in a hole. She commanded the blood to flow to her numb fingers. Just as she decided to move, a faint whimper came from inside the cell where someone or something shifted. Her skin crawled. Had the creature been in there long enough to work up an appetite?

She stood frozen as the gate creaked open. The motion caused a handful of dirt to crumble down the walls. She snapped out of her trance, and in a swift motion, she twisted, and her elbow connected with the body behind her. She swung her bound hands downward in the opposite direction but missed her target. With a forceful shove to the shoulder, she found herself sprawled on the ground inside the cell. Pain cut into her bound hands, and her chin bounced off the floor. She shook her dazed head.

"Ya missed Tazman, girly." Mr. Dreadlocks chuckled.

Behind him Baldy's hands were planted on his knees, and he gasped for air. In the dirt near his feet lay his gun. *If I could have grabbed it, the soil would have benefited from new fertilizer.*

Lily pushed to her feet and rushed back to the now-closed bars. "You're right. Don't worry. Next time, I'll go for you first."

Mr. Dreadlocks, or as he called himself Tazman, flashed a brown-toothed smile and strode off.

"This isn't over." After shooting her a glare, Baldy followed.

Do something! What if they just leave you here to starve? "Where are you going you...you mentally challenged goats? Get back here!" One man climbed up the ladder, then the other. Desperation burst in her chest. "Your momma is a—"

Something shuffled behind her, and she spun around. The cell was shaped like a macaroni noodle, and whatever made that sound stayed out of sight in the shadow of the bend. The single light fixture caged in metal strips glowed several feet above her head. She took a step—*ping!* Lily glanced down. Water slopped over the sides of the metal bowl her foot had connected with. Next to it sat an empty bowl with crusted food around the edges.

"Here, doggy." She gave a weak whistle, hoping it wasn't Cujo. She lifted her chin and ignored the nervousness that dive-bombed into her stomach like kamikaze moths. *I have to face my fate head-on.* Placing one foot after the other, she rounded the bend. Her gaze met the back wall riddled with lengthy shadows. She swallowed and prepared to defend herself by lifting her bound hands in front of her chest. With a sidestep, she allowed for the light to filter past her and into the shadow near the ground. The sight robbed her of breath. A child with dirt streaked down his face huddled in the corner. His golden eyes widened as he released an ear-piercing scream.

• • •

Cooper rested on his knees, his arms stretched out by tight chains secured to opposite edges of the limestone wall at his back, inside a chamber about twelve feet in diameter. Blood and dirt covered his T-shirt and swim trunks. Pain knifed into his head. His left eye was almost swollen shut and hurt like the devil. The Samoan had thrown a sucker punch when Cooper had been chained, and for a few minutes the impact had made bile fill his throat. He knew more blows were to come, or worse, but he could deal with the physical pain.

Just thinking about William's senseless murder and Xavier's betrayal released a tidal wave of anger that threatened to shut down his brain. So he held it at bay. Right now he had to keep it together for Lily. He had to do something. He couldn't even fathom the thought of her being struck, raped, and other ungodly things. Was she calling for him— begging for help this very second? The possibility stole his breath, and anguish gnawed at his gut. He gritted his teeth and yanked repeatedly on the chains, but the bolts held firm. He collapsed, his back propped against the rough wall, and tried to ignore the burning sensation sawing into his arm muscles.

The hum of machinery and raised voices seeped through the wooden door. Two men spoke with heated words.

"Like I told your man, you cannot kill the Americans, but if you would have taken my call yesterday, I would not have had to hike out here and been eaten by mosquitos."

"You sweaty roll of lard, have you forgotten who secured your job as a superintendent of police for the Cayo Formation?"

Cooper tensed. Without question he recognized Maximo's smooth, sophisticated tones.

"You cannot kill the Americans," said the superintendent. "It will draw too much attention to the area. The girl is no worry. She's nobody and will rot away in prison…"

Their voices lowered, and Cooper leaned forward in an attempt to distinguish the words. The chains clanked with his movement, and he winced.

"I don't care that Deforest's father has international connections," Maximo said. "I pay you handsomely to deal with these kinds of things. I can't have witnesses roaming about, now can I?"

"Maxi, it will be a bigger problem when patrols search the jungles down the Macal River and stumble into your precious crops."

"Don't threaten me!"

Cooper lost the rest of the conversation to the rev of a motor from what sounded like a forklift. So he waited, hoping like crazy that the superintendent, although corrupt, had talked Maximo out of killing them. Cooper struggled to see through the swollen eye when the wooden door creaked open and an armed guard stepped aside. Dread lurched in Cooper's stomach as Maximo entered, dressed in a white button-down shirt and gray slacks. The drug lord lifted his hand to his nose as if to block the stink of blood and sweat inside the room. The Samoan closed the door, leaned against the rock wall, and crossed his bulky arms.

"Doctor, I wasn't expecting us to meet again so soon. I must say your eye is an interesting shade of blue, or is that purple?" Maximo arched a thick brow and glanced at his head of security. "I see you two have been chatting."

The Samoan shrugged a massive shoulder. His shaved head almost touched the overhead light screwed into the low stone ceiling.

Maximo refocused his attention on Cooper. "Excuse my manners, Dr. Deforest, for making you wait so long." He stuck his hands inside the pockets of his slacks. "It seems you have had an unfortunate turn of events."

"Nothing that..." Cooper cleared his dry throat. "We can't work out."

"Always an optimist, aren't you?" Maximo frowned. "Unchain him."

The Samoan handed his weapon to Maximo and did as instructed.

The locks released from his wrists, and Cooper fell to the ground. *Come on.* He commanded himself to sit up, to face whatever was coming head on—like a man. After a few failed attempts, Cooper propped himself up against the wall.

Maximo relinquished the weapon to the Samoan. "Your work must be important if the government issued you a permit. Those can be impossible to secure."

The statement puzzled Cooper. Why did Maximo care about how challenging it had been to get his permit? Unsure if a response was wise, Cooper kept quiet.

Maximo continued, "The government believes you are a troublemaker, and they are ready to cancel the permit and ban you and your associates from the country."

Cooper stiffened. Maximo had the law in his pocket. Would he use it to ruin Cooper's chance to conduct research? No matter. He'd deal with that issue later. Right now his life and Lily's took precedence.

"But..." Maximo lifted his index finger into the air. "I am very well connected, and I believe a person has a right to pursue his dreams. I think your research must go on, and

I will even donate money to the cause."

Cooper slid a glance at the Samoan, who observed with detached interest, and then back to Maximo.

"You do want to continue your research, don't you?" Maximo snapped.

With lowered brows, the Samoan took a step closer.

"Yes." Cooper struggled to keep his voice steady and strong.

Maximo straightened the sleeve of his shirt. "Good, good. Then if that is the case, this is what needs to happen. You will forget about this misunderstanding and return to your research with a generous donation of ten thousand American dollars."

Another bribe. Cooper had expected a bullet, not a handful of cash, so this situation was definitely looking up. At least for himself. All because his father had served as a minister with Global Ministries at the United Nations and was on a first name basis with many Central American leaders, including the prime minister of Belize. Usually living in his father's shadow bothered him, but in this instance, he was eternally grateful. But would it also save Lily? His insides clenched into tight knots. "What about Lily?"

"She's none of your concern."

Like hell would he leave her with these monsters. "She comes with me."

Maximo laughed. "Without a doubt you have guts, but you don't give the orders." His expression instantly sobered. "She stays."

Cooper tossed caution aside. "If you think I'll walk out of here and let you kill her—"

"Ah, now I see. Let me put your conscience at ease. I will

not kill her. She is wanted by the police for drug smuggling."
He made a *tsking* sound. "As a citizen, I have to turn her
over to the local authorities. It's out of both of our hands."

Cooper shifted his exhausted body, his gaze growing watery from his swollen eye. His first instinct was to fight, but
he was wise enough to know he had to use his wits if Lily
had any chance. He had a good idea of the location of this
cave. He'd awakened on the path, before entering through
the fake rock entrance, long enough to observe his surroundings and note the direction of the river's muffled roar.
After they released him, he would double back for Lily. Or if
he was close enough to a dwelling or lodge, he could phone
the police. Cooper rubbed a hand over the raw skin on his
wrist. He'd best not be completely agreeable, or he'd make
Maximo suspicious. "So you're just going to let me go? How
do you know I won't go to the authorities?"

"Because you aren't a stupid man, and you're wise
enough to know when things are out of your power and
can't be changed." Maximo pursed his lips and let the silence
stretch. "But just so you know the severity of the situation,
I'll make you a promise. If you say a single word about what
has occurred, not only will Miss Sanborn meet with a violent
death—"

A burst of adrenalin had Cooper on his feet. "If you so
much as touch a hair on Lily's head—"

In a quick motion, the Samoan had the barrel of the
pistol pressed to Cooper's forehead.

Cooper's legs shook as he stared straight ahead.

"If you talk to the police," Maximo said in a matter-
of-fact tone, "Your beloved villagers—men, women, and
precious children—will be executed by a rogue band of

rebels. Very tragic, and the police will find no leads. Do you understand?"

Cooper's heart clenched. "Clearly."

The Samoan stepped back, lowering the pistol to his side.

Cooper's legs gave out, and he collapsed onto the ground. He clamped his eyes closed to fight the nausea sloshing in his stomach.

"Well done. See, this was very civil," Maximo said, his voice strangely sounding as if he spoke in a tunnel. "Did you blindfold him en route to the cave?"

"He was unconscious," the Samoan said, his voice sounding distant.

"Good. Then that's how he shall exit."

Cooper released a breath and peered up just as the Samoan's massive boot connected with his head.

Chapter Nine

Lily rested near the gate of the cell while Jaime slept in a huddled form across the narrow cave. The poor boy had hollered so long, he'd worn himself out. Hours had passed, and not one of the guards had checked on them. Now that she'd found Jaime, her worries bounced between Cooper and finding a way to escape. She licked her dry lips and glanced at the remaining water she hadn't spilled out of the bowl. If it were just her in here, she'd drink it, but Jaime would need hydration.

The boy stirred, whimpered, and rubbed his small fists against his eyes.

Lily held her breath.

After yawning, Jaime's gaze locked on to hers.

"Shh, shh. I'm not going to hurt you," she said, only for Jaime to start crying. "Don't you remember me?"

He wrapped his thin arms around himself, pressing his little body closer to the abrasive rock of the cave. "I want my mommy!" he howled louder.

"I know, sweetie. Do you remember me from the lodge?" With her hands still bound in front of her, Lily teetered to her feet. She moved forward, allowing the overhead light to shine over her features. "Jaime, remember you came to my patio and wanted to play dinosaurs? Your fath—" She chided herself. *You idiot! Don't talk about his father! Jaime may have witnessed his murder.* "And at breakfast we saw birds."

Jaime's cry cut off, and little tear trails migrated down his dirty cheeks. He nodded, sending the unruly brown locks floating about his head. "Bird eat me."

She smiled and subtly stepped toward him. "A bird won't eat you. You're big. How old are you?"

He stuck his thumb in his mouth and held up four fingers with his other hand.

"Wow, four! You're a big boy." She conducted a visual assessment of his person.

Jaime didn't look hurt, and although he was dirty and appeared to be treated no better than a dog, at least he'd been given food and water. He sat on top of a thin blanket. She worried her lower lip. What did the drug lord want Jaime for? And the bigger question: how was she going to get them out of here? She didn't even know where Cooper was. Her heart constricted, and guilt flooded her mind at the memory of his bleeding, unconscious body.

Lily gathered her loose strands and pulled them across her shoulder. "May I sit down next to you?"

Without removing his thumb from his mouth, he vigorously shook his head.

She sighed. *And I thought I'd made progress.* "Well, okay, but I hope we can be friends. Like when you visited me, and we saw the caterpillar."

The sound of approaching footsteps caused Lily to plant herself in front of Jaime. He released a whimper. "It's okay, sweetie, I won't let them hurt you," she whispered. She twisted her body trying to get her bound hands to her rear pocket. If only she could grab the pocketknife. All she managed to do was send a shooting pain into her lower back. Frustrated, she straightened.

Jaime! Just as she started to ask him to get the knife from her pocket, the iron gate squeaked open. Lily's heart thundered in her chest, and she fought to swallow. Armed with a scowl and a gun, the Samoan ducked his head to enter. She met his scowl and widened her stance. A man dressed like a banker also stepped inside. The Samoan leaned against the wall, his black eyes watching. He kept the barrel of the gun aimed at her. *Thank God I didn't pull out the pocketknife.* The dandy in the dress clothes stopped just short of her. His clear, brown eyes appraised Lily from the top of her head to her dirty sneakers.

This must be the drug lord. He doesn't stink like the rest of them, and he struts like a rooster. The angles of his face and lighter skin color leaned toward Spanish heritage. With close-cut brown hair, he was handsome, if you were into sociopathic drug dealers. She scowled. To her he was as appealing as a heap of steaming manure.

"Well, I wasn't expecting you to be such a beauty, Miss Sanborn, that is once you rinse off all of the dirt," he said, his accent very smooth. A faint smile tilted the corners of his lips, and his nose scrunched up.

Lily wanted to tell him to go screw off, but she had Jaime to think of, so she kept silent.

"Let me introduce myself. I'm Maximo." He gave a slight bow.

Did he expect her to applaud? Anger simmered in her belly. "Are you the man who kidnaps babies and locks them in cages?" As soon as the words flew out of her mouth, she wished she could reel them in. *This man is unpredictable, and in a snap, he could hurt Jaime.*

Maximo tensed, his mouth tightening.

Lily stepped closer to him and plastered on a smile. *Go for the ego.* "You look out of place amongst this riffraff. Kind of like a…" She racked her brain for a comparison. "A peacock amongst sparrows." That hadn't come out right. *Shut up, Lily!* She took another step and forced her eyes to gleam.

The Samoan straightened. "That's far enough."

Maximo rubbed his jaw with a hand missing two digits. Lily battled against the urge to poke out his eyes as they lingered on her breasts through her green tank top.

"You'll have to excuse my bodyguard. Safety supersedes manners, I'm afraid."

This man was delusional. He spoke of manners when his bodyguard had killed William in cold blood. The image sent a chill down her spine. *This isn't a game. Be smart.* "Mr. Maxim—"

"Please, it's just Maximo."

Ugh! "Maximo, I want to go home. This is your country and none of my business. So if you'll just let Jaime, Cooper, and me go, we'll be on our way."

"You know the child?"

"Yes. We're related."

"Really, you're different ethnicities."

She clenched her teeth. "I'm adopted."

His body shook with laughter. "I love watching a woman's manipulative mind in action. But you had best avoid a lying tongue; it will wrap around your neck and strangle the life right out of you." The smile dropped off his face. "I know for a fact this boy is not related to you. His deceased father, who met an unfortunate end for being a spy, was once married to the sister of my competition in Guatemala. So you see, the leverage of a nephew will be useful for future business dealings."

Lily struggled to digest this news. She'd risked Cooper's and her lives to save the child from a drug lord only for him to return safely to his own drug lord family. *What is wrong with these people?*

Maximo angled his head, tapping his index finger against his mouth. "You said Cooper? Would that be Dr. Deforest?"

"Yes." Lily decided it didn't matter that Jaime came from a drug lord family. She still had to get him out of this situation. Maybe he could be taken someplace safe, like an orphanage, although that thought didn't sit well with her.

"I already released the doctor."

Tension eased out of her shoulders.

The hint of pity that reflected in Maximo's eyes made her uneasy. "Once I offered the doctor a generous monetary donation, which I might add is not the first time he's accepted money from me, and reassurance his research permit wouldn't be withdrawn, he was more than willing to forget about this misunderstanding."

A crushing pressure built up in her chest. No! Maximo was lying, Cooper wouldn't accept a bribe.

"He looked relieved when he left. Research is his life after all. Sometimes we men allow our priorities to be swayed by beauty."

The truth pierced Lily's heart like an arrow: the most important thing to Cooper was his research. Tears pricked the backs of her eyes. The bitter taste of his abandonment clogged her throat.

"However, it would take a bigger bribe than ten thousand American dollars to tempt me to leave a beautiful woman to her dark fate." Maximo approached and captured a strand of her hair. "As I imagined: silky." His hand dropped, triumph gleaming in his eyes. "I'm going to make you a promise. I won't leave you in prison for long before I stop by with a proposal."

Prison? Why would I go to prison?

Before she could voice the question Maximo continued. "And if you can satisfy me in bed—"

She stiffened. "The only thing that satisfies a pig is shitty mud." The words flew out before she could stop them.

In a split second, Maximo's hand wrapped around her neck and squeezed. The pressure cut off her breath, forcing a faint gasp to rush from her throat. She grew lightheaded, and tremors rioted across her body. Her short nails clawed at his wrist. He loosened his hold, and she took in a sharp breath.

Maximo leaned closer to her ear and whispered, "I hope prison doesn't take all that fight out of you. I look forward to breaking your will." His thumb brushed against her lower lip. Desire flared in his eyes.

"Let go of me," she said with bravado she didn't feel. Behind her Jaime whimpered.

"Until then." Maximo winked, told the Samoan to untie her, and left.

• • •

Cooper struggled to open his eyes and only one seemed to work. The other felt sealed shut by cement. Pain jabbed inside his head as if prodded by spears. He touched his face and flinched. After a moment his vision cleared in his uninjured eye. A breeze cooled his skin. Above him the outline of trees reached toward a gray sky. Gradually the sky lightened. After the confusion had subsided, he realized he lay on a granite slab just outside of the village.

It was morning. He struggled to recall the day. It had to be Thursday. That meant he'd been unconscious twelve hours. He vaguely remembered waking a few times to pitch black only to fall asleep again. Memories of his encounter with Maximo surfaced. *Lily!* Panic surged through him, but his sluggish body struggled to move.

What had he been thinking taking her to that cave? Okay, he hadn't known she wanted to take on the Samoan, but he'd known whoever it was had murdered someone and kidnapped a child. Cooper was a scientist, and he'd let the determined glint in her lovely eyes sway his good judgment. He should have protected Lily, even from herself. If he had, she'd be with him right now, and he'd be kissing the feistiness right out of her.

After several failed attempts, he staggered to his feet. Nausea sloshed in his stomach, and he fought a gag. Cooper closed his eyes. *Breathe in, and breathe out.* It didn't help. His stomach convulsed, and he bent over and vomited. Only his grip on a tree trunk kept him upright. After the sick feeling retreated, he ventured down the dirt path sprinkled with clumps of grass. Each step taxed his battered body.

He touched the side of his head and winced when he came in contact with a bump the size of a golf ball. He paused and waited. *Come on, I can do this.* After it took what seemed like an hour to walk two blocks, the first shacks lifted from the ground by stilts came into view. If his guess was correct, his last encounter with Maximo had been yesterday. Maximo's men must have dumped him on the rock as an offering to the nocturnal creatures. Luckily a jaguar hadn't caught the scent of the blood and eaten him as he lay defenseless.

He struggled to keep moving. His pace slowed as if he'd stepped in quicksand. A cold lump of dread lodged in his belly. He needed to get to Lily, but how? He'd already lost two friends to murder and betrayal. Who could he trust? Just as he entered the heart of the village, his knees buckled, and he fell to the ground. Cool dirt connected with his cheek. His labored breathing shot pain into his lungs as his vision distorted.

"Oh, no, Cooper!" A female voice came from nearby and then the sound of rapid footsteps. Someone turned him over, and smooth fingers touched his neck.

"Is he dead?" a man asked.

"No. He's alive. Cooper, can you hear me?" He recognized that soft voice. As hard as he tried, his fogged brain couldn't conjure a name. He tried to talk but only produced a groan. Then he was lifted. He released a sigh of relief when his body met a soft surface and everything faded into nothingness.

• • •

"Cooper, please wake up." A smooth hand touched his cheek.

He pried his eyes open only to snap them shut at the pain. Cooper drew in a deep breath and looked again. "Mary?" *Is that my voice?*

Concerned, brown eyes peered down at him. "Oh, thank goodness." She tossed her thick braid over her shoulder. A woman of efficiency, Mary already had a glass of water with a straw to his mouth.

He drank. His dry throat absorbed the first mouthful, so he drank more, only to choke. She removed the glass, and he licked the water that dripped down his lip. Glancing past Mary, he realized he was in his tent. "How did I get here?" Some of the gravel had left his voice, leaving him sounding more like himself.

"You collapsed this morning outside my restaurant."

He frowned, racking his memory. If he'd walked into the village, where had he come from?

"I had *the piai-man* look at you, and he gave you healing herbs. It took forever to get the tea down your throat."

Cooper groaned. Great, just what he needed: some concoction swimming around his stomach from a local priest-doctor.

"Do not be like that. You look horrible, and he is the best we have. What happened to you? You disappeared after the gunmen came two days ago…and I…and I thought…"

He reached out and squeezed her hand. "A lot has happened. I have to go…Lily!" He needed to get to her. Cooper sat upright then wished he hadn't. He grabbed Mary as the inside of the tent spun. He grimaced and gulped in mouthfuls of air in an attempt to keep the nausea at bay.

"Lily is not here. I sent William to find you, but he never came back."

"He's dead."

She gasped, her hands flying to her mouth. "William? Are-are you sure?"

He peered into her widened eyes and read the horror. "I'm sorry, Mary." *I am such an ass. How can I have been so thoughtless?* Although on the verge of collapse, he wrapped his arms around her. "Yes, I'm sure." He fought to push the graphic image of William's dead body from his mind. "Someone shot him."

"Oh, no. He is...was so..." Her sob shook his body. "He was good and considerate. Not like most of the young men in the village."

"I know. I'm sorry, sweetheart." His eyes blurred as he rested his head on top of hers. He would have to call the university. He would have to tell William's parents, whom he'd met once at a fundraiser for the department. Sorrow twisted in his gut. Time stretched out. Maybe this would all be a bad dream, and he'd wake up. The only thing he wouldn't change was meeting Lily. Someone called Mary's name from outside the tent. He lowered his arms. She swiped at her cheeks and slipped out. Cooper's energy drained, and he fell back onto the cot. She returned with a bowl of steaming soup. Through the slit of the swaying tent flap, he noticed how gray it had gotten outside.

How had it become so late? Panic set in as he struggled to get up. "I have to leave. My boat! Is it still on the dock?"

She narrowed her red-rimmed eyes at him. "No, it was stolen. Now, you have to eat this soup."

"I have to find Lily."

"And get killed like—" Mary sucked in a breath and set the bowl on the lid of a crate near the bed.

"I can't just leave her there. I need to contact the police and then…" He lifted a hand into the air.

Her brows drew together. "When Pedro returned from the hunt, I told him to go to the closest lodge to call the police. He just went to tell his mother, and then he'll leave. Pedro's fast and has a flashlight, but the police won't come 'til morning, so you can tell them then about William and Lily."

After her words registered, Cooper grasped her wrist. "How long ago was this?"

"Just now, before I came back in."

"Stop him. Tell him not to call the local police. They're bad. He has to call the headquarters in Belmopan and ask for an inspector. Tell them the American, Dr. Deforest of Berkeley University, said the local police are taking bribes, and his life is in danger." Would the inspector care? He didn't know.

A crease marred her forehead.

"And I need to use your gun," Cooper added.

"Is that wise?"

Mary had never questioned his request—but then again, he'd only been using it as protection on days he went deep into the jungle. "Please just tell Pedro and bring the gun."

"I will see to it." With that Mary slipped out the tent flap.

Cooper glanced down at the *escabeche* soup. He spooned in several bites. Usually he enjoyed the flavor, but he barely tasted the chicken in the white sugarcane vinegar. Did he have the strength to hike back to the cave? Even without the difficulty of traveling at night, he feared he wouldn't make it on foot. The two rivers and dense forest made reaching the village by vehicle impossible, so having someone pick him up was out. The isolation lent to the charm of the village, but right now, it just created more problems. He only had one choice: he could make it to the closest lodge in the footsteps of Pedro and pay someone with a four-wheel-drive vehicle to take him over the creviced dirt road that ended about five miles from the suspected cave.

It doesn't matter how long it takes. I'm going back for Lily. Within five minutes he peeled off his blood-covered T-shirt and dropped it onto the floor. After donning a clean, sand-colored shirt and gray cargo shorts, he snatched a flashlight and strode out of the tent. His hiking boots felt as heavy as bricks, and sweat trickled into his eyes. The evening air was cooler, so why was he so hot? He clicked on the flashlight, and the beam lit a wide span. He'd made it to Mary's just as she came out of the door with the gun pointing toward the ground.

"I told Pedro," she said.

"Thanks." He accepted the gun, slipped it in his rear waistband, and walked down the dirt pathway.

"Please don't do this," Mary said from behind him.

"I have to go," he rasped and kept moving. He fought to place one foot in front of the other. *Come on, damn it!*

"Cooper, stop!" Mary said again.

He staggered. Before him, the road turned to dark liquid, and he felt himself falling.

. . .

Lily woke up with a start on the cool, hard ground. The iron bars slammed before her, and the figure of a short man retreated into the shadows of the corridor. A freshly emptied tin pot wobbled a rotation before settling. Yesterday they were given that luxury to use after she'd demanded to relieve herself. Prior to this, Jaime had proudly informed her he'd just peed on the cave walls. That explained the potent odor.

Without a light source, Lily could only guess about the time of day. She assumed the man wouldn't empty their pee pot in the middle of the night, so it must now be sometime Friday morning. Her pulse throbbed against her temples. Would she and Jaime die in this cell? Hurt and anger twisted through her. Cooper had ditched her—been paid off—and just left her to rot in this hellhole.

Jaime stirred in her arms, and she lifted the thin blanket up to cover his narrow shoulders. Earlier when he'd gotten tired, he'd surprised Lily by plopping down on her lap, sticking his thumb in his mouth, and drifting to sleep. She sighed and brushed a wayward lock out of his face. His little thumb lay halfway out of his lax mouth. *Poor baby. No child should have to endure such cruelty.*

Her stomach growled, reminding her of the meager dinner they'd been given in bowls. She and Jaime had scooped up the runny, peppered-looking mud with relish. If she hadn't been so famished, she would have thrown the bowl, food and all, at the smirking guard's head. *How dare they treat them like animals!*

They needed to escape today before she and Jaime were separated. Lily considered the knife still in her back pocket. Thrusting the blade into the guard's neck would surely kill him. But could she kill the guard in front of Jaime? As an embalmer, she lived with death day in and day out, but taking a life was not the same thing. Weariness settled over her.

At this point, if they were to live, she didn't have much of a choice.

Jaime stretched his arms, and his golden eyes blinked up at her.

"Good morning, sweetie."

He sat up and stared at her.

What could be going on in that mind of his? Her suspense didn't last long.

Two seconds later his eyes teared up. "I want my mommy."

She patted his shoulder. "I know. Hopefully soon."

His little lip quivered. "I want my daddy."

Lily ran a hand through her knotted hair, unsure of how to respond. In the end, she decided to go with the truth. "Your daddy's in Heaven." Okay, maybe it wasn't the truth. Who knew? But she wasn't going to tell this little guy his dad was frying like a greasy slab of pork in Hell.

"Daddy hurts. The wope choked Daddy here." He pointed to his neck as a tear trickled down his cheek.

Her heart broke, knowing he'd witnessed his father's murder. "I'm sorry. Those men were bad."

More tears slid winding paths down his somber face. Lily kissed the top of his head, his soft brown curls tickling her nose. She eased back and forced a smile. *Time to change the subject before I start crying along with him.* "Where's your mother?" How much did a four-year-old know? Could he tell her the name of his hometown? She waited, but he didn't respond. "Jaime, do you know where your mom is?"

He nodded.

"Good, where?"

"Home."

"And where's that?"

He lifted a hand into the air and pointed.

"In the cave?"

His face scrunched up, and he looked at her as if she didn't have all of her crayons in the Crayola box. "Nooo, not the cave! Mommy is at my *house*."

Okay, next question. Nothing like being made to feel like a half-wit by a kid who'd barely earned his potty training certificate. "Do you have any brothers or sisters?"

Jaime nodded, picking at a scab on his shin.

"How many?"

He held up all of his fingers.

Lily's eyes widened. "Ten? You have ten brothers and sisters?"

"Ummhmm."

"What are their names?"

"Don't ya know? Everybody knows that," he said with a frown.

"How can I know their names when I haven't been to your home?" She poked him softly in the stomach, and he released a giggle. "Tell me their names."

"Feeodore, Sonya, and Patches."

Lily pursed her lips. "Is Patches your brother or sister?"

He laughed at that. "He's gotta tail."

"Sounds serious. Has he seen a doctor?"

Jaime shook his head. "He's a dog."

Lily made a dramatic swipe of her forehead. "Thank goodness. I was afraid you were going to grow a tail, too."

His big grin caused her heart to swell.

"No, I'm a boy." He stood and brushed off his knobby knees below his blue shorts. The face of the Mickey Mouse character on his T-shirt was as dirty as Jaime's.

Lily had just gained her feet when approaching footfalls sounded. She knelt in front of Jaime and whispered in his ear. "Go to the back of the cave, and be very quiet. When I call you, I want you to come to me really fast, okay?" He nodded and scurried to the rear of the cave. Keys clanked together, and the gate pushed open. Lily recognized the single guard who held a pot in his hand with a spoon resting against its side. Baldy. The same man she'd elbowed in the midsection. From the hostile look in his narrowed eyes, it appeared he still had hard feelings. He was about five inches taller than her with a slight frame. *I can take him. I have to do it now; I'll never have a better chance.*

As inconspicuously as possible, she reached into her pocket and removed the knife. Nimbly, her fingers opened the concealed blade. He stepped inside and kept his hard gaze glued to her. His mouth spread into a thin-lipped smile. *Plop!* He dished out a scoop of white slop, allowing more to land in the dirt than in the bowls. Lily wanted to slap the smirk off his face. He was only two feet away from the open gate, how could she get him to come closer? If she rushed him now, he'd most likely make it outside the gate before she could reach him.

The man straightened and tapped the spoon against the pot. She ignored the loud call from her growling stomach. "You hungry, girl?"

"Yes."

"How bad do you want the food?"

"Bad." *What is he up to?*

He set down the pot. "Take off your shorts."

This pig must think he had some really good oatmeal. She tried to calm her skittering pulse. "Isn't there another way?" She made her lip quiver.

"As I see it, you owe me. I should beat you but…" He grabbed himself and made a grinding motion with his hips. "You just make me happy, and I will feed you real good." He stepped closer, his gaze feasting upon her bare legs and resting on her breasts.

She tightened her grip on the knife handle. *This guy is a good candidate for my first attempt at castration.* He stopped a hairsbreadth away from her. The smell of his unwashed body caused her gag reflex to yo-yo.

"So ripe," he murmured. His hand squeezed her breast, and she tensed.

With a growl, she kneed him in the balls and plunged the blade into his upper back.

He doubled over and grabbed at his shoulder, yelling in pain.

Someone's going to hear him. Panic pumped through her veins. She swooped down and snatched the tin chamber pot. She drew back and whacked him in the head. *Ding!* He hit the dirt floor with a thud. Lily panted, staring in astonishment at his sprawled body. Seconds stretched out, but he didn't move. Then Jaime started crying.

Snap out of it! She dropped the chamber pot. She started to retrieve the knife from the loser's back but then thought better of it. She couldn't bring herself to traumatize Jaime further. "Come on, sweetie, hurry. Let's go find your mommy."

He was at her side in a flash. She grabbed his hand, and they rushed out of the cell. After locking the gate to buy them time, she glanced at Jaime, who looked on the verge of hysteria.

She leaned down and whispered into his ear. "If we're quiet, we can go find your mommy, okay?"

He sucked in his breath and nodded. She peered up the ladder. *All clear.* With Jaime securely in front of her, they progressed up the ladder at snail speed. More than once she had to pry his death grip from the wooden rungs. At the top she poked her head up and glanced in both directions. *No one about.* They made it to their feet and pressed their bodies near the edge of the tunnel. The plant drying room would come first. The chances of a guard not being at the post were slim, and she prayed she didn't run into a worker.

The limestone scratched Lily's bare arms as she slunk along. With his hand still in hers, Jaime kept up his pace. The archway of the drying room came into sight. She crept closer. The guard dressed in army green had his back to her, eating. She scooped Jaime into her arms and rushed past. Jaime's legs wrapped around her waist, and he started to speak, but she covered his mouth in time to muffle his words.

"Shhh," she whispered into his ear.

She glanced back, but the guard hadn't appeared. Perspiration beaded across her forehead, and tension stiffened every muscle in her body. The musty smell like wet grass teased her senses. The other tunnel that had earlier been filled with workers was near, but this time she didn't hear the sound of machinery, just the low murmur of voices. Jaime buried his face in her neck. She shifted his light frame in her arms.

Pausing at the opening, she peeked into the beer-belly shaped cavern. She blinked against the bright light. The false door stood wide open. The workers on the far side of the room carried crates onto several trailers towed by quads.

Delivery day? Lily took a deep breath, and when she was sure everyone's focus was toward the outside, she scurried by.

"Almost done, sweetie," she whispered.

The faint glow from the lamps adorning the cave walls now seemed like search lights beaming down on her. A twig cracked under the weight of her shoe, and she winced. She crept toward the opening of the tunnel. Sunrays slanted inside. Her nerves fluttered about. *I can do this. Please, God, don't let armed men be posted in front.* Water licked at her ankles as she hurried across the stream. Pressing her body against the cave wall, she patted Jaime's shoulder. As she leaned out to peer through the roots draping from the cave's entrance, she collided with a man.

Chapter Ten

Cooper clamped a hand over Lily's mouth to muffle her gasp. As she stumbled back, he tucked the gun into his rear waistband with barely enough time to steady her. Her eyes widened in horror for a split second, but upon recognition, she visibly relaxed. Relief washed over him. Other than smudges of dirt, dark rings under her eyes, and the scrape on her forehead, she looked no worse for wear.

Rescuing her had been easier than he'd imagined. A bit of disappointment surfaced. His inner macho man had envisioned himself dodging bullets in a flurry of action, tossing her limp body over his shoulder, and with a kick, knocking a hole in the cave wall to escape through. Instead after he'd dealt with a single guard, she'd strolled right up to him. He'd written scientific reports more difficult than this. The realistic side of him pointed out that he had zero training in self-defense and counted his blessings that, for whatever reason, Maximo's men were elsewhere.

The child in her arms whimpered, redirecting Cooper's attention. *Please don't cry kid, or we might as well sound a blow horn.* He dropped his hand from her mouth. "Hurry."

They rushed out of the cave's opening. She glanced at the downed man sprawled on the ground.

"He's not dead. Come on." He felt like hell for knocking the man in the head with a thick branch, but it couldn't be helped.

With her arms filled with the boy, Cooper could only grasp her elbow. Together they jogged through the lush broadleaf jungle. With every breath, humidity coated his lungs. The path narrowed, and he took the lead. Crooked branches snagged his clothes and scratched his flesh. He closed his mouth and sprinted through a swarm of gnats hovering near a plant with flowers resembling lobster claws. He paused and waited precious seconds for Lily to catch up. The urgency of the situation made Cooper's jaw muscle tick. His grandmother, cane and all, could catch them at this pace.

"Let me take him."

"He's quiet. Let's keep moving," she said.

Cooper wanted to argue, but she passed him, so he continued onward. The woman was stubborn, plain and simple.

"I'm surprised you came back."

"What's that supposed to mean?" He frowned as he skirted a spot of moist soil on the ground, cautious not to leave a footprint.

"Maximo was very forthcoming about the bribe you accepted and how easily you were willing to abandon us."

Cooper tensed and held a branch out of her way.

"Did he lie?"

"Does it matter that he offered me money? Did you

ever think maybe I had a plan to rescue you?" His teeth ground together. It stung that she didn't have faith in him. "Why do you have to always jump to the worst assumption? I'm here aren't I?" He cut her off when she started to speak. "Don't. Let's just move."

Soon they came to a steep ravine and descended with sideways steps. Next to him, Lily slipped on the loose dirt. She swallowed her gasp, and Cooper barely caught her in time. The boy let out a startled cry. Cooper held on to Lily as she struggled not to drop the boy and regain her balance. She stopped sliding and pinned him with an expression of such unguarded vulnerability, if he hadn't been furious at her, he would have leaned in and kissed her.

"Are you okay?"

"Yeah," she said. "I think just the lack of food has drained my strength."

"Understandable. We'll get you both something to eat soon." Cooper glanced up the hillside, wiping the sweat from his brow. Returning his attention to her, he sighed. Lily was too petite to be running while holding a child.

"Cooper, I'm sorry for believing you abandoned us. It's just when Maximo spoke about bribing you, I felt scared and angry and hurt. " She visibly swallowed.

"You had every right to be afraid of him—but you need to have a little more trust in me."

The boy wiggled in her arms.

"Let me carry him. We'll move faster." Cooper touched the boy's leg.

The shriek that followed could have raised the dead. The dreadful sound cut off as he buried his little face against Lily's shoulder.

"Shhh, sweetie." She patted his back and peered up at Cooper. "He won't budge; he's practically glued to me."

In the distance came the sound of a revving motor. *Oh, crap! Please be a chainsaw and not a quad or motorcycle.* Cooper cocked his head and listened. "It's coming from the direction of the cave."

She stiffened. "Maximo's men have quads."

"We have an advantage since we're on foot. We'll keep moving and stick to narrow paths. Let's go." He kept a tight hold on her arm as they rushed down the last half of the ravine. The path leveled out. The fastest route, which unfortunately was blocked, required them to slip between a rocky hillside and a wall of thorn bushes. Cooper pointed up ahead to a mound of soil and partially digested wood.

"Watch out for that downed limb. It has a termite's nest." He assisted her while they climbed over another massive limb.

She shifted the boy to her hip in order to watch her steps. Lily's breathing grew haggard. She couldn't endure this much longer.

He shook his head, frustrated more at the situation than the kid. He couldn't blame the kid for being terrified of him. Cooper knew he looked like Frankenstein after being spit out of a meat grinder. Then an idea struck. "His name's Jaime, right?"

"Yes." Lily maintained a steady pace. The kid hadn't lessened his grip on her.

Cooper leaned down, keeping an eye on the path ahead to duck for low branches. "Hey, Jaime, you want candy?"

The boy's curly head popped up, and his light-brown eyes lit with interest. Cooper felt like a bad actor in a "beware of strangers" service message.

"You let me carry you, and when we get back to the village, I'll give you a handful of candy. Make that two handfuls."

With a big grin, the kid leaped into Cooper's outreached arms. "Candy! Candy!"

"Thanks, my muscles were starting to burn." Lily shook out her arms. Along with Cooper, she started to run, sending a group of squawking, long-billed birds searching for higher ground. With every stride, Jaime's head wobbled like a bobble head, connecting with Cooper's jaw on more than one occasion. Cooper heard Lily's lighter footfalls racing behind him; all the while, he scanned the area for trouble. *So far so good.* The rev of the engine hadn't sounded again. Hopefully Maximo's men were searching east in the direction of the river instead of inland toward the so-called dirt road.

"Candy, candy, I want candy," Jaime repeated over and over and over again.

Is the kid going to keep this up until he gets his reward? Cooper sure hoped not. "I'll give you another handful if you play the quiet game and don't talk."

"No talking? Like a wabbit?"

"Yep, pretend you're a wab-*rabbit*."

Thank God the kid stopped talking.

Twenty minutes later, Cooper weakened as rapidly as a tire with a hole in it. He slowed to a walk, his pulse ticking away in his ears. After doing a face plant in the village, he'd allowed himself time to eat a hasty meal and to get hydrated. Then, to his astonishment, one of the villagers known as Lefty had come blazing in on a "borrowed" dirt bike. Refusing to let Cooper commandeer it, Lefty had given him one hell of a ride. Cooper still had gnats wedged in his teeth, and he would have vomited if the bumps hadn't just knocked it back into his stomach. As if his thoughts conjured Lefty, the guy emerged from behind a knobby tree trunk.

Lily gasped.

"It's okay, he's with me." Cooper lifted Jaime higher in his arms. The heat from the boy's rapid breaths fanned across his neck. In a few strides, they stopped in front of Lefty, whose ebony skin was drenched with perspiration.

"Hey, I know this guy," she said, with a glower. "He caught me in a net and then dumped me in the dirt."

Cooper looked behind them for any signs of being pursued then glanced at Lefty, who just presented Lily with a blank stare.

"He's still wearing the same misprinted 'Capp'n Crunch' T-shirt," she said.

Cooper could give a flip about the guy's hygiene or misguided spelling. "Lefty's dirt bike is about a ten minute hike west. Give Jaime to him, and he'll take the boy to Mary in the village."

"Has your brain turned to mush? I am not letting this guy drive Jaime on a dirt bike."

"Lefty's a father of five, and he'll go really slow."

Lefty nodded and flashed a tooth-deprived grin.

She tugged Cooper a few feet away and whispered in his ear. "He only has sight in one eye."

"And it works really well," Cooper whispered back. "Here's the deal. I trust Lefty. Jaime can hold on to him in the front. If there was another way, I'd do it, but there's not. We're all in immediate danger."

Lily swallowed hard and rested against the trunk of a

papaya tree ripe with fruit. "I know, but what if he crashes and Jaime gets hurt?"

"I rode with him, and trust me, Lefty knows the location of every pothole and low hanging branch." Cooper left out *because we hit them all*. After all, he had demanded that Lefty drive faster.

She lifted her chin as if to argue.

Cooper picked a papaya dangling above her head and thrust it into her hands. "Eat. And trust me."

She took a big bite, glaring at him. Regardless of how annoyed he was with her distrust, he hadn't missed how sexy she looked, all dirty and spitting mad. He picked another papaya, and after waving it under Jaime's nose, the boy snatched it out of Cooper's hands. After Cooper lowered Jaime to the ground, the little guy devoured his fruit. Juice dripped down his chin. Anger stirred within Cooper, knowing the boy was half starved. Jaime's pink tongue licked a circle around his sticky mouth.

"I like it." His hope-filled eyes peered up at him. "*Sooo* good."

Cooper's heart melted like ice cream left out at a summer barbeque. After picking another piece of fruit, he handed it to Jaime. "Yes, they are good, but this is the last one, or you'll get a stomachache."

The boy took a big bite. "Hmmm."

Cooper scanned the area. "We have to get Jaime to safety, and we have no other option but with Lefty." He jerked a thumb over a shoulder. "You and I will meet Lefty at a granite outcropping a mile southeast of here. He has to take the long way to get over the river. So after we swim across, we shouldn't have to wait long for him to take you." By that time he hoped the police from headquarters would arrive to deal with Maximo, all without Cooper experiencing his first bullet wound.

Lily tossed the remains of the papaya into a bush and knelt in front of Jaime. "You go with Lefty, and he can get you more food."

The boy paused from licking his fingers and with widened eyes looked at the strange man.

"If you're really quiet, Lefty will give you that candy I promised." Cooper added, "Tell Mary, she'll handle it."

"Mr. Lefty," Lily said through tightened lips. "If Jaime so much as gets a hangnail in your care, I will find you and —"

"Thanks, Lefty." Cooper gave her a sharp look. "We need to move."

Lefty reached out a hand, and after a hesitant moment, Jaime allowed himself to be lifted. Ten seconds later, Lefty was out of sight, and Cooper dragged Lily in the opposite direction. They had slowed their pace out of exhaustion as they trotted through marshes, thorn bushes, and a clearing dominated by knee-high, wiry grass. Now and again Cooper tensed at the sound of a revving motor cutting across the muggy air. Finally they met the Macal River. He braced his hands on his knees, gasping for air.

Next to him Lily propped against a mangrove tree. Perspiration beaded across her forehead. She leaned into the shallow water and cupped her hand to take a drink. Water trickled down her neck, moistening her green tank top. Something possessed his gaze to brush over her small, firm breasts. His pulse kicked up, and it had nothing to do with running. He forced himself to focus. "We need to cross. Can you make it?" The last thing he wanted was for her to be too weak to fight the current and drown.

"Yeah, I can make it," she said breathlessly. "Just give me a minute, and I'll be fine. What about you? You took a lot of knocks to the head."

"I look worse than I feel. I'll make it, no *problema*."

After taking a drink of bitter, yet refreshingly crisp, water himself, he helped her to her feet. He scanned the river, and once satisfied there were no threats, they entered the river. His shoes sank in the mud. He held on to Lily as the level of the water met their waists. "Watch out for rocks," he said, earning an eye roll. Hey, she might dismiss the last river crossing where she'd almost bashed her brains out, but it had scared the life out of him. Scanning the steady flow of water, he was grateful no rapids were within sight. "Here goes. If you get tired, float awhile."

He released her hand and started swimming. With his head partially submerged, his hearing was muffled. The cool water glided over him, soothing his aching body. He flipped over onto his back, relieved Lily kept pace. He scanned both directions, but nothing seemed amiss. The sky rumbled. He glanced up at the dark, gray clouds as light raindrops fell, dimpling the surface of the water.

They needed to hurry, because if it started to downpour, the river could rise, and the current would become swift. Cooper flipped back around and continued swimming. It started raining harder as he increased his powerful strokes. Then a noise penetrated through the sound of his heavy breathing. He lifted his head. Lily heard it as well. Her head popped up, her gaze bouncing from one direction to the other. The high-pitched rev of an engine grew louder. A chill shot through him.

Crap! A boat. With a burst of adrenaline, they swam toward the bank. Lily was so close they were touching. He feared any second a barrage of bullets would strike them down. His feet met the river bottom, and he grabbed her waist to keep the current from sweeping her away. Just past the bend, Cooper caught a glimpse of a boat heading up-river. His heart thundered in his chest.

"Hurry!" He scanned for a hiding place. Of course the nearest bank had to have a sandy beach that gave way to knee high grass. No good. Farther down a clump of bamboo pointed skyward, but they'd be seen between the gaps. Then he saw it: a massive mangrove tree about eight feet in diameter, half in the water and half growing into the bank. The stilted roots reached into the river like arthritic fingers. The plentiful, green, waxy leaves that fell in waves over the tree would provide the much-needed cover. They could fit. They had to.

Cooper grabbed her hand, shoved with his feet off the bottom, and gave her no other choice but to follow.

"What…oh, hell no," Lily's voice rose to a squeak. "Something's bound to be living in that crevice and kill us. We have to run for it."

"We can't make it, and something out here will kill us for sure. Come on, I'll swim in first. If something eats me, I'll put up a fight so you can get away."

"No—"

With a firm grip on her hand, he maneuvered through the labyrinth of roots and entered the darkened crevice. The potent rotten-egg smell hit him full force. The bark of the hollowed trunk brushed against his head as he lowered himself to his knees. He tugged her close to him. The water lapped up to his chin, and something tickled his ankle, but he didn't dare move. The boat was on them now. In such a small space the noise from the motor came across as deafening as a NASCAR race.

Lily trembled. He tightened his hold and kissed the back of her head. *Please God, let their motor stall out and the current sweep them downstream.* In a long stroke something brushed against his ankle again. A streak of ice cold shot up his spine. Whatever it was, it was long. Snake. He closed his eyes and mentally counted to ten.

The motor cut off, and voices came from nearby. The men must have pulled the boat onto the sandy bank. Cooper peered through the sliver of an opening and determined the rain had lessened. The men could be searching for their tracks in the sand or just needed to empty the water collected in their boat and be on their way. He prayed for the latter. His gun! Regardless of the lurking water creature, he reached back into the waistband of his shorts. Nothing. He ground his teeth. He'd lost the stupid gun! Great, some rescuer he'd turned out to be.

Then to his ultimate relief the engine revved to life, and the sound faded upriver.

"Can we get out of here now? Something swam up my shorts," Lily hissed.

"Big or small?"

"Small."

Good, not a snake. "Lead the way. Best not to rush out."

She peeked out of the long roots. "All clear." She waded the few feet to the bank.

He followed, his clothes clinging to his skin. He clasped her cold hand, and their shoes sank in the sand as they raced across the beach.

"Hey!"

The deep voice caused Cooper to whip around. To his horror he locked gazes with the Samoan as the current carried the boat downstream. Behind him sat the dreadlocked man clad in a wife-beater T-shirt, struggling to start the motor. The Samoan lifted a gun.

"Get down!" Cooper shouted. A shot exploded just as he tackled Lily.

• • •

Lily screamed as another bullet plunged into the dirt near them. Cooper's arm pressed her upper body into the ground. Panic rioted within her. *This is bad. No blade of grass is going to stop a bullet.* But if they bolted, they'd be totally exposed. They needed cover before the Samoan gave chase and planted bullets in their heads.

"Army crawl!" Cooper ordered.

In a flurry of motion, he crawled like he was just out of boot camp. Lily followed suit but spent more time scooping up dirt with her mouth than keeping up with him. Pebbles and sticks cut into her elbows and knees, but she continued with her pathetic attempt to crawl without lifting her backside.

"Lil, move it," he urged, two body lengths ahead of her.

"I'm trying." She spared a glance over her shoulder but only gained a glimpse of the gray sky.

Once they reached the edge of the vegetation, they veered behind the girth of a mahogany tree. Cooper grabbed the waist of Lily's shorts, lifted her, and dropped her with a *plop* beside him. After peering toward the river, he rested firmly back against the bark. "I think they're having engine trouble. The dreadlocked guy kept trying to start the engine, but now the boat's out of sight. The Samoan wasn't with him. He must be swimming or on foot." Cooper pinched the bridge of his nose. "We need to move. Keep low."

They gained their feet and ran deeper into the vegetation. Hit by a wave of lightheadedness, Lily forced herself to keep moving.

"Give up, and I won't kill your boyfriend."

The Samoan's shouts shot ice rockets through her body.

"If you make me find you, and I will find you, Dr. Deforest will die a painful death."

What if he captures us and kills Cooper? Maybe I should... Lily's steps faltered.

Cooper's large hand grabbed hers. "Don't even think about it," he said in a hushed tone and made a beeline for a cluster of pine trees with vines draped across the trunks and outreached branches. He pressed her into a gap amongst the nestled trees and squeezed in with her. The dense vines provided cover on all sides except for the way they'd entered. He leaned in and whispered into her ear. "Get down and stay down."

"What—"

He pressed an index finger to her mouth and shook his head.

She didn't like the wild glint in Cooper's eyes. Why did she have the sinking feeling she was never going to see his dimpled smile again? Her breath suspended in her lungs. All she wanted to do was to latch on to him and beg him to discard whatever harebrained idea he was plotting. He was going to get himself killed, and then all those kisses she wanted more of, his years of working on the vaccine, and those boards of dead bugs would be for nothing. She sank to the ground, pressing against the length of the tree, while he remained standing.

"Little pig, little pig, I'm going to skin you alive and leave you for dead!"

Lily jerked in reaction to the deep voice, her heart thumping. The Samoan had to be mere feet away. *Does he know where we're hiding?* She squeezed her eyes closed and clamped her jaw shut to keep it from shaking. Seconds ticked by. The crunch from his footfalls came closer. She feared if she inhaled, the Samoan would hear, and bullets would shred their bodies. Next to her, Cooper hadn't moved. Then the sound of the footfalls passed, and she opened her eyes in time to see Cooper launch himself out of the cluster of trees. He landed on the Samoan's back, and they both crashed to the ground.

"Run, Lily!" Cooper maneuvered on top and landed a punch.

The Samoan bucked, knocking Cooper off. Several feet away, Lily noticed a gun on the ground. Cooper must have knocked the weapon out of the Samoan's hand. She left the safety of the pine trees, her gaze bouncing back in time to see Cooper double over from a blow to the midsection. The Samoan glanced her way. A sense of dread spread across her chest. As if reading her mind, the Samoan's dark eyes scanned the ground. In a burst of energy she raced to the gun. The cool metal had just touched her palm when the Samoan's beefy hand clamped onto her bicep. She lifted the gun, preparing to pull the trigger when his fist struck her cheek. He released her as the weapon flew out of her hand, and she slammed to the ground. For a moment she lay dazed, her face throbbing, her ears buzzing in stereo. Then her blurry eyes cleared. Nearby, the Samoan searched the grass.

"You son of a bitch!" Cooper hollered, his features dark and tight.

The Samoan jerked around in time for Cooper's head to ram into his solar plexus. Both men toppled over. In a series of punches and grunts, they wrestled. She wobbled to her feet, scanning the thick mat of grass. *Come on, come on.* A glint of metal caught her eye. In a rush, she grabbed the gun, turned, and widened her stance. The Samoan pressed his forearm across Cooper's neck and, with his free hand, slipped a long blade from his belt. Her blood ran cold. She aimed the gun at the Samoan.

Indecision pulled at her as her breathing grew haggard. If she shot the Samoan, she could kill Cooper, too. Just as the Samoan arched the knife backward, Cooper twisted and kicked the man off him. Using cat-like reflexes, the Samoan leaped to his feet, the knife blade in his hand glistening. She sidestepped, and that was all the clearance she needed. *Bang! Bang!* The gun jerked as she fired two rounds into the Samoan's chest. As he staggered back, his sights honed in on Lily. In slow motion, the blade in his hand whipped back and flew straight at her.

· · ·

Cooper had lost a hundred lives and then some. In his mind, the image of the blade ripping through the air toward Lily was on instant replay. His body grew chilled, and he couldn't seem to complete a breath. On shaky legs, he stood beside her, and his vision tunneled as disbelief swam in his head.

"Snap out of it!" Lily urged. "You can go into shock later. Just pull out the knife." Beams of filtered sunlight slanted across her silky black hair pinned to a tree trunk by the blade. Her head tilted at an odd angle.

"Two inches closer and it would have plunged into your neck."

"Please focus." Her widened eyes stared up at him.

Mentally he gave himself a shake. "You're right. Here goes." He propped his foot against the tree trunk for leverage and tried to pry out the knife. It didn't budge. A continual cycle of bird chatter played in the background as he made several more attempts.

"Cooper, hurry!"

"Well, sweetheart, if you think this is easy, think again, this thing's in here tight."

Crack.

"Darn it! The handle broke off." Cooper frowned and tossed the pieces into the grass. "The blade's stuck. I'm going to have to just pull your hair, see if I can get the strands free."

"Okay."

He grasped a hold of her hair and yanked, trying not to hurt her. She gasped and clamped her eyes shut.

He paused. "Sorry, but a big chunk is stuck under the blade."

"Try again. It's okay. I know it's going to hurt."

He blew out a breath and tried again. Her every gasp and flinch released a sharp jab into his heart. He dropped his hands and stood. "This won't work." *Come on, think.* "Do you still have my pocketknife?"

Lily grimaced. "No. Sorry. Left it in a guard's shoulder."

Not exactly the answer he was expecting. *I don't want to know.* He glanced over his shoulder at the sprawled form of the Samoan. "Maybe he has another knife on him. I'll go look." He strode several feet away to a cluster of pines. Cooper knelt, trying to ignore the pooled blood and the dead man's sightless stare. A tremor ricocheted through his bones as he patted down the pockets of the camouflage cargo pants. Cooper's hand hit an object, and relief struck as he withdrew a folded blade.

"Got one. Small but it should work." As he rushed toward Lily, he noticed the birds had stopped chirping. A rustling noise registered just as two men stepped out of the dense foliage.

Gun in hand, Maximo advanced; his slacks were wrinkled and wet sand coated his Italian loafers.

"I told you I could track them," the dreadlocked man said, and Cooper recognized him as the driver of the Samoan's boat. The man held his gun in a lax grip. Could Cooper grab it? With Lily unable to move, it was too risky.

"*Tsk, tsk.* Miss Sanborn, I turn my back, and you just keep getting into more trouble." Maximo smirked.

Cooper stepped in front of Lily.

"And you, Doctor. As I recall, we had an understanding. I guess the lives of the villagers don't mean much to you."

Anxiety clawed down Cooper's spine. "Keep them out of this. They are just trying to live in—"

"How dare you tell me what to do?" Maximo pointed the barrel of the gun at Cooper's chest. "Times up."

Chapter Eleven

Lily's stomach plummeted as Maximo aimed the gun at Cooper.

"Wait! I'll make a deal with you!" She struggled to glance around Cooper to meet the drug lord's dark eyes.

Maximo shook his head, and a low laugh emitted from him. "Leave it to you, Miss Sanborn, to think you can negotiate with zero leverage."

She tugged at her hair. Pain splintered jagged lines into her scalp. She dropped her hands, her mind racing for some way to save their lives. "Cooper had nothing to do with my escape. I just happened to run into him at the river."

Maximo stepped to the side only for Cooper to mimic the movement. Why did Cooper want to protect her? If it wasn't for her, he wouldn't be in this mess. From a distance came the faint sound of a revving motor. *Oh, no, please don't let it be more of Maximo's men.* Somehow, probably because of all the drama trying to get her hair free, she'd missed

Maximo's approach. Hadn't even heard an engine.

"Really? Interesting. So tell me then, where's the boy?" Maximo asked, his tone calm.

"He ran away when the Samoan came," she said. "I don't know where he is." *Thank goodness Cooper sent him away with Lefty.*

"Find him," Maximo said to Tazman. "And check on that boat. If it isn't one of ours and they beach, kill them."

Lily swallowed hard.

"Um, boss, I found the Samoan," Tazman said before he slipped away.

Okay, one down. But getting away from Maximo would be the greater feat. Especially because her stupid hair was pinned to a tree. When she got home she was cutting her hair short, really short.

Maximo stepped back, never lowering the gun. He reached the bloody body sprawled in the tall grass.

"Cooper, run now," she whispered.

His gaze never left Maximo. "Not without you." Cooper reached back and handed her the pocketknife. "Start cutting."

She opened the three-inch blade and sawed at her hair. "He'll kill us both."

"You die, then I die." He widened his stance, blocking Maximo's view of her. This would've been the perfect time to run if it hadn't been for her. Lily sawed in a frenzy. A few strands gave way. Why did her hair have to be so thick? More strands broke free.

"You shouldn't have killed my head of security, Doctor. You will suffer before you die."

She hid the knife and peered around Cooper to see

Maximo approach, anger ablaze in his eyes. *Not good.*

In a split second, Maximo lowered his aim and fired.

She screamed as Cooper fell. "Stop! I killed the Samoan."

Another man rushed out of the jungle and started arguing with Maximo, but she was too focused on Cooper's writhing form to care who he was. Lily's outstretched hand could barely reach Cooper's back. He groaned holding his foot.

Her pulse pounded in her throat. They had to get out of there! The next shot could be deadly. With all her strength, she whacked at her remaining pinned strands, and they fell away from the trunk. She glanced over at the heated argument that was buying her some time. Her eyes widened at the man Maximo now threatened: Superintendent Castillo.

"I already told you I'm arresting the Americans," Castillo shouted.

Hopefully the two stupid pigs would just shoot each other, and she'd be rid of them. She rushed to Cooper. Blood covered his hiking boot.

"Run, Lil, now!" Cooper growled, pain lacing his words.

She tightened her grip on the pocketknife. "Get up, you're coming, too."

Cooper pushed to his knees. "Run, I'll be close behind."

Then the place exploded into pandemonium. Gunshots rang out from nearby. Lily fell on top of Cooper, only for him to pull her flat onto the ground next to him. Maximo and Castillo ducked, waving guns about as if trying to decide where to shoot.

"This is Senior Superintendent Zepeda of the Police Crime Investigation Division. Drop your weapons, or you will end up dead like your friend who fired at my men." The bullhorn cut out.

Maximo's expression hardened as he gestured for Castillo to head into the jungle. With sweat pouring down his face, Castillo glared at him before leaving. Maximo pointed the gun at Lily and jerked her to her feet. The movement caused the pocketknife to slip from her hand and tumble onto the ground.

"No!" Cooper bellowed and grabbed for her.

In a swift motion Maximo had her in a headlock with the gun pressed to her temple. "You misunderstand the situation, Superintendent," Maximo yelled, his body tense behind her. "I have hostages, two Americans I will kill if you don't leave the area!"

Lily briefly closed her eyes, struggling to keep panic at bay. If she didn't play this right, she'd be dead. Then Maximo would kill Cooper. In her peripheral vision she noticed Cooper slowly lean over and pick up the knife. She wanted to scream for him to stay still but couldn't risk drawing attention his way. Maximo spun in a semi-circle and shouted. "Did you hear me?"

Lily flinched at the volume, her heartbeat pounding erratically. A gun blast sounded in front of them, causing Maximo to fire into the jungle. Shots plunged near their feet. *Hell! The police are shooting at us!* She sank her teeth into Maximo's forearm, and he yelped and released his hold of her neck.

Cooper slammed into Maximo's side, and the men crashed to the ground. Maximo maneuvered on top and struggled for control of the gun. The barrel waved close to Cooper's head and fired into the dirt. Lily screamed and started to plant a kick to Maximo's ribs, but Cooper flipped their positions, and her leg met air. The momentum sent her into a stumble, and she landed on her knees. With gritted teeth, she zeroed back in on the fight. The men were on their feet, arms and legs a blur of motion. Maximo threw a punch, knocking Cooper back a few inches. In a split second Maximo leveled the gun at Lily and fired. She dove headlong into the grass—the impact slamming the air out of her lungs.

"Lily!" Cooper released a pain-filled roar.

She blinked and inhaled a shaky breath. Quickly she took inventory of herself. *No blood, that was close.* Her mouth pressed into a tight line. She rolled to her feet as Cooper plunged the knife into Maximo's throat. The momentum sent them sprawling onto the grass. The gun slipped from Maximo's hand as he clutched Cooper. Blood spurted out of his neck, and he made a gurgling sound. Lily rushed over and snatched the gun.

Still on top of Maximo, Cooper released another anguished cry.

"Cooper! Stop, he's dead." She shook his shoulder.

His head whipped around, a wild look reflected in his blue eyes. He visibly swallowed. "Lil? You're not hit?" He stumbled off Maximo's still form as he assessed her. Blood coated his hands and was smeared across his T-shirt.

"No. I'm okay."

"I thought that he…that you were…"

A crushing pressure built up inside her chest. Tears welled in her eyes. "No, he missed." She launched herself into his open arms.

His breathing was just as labored as hers. "Thank you, Lord. I thought you were dead. I…" He stared at Maximo's body. "I killed a man. I just took his life."

"You had no choice." She touched his cheek and forced his gaze back to her. "It was self-defense."

"Freeze!" A voice boomed from nearby. They broke apart. Police surrounded them with weapons drawn. "Drop the gun!"

The spit in her throat dried up. Were these police corrupt, too? She counted five of them as she tossed the gun into the weeds.

"On the ground, now!"

Cooper and Lily flattened themselves on the grass. An officer picked up the weapon, and they were both handcuffed.

Disbelief swirled in her head. *We're being arrested?* She was lifted to her feet and then pushed down to sit on a granite rock.

They lifted Cooper. He groaned and would have dropped to the ground if not for the officers.

"He's shot!" She hissed. "Can't you see the blood?"

"Just sit him up," said a barrel-chested, dark-skinned older officer. His pencil-thin mustache matched the downturn of his mouth. "I'm Senior Superintendent Zepeda of the National Crime Investigation Branch out of Belmopan. Are you shot anywhere other than your foot?" His thick accent could have easily been mistaken as Jamaican.

"No," Cooper said.

A young officer with a curl on his forehead like a member of a Latino boy band checked the Samoan's pulse. "This one's dead, too," he announced and brought a first aid kit to the officer with Cooper.

Cooper leaned back and shut his eyes as his hiking boot was removed. One officer held his leg as the other irrigated the wounds with saline. A wave of concern hit her at the sight of his grossly swollen foot. The entrance wound was near the top of the foot with the exit wound close to the bottom of his ankle. Lily bit her lip. *So much blood.* "Please let me sit with Cooper," she begged, unable to peel her eyes off of him.

"I'm fine." Cooper's mouth flattened as he met her gaze.

"But you're not used to being shot; you're a scientist. You need me."

Cooper flashed a tense smile. "I do need you. But not much you can do right now, sweetheart."

An aged officer snapped pictures of the dead bodies and jotted notes on a small pad.

Zepeda batted a mosquito away and cleared his throat. "Ma'am, what's your name and country of origin?"

"I'm Lily Sanborn of Las Vegas, Nevada, USA."

Zepeda asked Cooper to identify himself. Cooper responded as his foot and ankle were wrapped. In spots, the fresh, white gauze quickly turned crimson. She fought to steel herself against a barrage of emotions.

"How long have you been working for Maximo?" Zepeda asked Lily.

Movement from near Cooper distracted her. Two officers knelt and interlocked their wrists, making a fireman's chair. Now uncuffed, Cooper rested in a sitting position in their arms and held on to the officers' shoulders. She frowned at the trio. How could they carry him? Cooper outweighed both of the men.

"Where are they taking Cooper?"

Zepeda crossed his arms, feet spread apart. "To the boat, then to the hospital."

"Where will Lily be?" Cooper questioned.

"Headquarters in Belmopan," Zepeda said, a sheen of perspiration glistening his wrinkled forehead.

Cooper started to speak, but when the officers attempted to lift him, they stumbled. His words ended in a groan as his injured foot brushed against the ground. The officers righted themselves.

"Be careful!" Lily shot to her feet. A firm hand forced her to sit back down. She glared at Officer Boy Band and then spoke to Zepeda. "Don't you have any bigger men? My grandmother outweighs those two."

"Don't leave the police station. Wait for me," Cooper's words rushed out.

Zepeda jabbed a finger in the air. "Neither Dr. Deforest nor you are giving the orders here."

Her mouth tightened as she watched Cooper carted off toward the river. The aged officer who'd taken the pictures followed.

"Miss Sanborn, how long have you been working for Maximo?" Zepeda repeated.

Mentally Lily counted to five and fought to clear the emotion from her head. *Everything's going to be fine. Cooper will be fine.* She lifted her chin and looked Zepeda straight in the eyes. "I don't work for Maximo. I just met him two days ago after his man shot and killed someone in cold blood and kidnapped us. And by the way, I have to tell you my vacation in your country really sucks."

Zepeda shifted his weight. "Who was killed?"

"Cooper's assistant, William." The muscles in her stomach tightened. She inhaled a deep breath. "He's buried by a waterfall near Che Chem Ha Cave."

"And why were you by the cave?"

She pointed to the dead body. "Because the Samoan kidnapped Jaime, the son of the murdered man at the lodge, and the police are corrupt." She lifted her chin in response to the sternness of his expression. "Cooper and I went to find Jaime. We were taken at gunpoint to a drug cave. I don't know what happened with Cooper, but I was locked in a cell with Jaime like an animal."

"And how did you end up here surrounded by bodies?" Zepeda made a wide gesture with his outstretched arm. She was starting to dislike this cop.

"Well, let's see. Since I was left to my own devices without any help from the police. I knocked the guard at the cave in the head and…" At the last second she decided to omit plunging a knife into the guard's shoulder since Zepeda seemed to be looking to fault her. "Um…knocked the guard in the head, grabbed Jaime, and we ran into Cooper, and the criminals followed us here."

Zepeda scratched his head. "That's quite a story. Where's the boy?"

"Back at the village…the one Cooper's from. Some guy named Lefty took him."

Tense seconds stretched out as Zepeda scrutinized her. "Miss Sanborn, are you aware there is a warrant for your arrest on drug charges?" Zepeda asked.

"What?" Lily jerked in response. Would her problems in this country never come to an end? "You can't be serious." She fisted her hands in her lap. "Whatever stupid charges Castillo slapped on me are to cover his own ass. What kind of police force are you running, Superintendent?"

Zepeda gave her a hard look. "Bring her."

· · ·

Cooper was lifted into a waiting ambulance by the time the boat Lily rode in reached the small town of Cristo Rey. Officer Boy Band helped her onto the dock and clasped one of her arms, which were now cuffed in front.

"Where are they taking him?" she asked.

The dock swayed as Zepeda stepped onto it. "To the Western Regional Hospital in Belmopan."

The paramedic disappeared inside with Cooper, and the driver closed the doors.

Worry swept through her. "Wait! I want to go with him."

"Miss Sanborn, calm down." Officer Boy Band's grip halted her forward movement.

With flashing lights, the ambulance drove onto the highway. Lily never took her eyes off the bend where it had been swallowed up by the tree line. Sharp tips of pain threaded through her chest. *Will I ever see him again? Will he end up in prison because of me?*

A handcuffed Castillo and an inspector she didn't recognize were placed in the rear of a police vehicle. Seconds later it drove away. Satisfaction spread through her. *What comes around, goes around.* Castillo deserved to go to prison.

"We'll have a doctor take a look at that scrape on your forehead and bruise on your cheek before we go to the police station," Zepeda said.

What bruise? Then she remembered the Samoan hitting her right before she pulled the trigger and bullets had plunged into his chest. She inhaled and exhaled rapidly. Officer Boy Band assisted her into the back of the waiting police truck. An hour and a half later, she'd eaten, been seen by a doctor, been treated for minor cuts and scrapes, and been allowed to wash up. As soon as she stepped out of the room, a nurse informed her that Cooper was still in surgery. As she stood with Officer Boy Band in the busy hospital corridor waiting for Zepeda, her gaze locked on to a Caucasian man in his late forties dressed in a Hawaiian shirt. He was tall with a shaved head, and he held a briefcase. Zepeda approached, and the men shook hands. They spoke in low voices and headed her way.

The tourist wannabe stopped in front of her. "Miss Sanborn?"

"Yes." She shifted her stance, her handcuffs clanking together. Uneasiness danced in her stomach.

"I'm ACS Officer Vaughn with the U.S. Embassy." He flashed photo identification. He sounded American. Texas maybe?

"ACS?" she asked.

"American Citizen Services."

"Oh." Okay, this was a good thing.

His blond eyebrows furrowed as he looked from her face to her lopsided hair. "I've been informed that you've been provided medical care."

"Yes…How did you know we needed help?"

"I received a call stateside that you were in need of assistance. Superintendent Zepeda has agreed to let me ride along with you to the police station."

Had G-ma called? Rae? It was on the tip of her tongue to ask when Zepeda announced they needed to head to the police station, and she was escorted out to the dirt parking lot.

The grip of an invisible hand tightened on her heart the farther she got from the building. Lily came to an abrupt stop and faced Zepeda, almost causing Vaughn to bump into her. "I need to be with Cooper. Can't I just stay at the hospital and answer your questions? You'll have my complete cooperation."

"No." Zepeda frowned. "I have five deaths all involving you. One was an officer of the law."

A lump formed in her throat. "You can't seriously hold me responsible." Mentally she counted all the incidents. How did he get five?

Zepeda pointed a dark brown, stubby finger at her. "Don't tell me what I can do, Miss Sanborn. Now move."

"Dr. Deforest is in good hands," Vaughn said. "The best thing you can do is get this all cleared up."

Lily pressed her lips together and got into the police vehicle. Vaughn sat with her in the rear seat. This guy acted like she had a bad case of acne rather than the possibility of facing a firing squad for murder in a third world country.

Her breathing quickened. They didn't really do that here, did they? "Are you going to help me get home?"

Vaughn paused and narrowed his gaze, making the lines around his eyes more pronounced. "Please remember the investigation and prosecution of crimes are solely the responsibility of local authorities. However, I'm here to ensure full observance of the citizen's rights under Belizean law and to find an attorney if needed."

Okay, that didn't sound promising. From the front passenger side, Zepeda stared at them through the lowered mirror of the visor. She pressed a hand to her temple. *I've been accused of being involved in multiple murders. What am I going to do?*

"Would you like your family to be contacted and informed that you are safe and currently being held for questioning?" Vaughn asked.

Lily nodded. *Poor G-ma. She must be worried sick.* Lily felt some relief knowing Rae was with her. Vaughn lifted a briefcase by his foot and opened it. After having her sign a Privacy Act Waiver to provide authorization for the U.S. Embassy to be in contact with others regarding the arrest, he returned his briefcase to the floorboard. They traveled a few blocks, and the vehicle came to a stop in a parking lot.

She studied the side of the two-story, cement structure with air conditioners, most of which were in disrepair, propped into about every window. The structure looked as if it had survived an atomic blast. "Where are we?"

"Police headquarters," Zepeda said as they stepped out of the truck.

A few other vehicles of various makes and models sat parked in the rear lot. Vaughn gripped her elbow, and they walked past chipped cement planters that sprouted an array of weeds. Officer Boy Band opened a side door with a key. Zepeda flanked her on the other side and waited for her to precede him through the doorway.

Her body trembled as she entered a stiflingly hot space in a flurry of activity. The large room with scuffed, cinder block walls was packed with cops, cheap desks, and a raggedy band of children who all had the same yellow bandanas hanging from their pockets or worn as headbands. An officer asked one of the younger boys about a robbery. The oldest member of the gang had to be twelve, tops.

Vaughn guided her by the arm, and she started walking

again in the footsteps of Officer Boy Band. The attention of a few cops gravitated their way.

When Zepeda stopped to talk to someone, Vaughn released his hold of her and leaned down to Lily. "Answer his questions. Don't be a smart mouth, and I'll do my best to get you on a plane home ASAP."

She nodded.

"Miss Sanborn, you will be placed in an interrogation room," Zepeda said once he approached.

"May I sit in on the questioning?" Vaughn asked.

"As long as you do not interfere." Zepeda escorted her across the hall and into a room with peeling paint and no windows. A fan perched in the corner pushed the heavy air around. "Sit. I will be with you shortly." Zepeda shut the door.

Lily sat in a chair on one side of the scarred table and waited. Through the narrow, rectangular window she could see Officer Boy Band standing guard as the plastic clock on the wall ticked off the passing time. She rested her head on her palms and allowed her eyelids to droop, surrendering to the numbness flooding her brain. The door opened, and Lily jerked upright as Zepeda and Vaughn stepped in. A glance at the clock revealed forty minutes had passed.

Zepeda sat across from her, and Vaughn took the spot next to him. Officer Boy Band entered with a tape recorder and notepad and handed them to Zepeda. He then stood in the corner.

"I need to record this conversation." Zepeda pushed a button.

Lily wiped her sweaty hands on her shorts. Vaughn gave her a slight nod, she guessed to reassure her. As instructed by the superintendent, she gave her name, age, country of origin, and how she came to Belize.

"You're Asian. Were you born in America?"

"Yes."

"You don't look American."

She rolled her eyes before she could stop herself. "And exactly how does an American look? Both of my parents were born in the U.S. My mother was full-blooded Mandarin, and my father has British ancestry. Haven't you ever heard America referred to as a 'melting pot?'"

Zepeda didn't respond, just set a passport on the table and studied it.

She peered over and saw her photo. "You have my stuff from the lodge?"

"Yes." He flipped pages. Other than a stamp from a trip to Mexico two years ago and the Belize City entry stamp, the pages were blank.

In detail, Lily retold the story of stumbling upon Jaime's father hanging from the ceiling fan.

"What happened to Inspector Reimer?" Zepeda questioned.

"Someone shot him."

"I know that."

Lily shifted in the hard seat. "Reimer found me on the trail walking back from the river and warned me that Castillo and other police officers were in Maximo's pocket. He said he called an old friend at headquarters for help on the case. Then someone shot him multiple times from a distance. I ran and ended up at Cooper's village."

Zepeda instructed her to give an account of William's death, and then she explained how she shot the Samoan after he attacked her. "You saw what happened with Maximo," she said, her voice sore from talking so much. "He shot at Cooper and me. Cooper had no choice. It was self-defense."

"I read the police report, and it clearly states it," Vaughn assured, his elbow propping on top of the table as he leaned forward.

Lily wiped her damp forehead and released a breath. Another hour had slipped by.

Zepeda turned off the tape recorder. "I do not hold the doctor responsible, since I saw the altercation myself, and the charges for drug smuggling against you have been dropped due to the questionable involvement of illegal activities by Superintendent Castillo."

"Thank you," Lily said in a rush.

"Do not thank me, because that is the least of your worries." Zepeda wrote on a pad of paper and pushed it toward her. Scrawled in blue ink were three names. He reached over and circled the first two. "I need confirmation that you shot the Samoan in self-defense and to verify your account of what happened to Doctor Deforest's research assistant."

"Is Superintendent Castillo still refusing to cooperate?" Vaughn asked.

Zepeda nodded.

Vaughn straightened in his chair. "Dr. Deforest should be able to corroborate the events leading to the deaths of those men. Have you questioned him?"

"No. As you are well aware."

"I just want to make sure Miss Sanborn is being treated justly."

"Treated justly? A friend of mine, a fellow officer of the law, is dead. I had to tell his wife and children." Zepeda's mouth tightened as he turned to Lily. "Other than your word, I have no evidence to dispute you did not cause the death of my inspector." His pen jabbed the paper next to Reimer's name.

Emotion clogged Lily's throat. "Reimer was a good man. Justice was important to him. That's why he told me about Castillo and Maximo being cousins. He wanted Mr. Flores's murderer found." She met Zepeda's hard gaze. "You were the old friend he called about the case, weren't you?"

He didn't respond.

Lily pressed on. "He said you agreed to discuss the issue with the assistant commissioner and would try to get jurisdiction of this case."

Zepeda stood, his expression grim. "I will be detaining Miss Sanborn for suspicion of committing or being an accomplice in three homicides until I have had time to conduct further interviews." He turned to the officer. "Take her."

"You can't be serious. I did nothing wrong!" Panic slammed into her and she smacked her fists onto the table. The clang from the cuffs echoed in the small space.

Officer Boy Band stepped forward, his hand on the holstered gun.

Vaughn stayed in his seat but lightly restrained Lily's hands against the table. "You're just being held in a detention cell. No charges have been filed. Just sit tight."

Lily's eyes widened. "What? I'm going to spend the night in jail?" Disbelief flooded her brain as Officer Boy Band entered and ushered her into the hallway.

"Lily!" a deep voice called. "Where are you taking her?"

"Cooper?" She whipped around, throwing Officer Boy Band off balance before he righted himself.

In a wheelchair with his leg outstretched, Cooper

barreled down the hall. His left eye was a deeper hue of purplish-blue and almost swollen shut. He'd cleaned up, his hair was freshly washed, and he'd changed into a new pair of shorts and a blue T-shirt. He'd almost reached her when two officers hopped from their desks to halt his progress.

"Are you okay? Shouldn't you be in bed?" Joy leapt in her chest, and she rushed toward him only for Officer Boy Band to halt her progress.

"Dr. Deforest." Zepeda's face wrinkled in a glare. "My men were to bring you to the station after your discharge tomorrow morning."

"I'm not going to just sit back while all this is happening to Lily. I grabbed a taxi."

Lily bit her lip from the onrush of emotion. He'd come for her. Judging by his slurred speech and glassy eyes, apparently the drugs hadn't worn off. After a closer look, the signs of fatigue on his way-too-pale face concerned her.

"Are you okay, sweetheart?" Cooper asked, his brows drawn together as his squinted gaze assessed her.

"Better now that you're here." Lily was touched he'd taken such lengths to be by her side, but she refused to be selfish. He mattered too much to her. "You need to return to the hospital. Make sure everything's all right with your foot before it falls off."

"Not with you here."

"Leaving with a gunshot wound before the doctor released you was not wise, Dr. Deforest." Zepeda glanced at the officers holding the wheelchair. "Take him back."

"No!" Cooper shouted. "I need to know what you're doing with Lily."

"She is being held as a murder suspect until I have had

time to conduct further interviews. One will be with you," Zepeda stated. "Once the drugs have left your system."

"You can't seriously consider her a suspect."

Zepeda's thin mustache straightened as his mouth pressed into a straight line.

Vaughn approached and crossed his arms over his Hawaiian shirt. "You need to return to the hospital, Dr. Deforest. This isn't helping matters."

"And placing her in jail is?" Cooper's gaze sought hers. "Lily, I'm going to make some calls, and you'll be walking out these doors in no time."

She would give anything to go to him, but Officer Boy Band's grip held her back. "Okay." The knowledge that Cooper would be there for her, even if not close by, calmed her jittery nerves.

"Superintendent, my father, Reverend Deforest, previously from Global Ministries at the United Nations, is well acquainted with Prime Minister Barrow. I had dinner with the Prime Minister myself a few months ago."

"Dr. Deforest, do not think your connections can intimidate me."

Cooper shifted in the wheelchair. His focus stayed on Zepeda. "Will you honor my request that she be placed in a solitary cell and not with the general population?"

Her throat went bone dry. *How can this be happening?*

Zepeda inclined his head. "Agreed."

"And food, I can pay for whatever she needs," Cooper pressed on.

"It's already been arranged. The U.S. Embassy will make sure she has food and water," Vaughn said. "Time to get you back to the hospital."

"In a second. Can someone get her suitcase from the Hidden Paradise Lodge? Or maybe it's with the police in Cristo Rey," Cooper said, his words becoming more slurred. "She's exhausted, needs a chance to shower, and a change of clothes."

Lily fought to swallow the lump in her throat. She just wanted to go to him, feel his arms around her.

Zepeda scowled. "This isn't a hotel."

Vaughn murmured something to Cooper that she didn't hear.

Cooper nodded. "Lil, I'll be back as soon as I can. Just hold tight."

"Okay, but please stay in the hospital until the doctor releases you." Worry gnawed at her. Cooper looked ready to pass out.

The next thing she knew, another officer flanked her, and she was ushered away. She tried to shake their grasps loose, but it did no good. "I can walk on my own!" She glanced over her shoulder but lost sight of Cooper. Her insides twisted as a dreadful thought entered her mind: what if she never saw him again?

Chapter Twelve

"Time to get up," a female voice announced. Lily jerked awake. *Not my bedroom.* Her mind took a moment to lock on to her location. She shifted on her cot and rolled to her feet. Bars rattled, and the young female officer, wearing a service cap over her shoulder-length braids, entered the cell. In the background, Officer Boy Band observed with detached interest.

Lily straightened, wiping a hand down her face. *Right, I'm a jailbird. Okay, think positive. The police are going to tell you you're free to go, and they'll go to training to be better investigators.* Lily slipped on her sneakers and straightened the green tank top she'd worn for six days. It was so dirty, it could probably stand on its own.

"Ma'am, I need you to turn around and place your hands behind your back." It took a moment for Lily to comprehend the heavily accented words before she followed the female officer's orders. She cringed as her hands were cuffed. Her hopes of a release sank. "Where are you taking me?"

"To Senior Superintendent Zepeda."

Lily still couldn't believe she'd spent the night in jail. She'd been isolated from the others in an unused part of the building that had been closed down due to air conditioning costs. She'd been given a box fan, and the overhead light had glared down on her all night. "May I use the restroom?"

"Yes," the female officer stated. "The superintendent said you can freshen up before your interview. You have five minutes."

Lily was led out of the cell, down an empty hall, and into the restroom.

The officer removed her cuffs. "Your suitcase is up against the wall."

Lily blew out a breath. *What a beautiful sight.* "Thank you. Is Dr. Cooper Deforest here?"

The officer shrugged, the beads in her braids clicking together.

Even if he wasn't here physically, he still looked out for her. He'd taken care of Lily from the beginning. She'd never had a man do that for her before. Her hand shook as she picked up her suitcase. So much had happened since they'd first met, and she'd come to count on him. To care for him. Pain lanced into her heart. She hated that he'd been hurt and wished she'd been the first person he'd seen after he'd woken up from surgery. That she'd been there to pamper him and to make him follow the doctor's orders. Instead he'd come to rescue her—again. Lily stepped around the corner to a ten-by-ten open shower. She glanced around, relived to have the space to herself. She placed her suitcase against the wall, withdrew a small bottle of shampoo, a change of clothes, and since she didn't have a towel, a shirt to dry off with. After undressing, she turned on the lukewarm water. Goose bumps rose on her flesh, and she quickly washed.

Last night she'd barely slept partially because of fear of what today would bring, but also because she missed Cooper and that charming, unassuming way of his that somehow calmed her. The connection they shared was powerful. He made her feel special—and scared. Scared she'd do something to ruin it.

Five minutes later, she felt half human again, and Belize got a pound of its dirt back. She brushed out her lopsided hair and threw her soiled clothes in the trash. She decided, even though it was warm already, to skip wearing shorts and a tank top and slipped on a pair of jeans and a black T-shirt with *Las Vegas* written in gold script.

Back in handcuffs, Lily was escorted down the corridor toward the interrogation rooms. Her stomach knotted into a tight ball. Would Zepeda find her guilty, and she'd be locked away for life or sentenced to death? They veered right and came upon Vaughn leaning against the wall. He straightened when he saw her. He'd shed his tourist persona and now wore slacks and a short-sleeved polo shirt. He had a paper bag in his hand and a tight smile on his pale, clean-shaven face. The smell of food wafted up her nostrils, and her stomach growled.

"Good morning, Miss Sanborn. I have breakfast for you." Vaughn peered over her head at the female officer. "She needs to eat. Who knows how long Zepeda will question her."

Lily frowned. That didn't sound promising.

"She can eat in an empty interrogation room." The

female officer removed the cuffs.

"Lily!" The sound of the little voice warmed her like an embrace.

Lily whirled around to see Jaime, dressed in clean clothes and with a big grin on his face, holding hands with a petite Hispanic woman in her early twenties. Was this his mother? Then she noticed they shared the same golden eyes and had her answer.

"Hi, sweetie," Lily said.

He wiggled his hand free from the woman, and Lily crouched as Jaime ran into her arms.

Lily laughed and held Jaime close. She smashed down his brown curls that tickled her nose. He smelled sugary, and she noticed sticky stuff on his cheek. She eased back. "Did you have pancakes, waffles maybe?"

He nodded. "Yeah. Pancakes. Big ones."

She smiled back. "I can tell."

His face scrunched up as his expression turned serious. "Where you been?"

"Here. The police want to talk to me…a lot."

"I ride in a police car." He pointed back at the approaching Hispanic woman. "Mommy, too." Jaime beamed and patted the sticker of a police badge.

"Are you a policeman?"

"Yep. Mommy, too."

The mother had a matching sticker on her eyelet blouse. She looked young and innocent with her brown hair scooped into a ponytail. Lily would never have suspected she was a member of a drug cartel family.

"Hello, I'm Lily Sanborn." She stood and offered her hand. "You have a very special little boy." Tears swam in the mother's eyes, and seconds later she wrapped Lily in a hug.

"Thank you, Miss Sanborn, for saving my Jaime," she said with a faint accent. "He's my entire life, and I thought I'd never see him again." Jaime's mother stepped back and wiped her cheeks with her hands.

"He captured my heart the first time I saw him," Lily said as uncertainty tugged at her. Jaime asked to touch the female officer's badge, and Vaughn lifted him up. Lily lowered her voice so only the mother could hear. "Jaime will continue to be in danger if he has drugs and drug dealers nearby."

The mother held her hard look. "That is why I divorced Jaime's father, because he went to work for my brother. I moved back to Belize from Guatemala a year ago to get us away. But my ex-husband just used seeing Jaime as an excuse to move drugs. He had rights to see his son, so I could not say no."

Well, the loser was dead now, and knowing Jaime's mother left the drug life made Lily feel better about the little guy's future. Vaughn set Jaime down on the floor, and after saying good-byes, Lily was ushered into the interrogation room. The cool metal of the chair chilled her skin. The female officer stood next to the door and blended into the cinder block like wallpaper.

"You might appear to be tough, but you have a big heart." Vaughn slid into the chair across from her.

"No, I don't. Anyone worth their weight in spit would protect a child."

"That's an interesting way to put it. Although I have to disagree with you. You'd be surprised how selfish people can be."

"Talking about being worth your weight in spit." Lily took a deep breath. "Besides observing my downfall, what are you doing to help?"

He had the nerve to grin. "I brought you breakfast, didn't I?"

"Well, yes, thanks, I really appreciate the food, but unless you plan to bring it to my cell for the next thirty years, I'm more concerned about my butt being in jail." She took an eager bite of the breakfast burrito.

Vaughn uncapped the bottled water and set it in front of her. "Trust me. I'm working on your release. And Dr. Deforest indeed has connections, because after his phone call, the assistant commissioner of police from Belize City graced us with his presence." He paused and tapped a finger on the table top. "You have to understand this is personal to Zepeda. He's grasping at straws on the murder charges, but he also has multiple homicides to sort through. Tourism is a big money maker, and they need answers and preferably an arrest."

The scrambled eggs caught in her throat, and she choked. She took a drink of water. "So that's me?"

"You need to be patient. The investigation is in full swing. Last night I sat in on the interrogation of the inspector who'd been with Castillo on the river. It took a while, but he finally admitted to taking a bribe for fear he'd be killed, and he confirmed Castillo was on Maximo's payroll."

Lily set her half-eaten breakfast down. "So why am I still being held? What more does Zepeda want?"

"That just proves the department's corrupt. Zepeda wants evidence on who committed the murders and, more specifically, Inspector Reimer's. You already admitted shooting one man, so Zepeda needs to deem the act as self-defense."

She dropped her face into her hands. "So, what now?"

"Right now Zepeda and the assistant commissioner are conducting interviews. Let's keep our fingers crossed that they get the answers they need to release you."

She straightened. "Who are they speaking to?"

"Yesterday Zepeda received an anonymous tip from the Hidden Paradise Lodge about two Americans being captured by armed men. His inspector located the caller and brought him in. The other person being questioned is Dr. Deforest."

• • •

"And then your men surrounded us, and here we are." Cooper pinched the bridge of his nose, relieved to have finished the play-by-play of what had happened after they'd been captured near the waterfall. He shifted in the uncomfortable wheelchair on loan from the hospital. With a soft hum, the fluorescent lights flickered above the stuffy interrogation room. He still couldn't believe the police locked up Lily. As soon as he'd been escorted back to the hospital, he'd bribed an employee, the same one who supplied his clean clothes, to let him make a call while the officer on guard flirted with a nurse. He'd called the prime minister's number and had spoken to his assistant. The man had remembered Cooper and of course knew who Cooper's father was. Cooper hated playing the connections card, but he'd do anything to get Lily out of there. He just wanted to hold her, protect her. The image of her inside a cell—scared and hungry—made him sick to his stomach. Hadn't she been through enough?

"So, Miss Sanborn fired the shots that killed the man known as the Samoan, and she had no other choice, correct? You believe her life was in danger?" The assistant commissioner of police asked, tenting his long, dark fingers against his marginal chin.

"Yes." Cooper forced an outward calm, even though his leg bounced under the table. He didn't know what he would do if they slapped a murder charge on Lily.

The assistant commissioner looked at Zepeda, who'd taken the backseat to most of the questioning. "Senior Superintendent, the evidence shows Miss Sanborn is cleared of any wrongdoing in those murders."

"I agree she had just cause to protect herself against the Samoan," Zepeda said. "And she had no involvement in the research assistant's death. But Dr. Deforest wasn't present during Inspector Reimer's homicide; let me bring in a witness." Zepeda stood, straightened his crisp police uniform, and left the room.

Cooper waited as the assistant commissioner scribbled on some paperwork. Why was Zepeda so determined to find Lily guilty for something? Cooper closed his eyes and prayed. *Please let this man see reason and release her.* He rested back in the wheelchair, his leg stretched out. His swollen foot, covered in a bulky dressing, hurt like hell, but he'd been really lucky. An x-ray determined no bones were hit. He'd been given a tetanus shot, had the wound irrigated, and had his foot packed with sterile gauze to absorb the drainage. His brain was still hazy from the painkillers he'd been given.

Zepeda opened the door, and Cooper craned his neck to

see who was with him. He tensed at the sight of Xavier being ushered in, noting his hands weren't cuffed. The older man kept his somber gaze trained on the floor. Cooper wanted to roar with anger. The wound still felt raw and fresh. William's death had been senseless. Xavier might not have pulled the trigger, but he'd willingly led a dangerous killer to those Cooper cared about: Lily and William.

Xavier and Yesenia had been considered family friends since he'd visited Belize as a teen. Cooper's parents would be devastated once they learned what their old friend had done. Xavier sat down on a metal chair. Cooper glared at him. How could he take money from a drug dealer? He thought he'd known the man.

After Xavier identified himself for the record, Zepeda asked, "Did you know Maximo?"

"Yes."

"In what capacity?"

Xavier swiped a hand down his white mustache and drew in a shaky breath. "Maximo's bodyguard, the Samoan, asked me to keep an eye on Mr. Flores, but I did not kill him."

"Do you know what happened to Inspector Reimer?" Zepeda pressed.

"Just before Inspector Reimer was killed, I saw the Samoan go in that same direction with a rifle."

"Why didn't you tell the police about all this?" the assistant commissioner asked.

"I was afraid."

"We cannot get rid of the criminal element if no one comes forward." Zepeda shook his head.

Cooper gave his old family friend a hard look. "The

local police were in Maximo's pockets." *As well as other people's.* "Xavier would have been killed." Cooper clamped his mouth shut. Anger clogged his throat. *Why am I involving myself? Because I've been taught about forgiveness my entire life. "Forgive as the Lord forgave you."* The Bible verse his father lived by. How many times had his father helped the natives of the third world countries after they'd robbed, threatened, or even burned down the Deforest residence? More than Cooper could count. *Well, I'm not my father.*

"Did you call in a tip about two Americans being held by gunmen near the Che Chem Ha Cave?" Zepeda asked.

Cooper straightened, confusion swirling in his head. Now why had Xavier done that?

"Yes."

"Why were you there?" Zepeda continued.

A lost expression played across Xavier's face. Cooper wanted to shout *because he's a traitor.* But something stopped him.

Xavier brushed tears off his wrinkled brown cheek. "Because I — "

Cooper interrupted. "He was looking for a special herb for his ill wife. It grows there."

Surprise registered in Xavier's bloodshot eyes.

What am I doing? William died, and Lily and I almost did. But he was desperate to save his wife. War raged inside Cooper as betrayal and compassion clashed. Xavier would die in the deplorable conditions in a Belizean prison. No question about that outcome. And then what would happen to Yesenia? He'd noticed she'd grown thinner but hadn't asked why. If her days were numbered due to heart problems, that kind woman deserved to have her husband by her side.

"I knew Maximo wanted Miss Sanborn." Xavier stared at Cooper, sorrow etched on his face.

"As all the locals probably did," Cooper said.

"I had no idea you and William were there until I saw you…or what Maximo planned to do with Miss Sanborn."

Cooper held his tongue and glanced at Zepeda and the assistant commissioner. Xavier had made a bad choice, but he didn't have it in him to turn his old friend in. A sense of peace settled over Cooper. Had he forgiven Xavier? Heck, no! But he could let it go.

"Well, I think we have all the information we need, Dr. Deforest. Charges will not be filed against Miss Sanborn," the assistant commissioner said.

Zepeda thanked Xavier, and both men stood.

Cooper closed his eyes from the onset of relief. *She's free to go.*

"Just so you know, Cooper, I have accepted an offer to sell the lodge, and Yesenia and I are returning to her family in Guatemala. I am in your debt."

"No, you're not," Cooper said, but Xavier had already exited with Zepeda.

Minutes later Lily rushed into the room with her uneven black tresses draped down one slender shoulder. Pressure spread through his chest.

"Cooper, oh God, are you okay?" She knelt by his side, looking tired and absolutely beautiful.

"Better now. Come here." He pulled her onto his lap and buried his face against her neck. Emotion cut through him. He'd almost lost her. Bullets. Jail. So much had happened, but she was all right. Her body shook as he pressed a light kiss to her bruised cheek and then her lips. He eased back. "It's over, sweetheart. We're free to go."

Her fingers caressed his jaw, and her mouth lifted in a small smile. "I know, I heard." Her expression did a one-eighty and transformed into a scowl as she glanced toward the door. "Why did they let Xavier go?"

Cooper blew out a long breath.

"You couldn't do it, could you?"

It should have surprised him that she knew him so well, but for some reason it didn't. "No. At least not and live with myself."

Her hand pressed to his chest. "You're a kind man, Cooper."

He grinned and winced as the movement shot pain across his swollen eye. "Amazing how a few days can change someone's perspective."

"Hmmm. Now don't let your head get too big; you still have to fit through the door."

"Ah, there's that feisty lady I remember."

"You two about done?" An amused Vaughn stood near the doorjamb next to the assistant commissioner.

Lily hopped off Cooper's lap and adjusted her clothes.

"You are both released from police custody," the assistant commissioner said. "Miss Sanborn, a flight has been secured for you in two hours' time, and a police escort will take you to the airport."

Lily stiffened.

"And Dr. Deforest, the surgeon ordered you not to travel for seven days because your swollen foot needs to stay elevated; after that time, you have twenty-four hours to report to Senior Superintendent Zepeda to be escorted to the airplane."

"What?" Cooper jumped to his feet and instantly regretted it. Burning pain shot through his foot making his eyes water. He groaned and fell back down. Spots danced before his eyes.

"You can't be serious," Lily blurted. "He has a permit for research—important research to cure meningitis A."

Meningitis B! Cooper would have spoken up if all of his energy wasn't focused on fighting the pain.

"And I have suspended it due to my concern for the safety in the area," the assistant commissioner said.

Cooper opened his eyes and inhaled a deep breath that did nothing to calm his racing heart. *This can't happen, not when I'm so close.* He cleared his dry throat. "I have two more weeks to locate all the areas the ashwagandha grows before the University of Belize sends over a research team for harvesting and replanting."

"As of now the project is on hold. The university will be notified."

Cooper tensed and leaned forward. "We can't afford that delay. We were given a permit, and we are this close to finding a cure." He held his thumb and index finger an inch apart. "The herb used in the successful trial vaccine came from the Mountain Pine Ridge area. You have to—"

"I understand the importance of your research, Doctor, but I cannot allow college students to roam the area until all of the criminals in connection with Maximo have been arrested. We also have to conduct an internal investigation into the department under Castillo's supervision."

Cooper ran a hand down his face. *I failed. I think I'm going to throw up.* What if he or his colleagues were never permitted to return to Belize? All these years he'd searched for a cure—while placing his life on hold—had been a waste.

The assistant commissioner interrupted Cooper's rampant thoughts. "If you think about it, the company backing the project may very well pull you based upon the death of your colleague."

True. Cooper hadn't notified the laboratory about William's murder. His head pounded.

"Miss Sanborn, we need to get going," Vaughn poked his head through the doorway again.

"Just give me a minute," Lily snapped. "Assistant Commissioner, you can't do this!"

"Actually I can, and I have."

"I plead with you to reconsider," Cooper said, his words coming out in a rush. "I'll deal with my employer. The village where I do my research hasn't had any issues outside of Maximo. Please understand the importance of this research. I just need—"

"I'm sorry. I will contact your employer at the address on the application when a decision has been made to either lift the suspension or cancel the permit." The assistant commissioner exited.

Anger boiled in Cooper's veins. He wanted to holler—to throw things. His purpose here had been to conduct his research, and he'd not only let others down, but himself. He leaned his elbows on the arms of his wheelchair and hung his head.

"Cooper, I'm so sorry." Lily reached out and touched his arm. "You must hate me."

"I don't hate you."

She dropped her hand and stepped away. "You don't

have to lie to spare my feelings. This is my fault, and I know you wish you'd never set eyes on me."

He stiffened and met her gaze. "Lily—"

"It's probably best I'm leaving first. That way I can't cause you any more trouble." Tears filled her eyes.

"Maybe you're right." Cooper couldn't believe she was doing this again. He struggled to process everything coming at him. He knew she wanted him to disagree, to tell her it would all be okay, but he just didn't have the strength, the energy. Instead, emptiness expanded, numbing him to the loss. "You're so ready to believe the worst again."

Lily drew in a shaky breath. "I'm not—"

"But you are. I'm constantly having to defend myself. Over Mary, over my character, over accepting a bribe to leave you behind. And every time, I've forgiven it, told myself you'd trust me eventually. Now you're accusing me of lying. You should trust me to be honest with you." He shook his head. "I've had enough. I just can't keep fighting you on this."

Zepeda stepped back inside. "Dr. Deforest, there is a young lady named Mary here to see you."

Cooper released a mirthless laugh. "A woman who actually trusts me."

Lily covered her mouth, turned on a heel, and rushed out. Cooper's lips flattened as he wheeled the chair out of the room to watch her walk out of his life, taking the shredded pieces of his heart with her.

• • •

"Would you like something to drink? Soda, coffee, water.

We also have alcoholic beverages," the flight attendant with a mouthful of pearly whites said after the plane had been in the air for an hour.

Lily scanned the list of alcohol. "White wine."

The attendant set a palm-sized bottle and a plastic cup on the lowered tray. Lily eyed it and frowned. "Better make it two."

After handing the attendant a credit card, Lily unscrewed the cap, poured it into a plastic cup, and took a swig. The floral, unoaked taste slid down her throat. Ever since she'd boarded the plane, Lily had been on the verge of tears. She hurt, a deep hurt like someone stomped on her chest. *"I've had enough. I just can't keep fighting you on this."* Cooper's words sliced into her. He was finished with her. She'd pushed him away too many times, accused him of things he hadn't done. It was her fault. And his comment about Mary stung because it was the truth; she took him at face value and trusted him completely. After another swig of her wine, she read the alcohol content of the bottle. *Maybe I should have gotten something stronger.*

The food cart rattled as it wheeled by. Lily stared at the cushioned seat in front of her as she listened to the high-pitched hum of the Boeing 737's engines. After a six-hour flight, the plane landed in Vegas to a pink-streaked, sunset sky. A taxi dropped her at her mobile home. Emotionally and physically exhausted, she paid the fare and wheeled her suitcase up the driveway. Lily had wanted to call G-ma before boarding the plane, but her cell phone was dead. She quickened her pace and passed the trickling fountain of a dragon on the small patch of lawn. She'd picked up her suitcase and climbed the wooden steps when she heard the sound of voices. Her mouth dipped into a frown, wondering who it could be. After quietly opening the door, she entered and set down her suitcase on the shag carpet.

"No crow—bad luck—go, go." G-ma's voice carried from another room.

Lily walked through the beige and green living room, aglow from the table lamp, and stopped at the entrance to the kitchen. Her adorable G-ma, with her wedge of gray hair and cheerful apron plastered with daises, glowered at Rae.

"I get it." Rae stood there in jean shorts and a Johnny Cash tank top with a hand planted on her curvy hip. "I just needed to drop off the groceries and check on you." Behind Rae on the fifties-style dinette table were paper bags with produce sticking out.

"You get out now. I have to get rid of bad mojo."

"I have other tattoos, too." Rae brushed aside her shoulder-length black hair and pointed to the tattoo on her other arm. "Don't orchids and bluebonnets stand for something good? Like life or beauty?"

"Orchid sign of fertility." G-ma narrowed her gaze and studied Rae's stomach.

"I'm not pregnant. I just have a couple extra pounds from too many Zingers."

"You will have lots of babies…with bad luck."

Lily couldn't stop the laugh from escaping.

Rae's gaze jerked toward the doorway and her hand flew to her throat. "Oh my gosh! You're home!"

G-ma gasped, worry heavy in her clouded eyes. "Lily!"

Seconds later she was in her G-ma's arms surrounded by the comforting scent of homemade Mentholatum.

"This girl." G-ma pointed at Rae. "Call hotel in Brazil.

They say you in jail."

Lily briefly closed her eyes and leaned down to kiss her grandmother's wrinkly cheek. "The hotel's in Belize, G-ma…and yes, I had some trouble, but I'm okay now. I'm sorry I worried you."

G-ma examined her. "You look bad. Color no good. Eyes red. Hair falling out." A *tsking* sound followed.

"I cut it off. It was a bit of an emergency." Lily had forgotten about her lopsided hair and bruised cheek.

"Get special tea, make you all better."

"Thank you."

With her mission set, her grandmother moved around the kitchen taking out ingredients.

Rae strode forward and engulfed her in a hug. "We were so worried."

As soon as her friend's arms wrapped around her, Lily just lost it. A tsunami of emotion rolled through her, swamping her under its weight. Her body shook hard, and tears fell unchecked.

Rae glanced at G-ma. "Come on. Let's get you unpacked." Rae picked up the suitcase, and they went to Lily's bedroom.

"You scared me to death," Rae said and dropped the suitcase on the vibrant red and shimmery gold comforter.

After closing the door, Lily blew out an unsteady breath and snatched a tissue off the black nightstand.

"The first time I called Belize you were missing, then you'd been arrested. You look like hell. What happened?"

Lily swiped at her cheeks, crumbled the tissue in her hand, and plopped down on the bed. Overhead a rush of cooled air pushed out of a narrow vent. "A lot. It wasn't a very relaxing vacation."

Concern reflected in her friend's green eyes. "I bet."

Lily gave a brief explanation of the kidnapping, Reimer's death, and the exchange with Maximo.

"Holy crap!"

A knot formed in Lily's stomach as she thought of Reimer and his determination to serve his people at any cost. She decided she would write a letter to his family, telling how he'd protected her. His daughters and wife deserved to know how heroic he'd been.

Rae's lips pressed together before she said, "I wanted to fly to Belize, but…"

"You had to take care of G-ma, and I can't thank you enough. Hey, did you call the U.S. Embassy?"

Rae scrunched up her pert nose and her gaze shifted to the floor. "No."

Lily wasn't sure if Rae was telling the truth or not. But why would she lie? Maybe Vaughn had been mistaken about the origin of the call being stateside. Lily made a *humph* sound, finding it odd, but still grateful. If Vaughn hadn't been there to monitor Zepeda's questions, heaven knows what could have happened.

Rae cupped Lily's chin and studied her face. "You're pretty banged up. Did you go to the doctor?"

"Yes. I'm fine."

"Well, that's over. You're alive and not seriously injured, that's what's important." Rae grabbed Lily's hand and squeezed. "Are you sure you're okay?"

Lily sighed and massaged her temple. *Cooper.* Her insides twisted painfully. Nope, she'd hurt a man she respected, desired, and deeply cared for.

Rae waved another tissue in front of her face. Great, she'd started crying again. She was pathetic.

"I'm fine. Just tired." Lily wiped her face with the tissue and tossed them in the tucked-away trash can next to the bed.

"Did...did something bad happen? What I mean is, were you violated?"

"No."

"You're face looks haunted. It's kind of scaring me. Talk to me."

Images of Cooper's handsome face bombarded her. Not with the expression of amusement he'd flashed at her so often—but with stunned disbelief that had shifted to anger.

"Do you need to talk to a counselor?"

Lily blew out a long breath and glared at her friend. "Will you stop? It's a man, okay? I met a man, a wonderful, passionate, kind of obnoxious, gorgeous man, and I screwed everything up." Lily realized she was yelling.

Rae laughed, earning a jab in the ribs from Lily. "Oh, this is an interesting development. Well, I'm waiting. Tell me about him."

Lily couldn't even begin to describe her relationship with Cooper. Although she hadn't wanted him to, the man drove her to distraction. She'd never met anyone like him before: the humor in his hooded, blue eyes, his ability to make her lose her composure, his passion to make a difference in the world, his courage. He'd faced bullets to protect her. And she couldn't lie to herself; the hard body and dimples that winked at her when he smiled didn't hurt either. Soon Lily found herself spilling her guts about meeting Cooper and dragging him across the Belizean countryside to rescue

Jaime and then losing him over her own distrust.

Rae shifted on the bed. "So he gets you out of the joint, and when his world is falling apart, you accuse him again of something he didn't do?"

Lily narrowed her eyes. "I thought he blamed me for his research permit being suspended. He's getting kicked out of the country! And he was right that Mary would be a better choice." Her stomach soured. He was right about everything. If she had trusted him in the first place, things might have turned out differently. Even after he proved over and over he was an honorable guy, she'd screwed up again and called him a liar. She was flawed, and he deserved a woman who could make him happy.

Rae snorted and crossed her arms. "Okay, so he's tired of defending himself, and your response was to turn and run."

"I didn't run—I walked quickly."

"Did it occur to you that if you'd given him a chance to cool down, you two might have worked the issue out?"

"His mind was made up. It wouldn't have mattered."

"Well, you'll never know sitting here crying your eyes out with me."

Lily stiffened. "I am not crying my eyes out."

Their gazes locked in challenge before Rae opened her big mouth. "So are you going to do something about this or just tuck your tail between your legs and accept defeat?"

Lily lifted her chin, and her hands flexed. "Oh, I have something in mind, and it involves my fist and your nose."

"You're not going to hit me." Rae waved a dismissive hand. "You have a big bark but a little bite, and you're angry at me because the truth hurts."

"You don't know what you're talking about." Lily jabbed

a finger in her friend's direction. "This isn't something that can be just made right. The damage is done."

"I love you like a sister, Lily. But I never took you for a coward."

Chapter Thirteen

Nine days later Lily, sporting a new sleek chin-length cut, leaned over the hydraulic, stainless-steel table and placed the finishing touches on her teenaged client. This morning had started with a long list of clients to get finished by the end of her shift, because a carload of teenagers had been drinking and driving. Lily lifted her shoulder and wiped the sweat from her brow. Three fatalities, two scheduled at Peaceful Memories for viewings that afternoon.

For the past three hours she'd used the process of restorative art to reconstruct the facial bones of the fifteen-year-old girl. Lily would do everything within her power to make the heartbroken parents' last moments with their daughter as easy as possible. Not a simple task when she flew through the windshield. With efficient motions she covered the scars and cuts with wax.

The ventilator hummed overhead, pumping in fresh air. After ending her vacation early, Lily had immersed herself in her work. The problem was she couldn't stop thinking about Cooper. She found herself worrying about him. Was he healing okay? How was he dealing with the loss of his research and William's death?

Lily glanced at her work and grimaced. *Focus!* She wiped off some of the makeup and reapplied a heavier opaque cosmetic to hide the bruises. She had to accept that she'd blown it with Cooper and move on. *He needs a woman who will help his career, not get his life's work canceled like a second-rate circus, all the while making him defend his own honor.* That woman wouldn't be Mary, because regardless of his angry words at the police station, Lily believed him when he'd said that she was like a sister to him. But some other woman would snatch him up and realize he wasn't just handsome but kind and talented. Lily scowled at the image of another woman in his arms loving him instead of her. She halted her wayward mind and paid close attention to the finishing touches on her client. After applying light color to the lips and eyes, Lily compared the girl to the vibrant photograph. Satisfaction spread through her. With a roll of her stiff shoulders, she looked at her next client, a man who'd died of old age—thank God.

The door swished open, and Rae entered. Her heels clicked across the floor before she stopped to study the teenaged girl. "You worked your magic again. I'm glad we didn't have to tell her parents it had to be closed casket."

"Me, too. Will you inform the director she's ready?"

"Happy to." Rae narrowed her eyes. "You look miserable. Why don't you just call him?"

"Why do you have to be so nosy?"

"Because, my friend, you don't sulk well. The neighbors

in the trailer-hood are afraid to cross your path."

Lily's lips pressed together as emotion clogged her throat. "Fine! I did, okay? He doesn't have a private number listed, so yesterday I left a message at his office and on his parents' answering machine."

"And?"

"He didn't call me back." Lily was disgusted with herself. She'd done something she'd sworn she would never do: act crazy over a man. She must have checked the volume of the cell phone ringer twenty times and had barely slept for fear she wouldn't wake for his call.

"Maybe he's not back yet."

"He had to leave Belize two days ago."

"Oh." Rae frowned. "This may require a face-to-face meeting."

"If he won't return my phone call, then he won't want to talk to me in person either. I screwed up. You're right. I should have stayed. But I panicked and—"

Rae wrapped an arm around her and squeezed. "If he really cares about you, he'll hear you out, but if you lose the man you love without even a fight, you'll regret it for the rest of your life."

Lily started to correct her about the love thing, but stopped herself. Maybe it was love. She constantly hurt and moped around. Her grandmother had even claimed Lily's mood had caused the freak thunderstorm last night. Bad mojo.

"I'll bring margaritas over tonight. You look like you need one." Rae pushed through the doors and left.

Lily tossed her latex gloves in the trash and sat down on a stool. If she concentrated hard enough, she could almost feel the humidity in Belize on her skin and hear the choir of annoying birds chirping. She thought of Cooper—that intent look in his eyes as he watched her, the gentle breeze ruffling his sun-streaked, dark blond hair.

"You're a lovely lady," he said, "I have a weakness for petite Asian gals who don't think twice about ripping a man to—"

"Please." Lily held up a hand. "You could probably talk a monkey right out of its fur, but your words are useless on me, so save them."

He burst out laughing. "Well, heck, the last thing I want is a bunch of naked monkeys climbing around."

"Okay, you're charming, I'll give you that. But I am not sleeping with you."

"Sleeping with me?" he questioned. "What do you think, I'm easy?" He shook his head. "Hey." He pointed at his face. "My eyes are up here."

A smile surfaced on her face, and just as quickly, it disappeared. She'd tried to pretend Cooper was just a Red Snapper, but she couldn't fool herself. She'd gone and caught a marlin, and she wanted to keep him, polish him with oil, stare at him constantly, unable to believe her good luck, and show him off to her friends. If it wasn't too late. She couldn't sit here and do nothing. Cooper might not forgive her, but she still had to try to make it right.

"So are you going to do something about this?" Rae's words echoed in her head. Yes, save his research. Lily chewed on her lower lip, racking her brain for a solution. She didn't have enough influence to sway a foreign government or her own. She stood and paced a tight circle on the linoleum floor.

She stopped and stared down at her elderly, male client.

"Any ideas? No? Me neither." She blew out a breath. "I mean, I could call the Vegas news station, but they probably wouldn't care. This is happening in Belize after all. Only if I…"

She blinked rapidly as an idea struck. She was already shaking her head even before the thought had finished taking form. She knew an investigative journalist. One who was highly respected in his field with his articles printed in major newspapers. No. She couldn't do it. She wouldn't ask that man for a pot of water if she were on fire. *But you would do it for Cooper.* The words whispered in her head and plunged into her heart in the same instant. This could be her only chance of saving his research. All she had to do was pick up the phone and ask something from the man who'd abandoned her and had broken her mother's heart. Lily washed her hands and retrieved her cell phone from her purse. She stared at it, sighed, and looked up her father in her contacts. He probably didn't even have the same number. It had been seven years after all.

Indecision tore at her. She pressed her lips together and hit the call button. With every ring the knot in her chest tightened. A barrage of feelings struck: rejection, anger, sadness, hope.

"Hello," said a gruff voice she instantly recognized as her father's.

She could still picture him the last time she'd seen him at her sister's high school graduation: still fit and attractive with a neatly trimmed, brown beard and a debonair air.

"It's Lily." Her muscles tensed, and her hand tightened on the phone.

Thick silence filled the line.

"Is everything all right?" he asked, his tone actually sounding concerned.

"Like you care." The words flew out of her mouth before she could stop them. She rubbed her temple. *Keep a leash on your tongue long enough to ask the man for something.*

"You're my daughter. I know I've been a lousy father, but it doesn't mean I don't love you."

She couldn't believe her ears. *Love me! Who's he trying to fool?* She took a deep breath and searched for her calm. "I didn't call you to argue."

He sighed. "Tell me what's going on."

Lily debated about the best place to start. She glanced at the double doors and then down at her client. She had work to do. *Just ask and end the call.* She clamped her eyes closed. This was for Cooper. *Swallow your pride.* "May I ask you a favor?"

"Name it," her father said in a matter-of-fact tone that instantly made her suspicious.

Why was he being so agreeable? Lily forced herself to focus on the reason she'd phoned. "Do you still have con-nections to the *New York Times* and the *Washington Post*?"

"Of course, I'm still a freelance journalist for both of them."

Lily wished there was another way rather than having to ask this man for anything. "I have a friend who is really close to finding the cure for meningitis…B. The herb used in the successful trial vaccine came from the Mountain Pine Ridge area, and the Belizean government suspended his research permit and has kicked him out of the country."

"And this is the only place this herb grows?"

Lily didn't miss the curiosity in his voice, and she could

imagine him pursing his lips in thought. "Yes. If he doesn't get back into Belize, lives will be lost."

A few seconds ticked by as she waited for his response.

"A cure for meningitis B would be big news. Does this friend of yours have a name?"

She straightened. "Dr. Cooper Deforest, Professor of Entomology and Ecology at the University of California in Berkeley."

"And who is this man to you?"

The last thing she wanted to do was share her life with her father, but she pushed the words out anyway. "He saved my life."

"Care to elaborate?" he asked, his tone hard.

"It's a long story."

"And I'm a patient man."

Lily rolled her eyes. *Since when?* "I went on vacation, and Cooper killed a drug lord before the drug lord could kill me."

"Good Lord. Were you hurt?" he asked in a rush.

"No, but Cooper was shot in the foot, and then he lost his permit. It's my fault, and I need your help." Bitterness filled her mouth, and she fisted her hand.

"I'll call him—"

"No. It has to be face-to-face. Soon. And I have to be there, too."

Silence stretched over the line as Lily thought of her reply if he said no.

"I'll clear my schedule and meet you in Berkeley in seventy-two hours."

• • •

For the umpteenth time Cooper reread the modified sylla-
bus for the fall Ecology 101 class. He'd come to his office at
the university to get some work done. Just in case his permit wasn't reinstated, he decided to speak to the department
chair about the possibility of returning a semester early
from his sabbatical. Sighing, he dropped the page on his clut-
tered desk. He shifted and adjusted the pant leg of his beige
Dockers and positioned his foot farther under the desk.

It had been twelve days since he'd been shot, and the
plastic boot bothered him more than the wound itself.
Through the open blinds, late morning sunlight spilled over
the upholstered chair opposite his desk and across the wall-
to-wall bookcase jam-packed with books and journals. He
stared at the phone on his desk, his fingers itching to return
Lily's call. He'd listened to her brief message yesterday. Just
recalling the vulnerability in her voice when she'd said she
missed him made his resolve to keep his distance waver.

He'd lost everything, well almost. He was still breathing,
had his parents and his professorship, but his quest to find a
cure had just dissolved like ashes in his hand. But for some
reason his mind wasn't occupied with that loss, but with the
loss of Lily. He'd meant what he said about the trust issue.
The memory of when she'd left still jabbed into his chest.
Part of him had hoped she'd stay, talk, work things out. But
the more he pondered the situation the more he realized it
was never going to happen. When times had gotten tough,
her father had left his family, and that's most likely where all
her trust issues rooted from.

Cooper stood firm on his assertion that parting ways was
for the best. *Sometimes you have to think with your head,
not your heart.* That thought should have brought comfort

to him, but it didn't. Regardless of her faults, he still wanted her, cared for her, and worried about her.

Light footfalls echoed in the otherwise quiet corridor before a knock sounded at the door. He frowned. Summer school was in session, but none of the professors in his hall were working today, and there wasn't a secretary here either.

"Come in." He removed his glasses and set them on his desk as the door opened.

A petite woman appeared in the doorway. His eyes widened as surprise struck straight into his chest. It took a second for his brain to register that Lily stood before him in a white sundress and sandals that tied at her narrow ankles. Her hair was now cut in a sleek line level with her jaw.

She inhaled a deep breath, not taking her gaze off of him. "Cooper, I need to talk to you." Her words came out in a rush.

For the life of him, he couldn't speak. At the sight of her, happiness spread through his chest before he tamped it back. *Think with your head, not your heart.*

She pushed the door closed behind her, but it didn't click shut. She cleared her throat. "How's your foot?"

He doubted she'd come all the way from Vegas to ask him that. He grabbed his aluminum crutches from the wall next to him and stood. "A Canadian doctor looked at it four days ago and said it was healing nicely." He lifted a crutch. "I should be off these in about a month."

"You were in Canada?"

"Yeah, after I left Belize, I flew into Vancouver for William's funeral."

Lily wrung her hands then dropped them by her side. "That must have been hard. I'm sorry."

"He was a good kid. It was the least I could do, and I needed to tell his parents what happened and give them his things. I gave them some pictures of William collecting samples and…" Sorrow seeped into his gut. "His mom hugged me and said she was touched. It was just pictures. I was expecting them to be angry, not grateful."

"You gave her a memory, one of her son doing something he cared about."

"Yeah, maybe." He sighed and maneuvered around his desk.

"I have something to say. Please let me get it all out, or I might miss something." She lifted her chin and visibly swallowed. "I miss you. I know we haven't known each other that long, but something happened when we met, and I've fallen in love with you. I can hardly stand to live with myself knowing what I did to you…knowing I ruined your research, and I treated you badly on top of it."

His heart pounded rapidly. Hearing her say she loved him tempted him to break his vow to keep his distance. More than ever he wanted to drag her into his arms and tell her he loved her right back. But his self-preservation warned him if he began a relationship with Lily, they'd be at this crossroad again, and next time it would hurt worse. He needed to put her mind at ease, at least where it concerned his work, and send her on her way. "My permit being suspended wasn't your fault."

"I feel like it was."

"Maximo was a wild card. He'd come to me, before you and I had met, warned me to stay away from his land holdings, and even came close to killing me." Cooper thought of the poisoned monkey, and his stomach churned.

Her exotic eyes widened. "The first time he'd offered

you a bribe?"

Cooper blew out a breath and sat on his desk, and papers shifted from his movement. "I wouldn't use the word offered, more like forced. I gave the money to Mary for her food bank."

"I remember she said something about that."

A moment passed as their gazes remained locked on each other.

"I left you a message."

"I know."

"Oh." The faint stirring of footsteps came from the hall. Lily glanced back before refocusing on him. She shifted her weight and didn't seem to know what to do with her hands. Very unlike her. It tore at him to see her display so much vulnerability, because he understood it wasn't in her nature. He decided she deserved to know the truth about how he felt.

"Listen, I didn't call you back, because after everything we went through, you were leveling accusations at me and still didn't trust me. Do you know how that made me feel?" He didn't wait for her answer, just plowed ahead. "Like nothing I could ever do would be enough to prove myself to you. You've constructed so many walls around yourself, no one can get past them."

"That's not true. You were hurting, and I thought you hated me."

"I don't hate you. But you have to admit you find reasons to hold people at bay. If a relationship is to have a standing chance, you have to learn to trust and communicate."

A tear streaked down her cheek, and she nodded. "I know, and I'm sorry."

A knock came at the door, and it was pushed open. A Caucasian man in his sixties, wearing a black sports coat and crisp jeans, entered. With his strong-featured face and confident demeanor, he could have been the clone for the "Most Interesting Man in the World" on the Dos Equis beer commercial.

"May I help you?" Cooper pushed to his feet. Maybe this man was a new professor, and Lily's and his heated conversation had spilled into the hall.

The man looked intently at Lily, but she just stared at the speckled linoleum.

"I'm Lucas Sanborn, a freelance investigative journalist for the *Washington Post* and the *New York Times*." He offered his hand to Cooper. "I'm here to request an interview about your research on the meningitis B vaccine and the country that very well may be standing in your way."

Cooper frowned as he shook the man's hand. "Are you two related?" They weren't even the same ethnicities. Maybe he was a distant uncle or cousin.

The man watched Lily as if waiting for her to speak.

"He's my father," she said in a monotone voice.

No way. Cooper would never had guessed in a million years that this man had sired Lily. They looked nothing alike, and he knew she wasn't adopted. She must completely resemble her mother. Cooper's mind struggled to grasp the fact that Lily and her father stood in his office. She held such deep resentment toward the man. This didn't make sense.

"He's very good at his job," she said. "And maybe his article will sway the Belizean government to lift the suspension and—"

Her father rubbed his hand over his grayish-brown

beard. "Lily, let's take one step at a time. Let me speak with Dr. Deforest and get all the facts."

She nodded.

The air sucked out of the room. Cooper's throat thickened, and he found it hard to speak. Why would she humble herself and contact her father just to try to save his research?

Lily strode to the door and glanced at her father. "Thank you," she said in a low voice.

Just as she passed the doorjamb Cooper regained his ability to speak. "Wait! Lil, don't go. I—"

"I'll just be down the hall on the bench next to the fountain."

Cooper stared at the door after she strode out then focused on her father. Anger tightened his jaw. This man had hurt her, and Cooper wanted to tell him exactly what he thought of his poor fathering, but he held his tongue. It wasn't Cooper's place to interfere in Lily's life.

Forty minutes later, the interview was over, and Mr. Sanborn gained his feet. "You have quite a story to tell, Dr. Deforest. I have a strong feeling that a newspaper will pick up the article, but I can't guarantee it."

"I understand. Thank you for flying out here."

Her father looked Cooper straight in the eye. "I didn't do it for you. Or for the story."

At that moment Cooper's phone rang, and he glanced at the readout. "Will you tell Lily I'll be right there? I have to take this call."

"Of course." Mr. Sanborn left just as Cooper snatched the phone.

Cooper kept his conversation with the department chair brief and learned that at this time there wasn't a need to add an additional class, but he'd be notified if anything changed. Cooper thanked him and ended the call. In two long spans with his crutches, he was out of his office, and after locking the door, he maneuvered down the corridor.

"You're absolutely right." Mr. Sanborn's gruff voice carried through the air. "It was easy to just send money every month for Jasmine's and your care. I wasn't there when you needed me. Hell, I don't even know where Jasmine lives now. I'm sorry I let you down. Believe it or not, this last year I must have dialed your number a dozen times but hung up because I was afraid to face you."

"You're sorry? Well, good for you," Lily said. "The damage is done. Mom's gone. Jasmine's a mess. It's too late to fix things."

Cooper hurried his pace. Not that he was afraid anyone would hear since the building appeared deserted, but because he hadn't missed the hard edge to her voice.

"I want you to know I'm not the same man as before," her father said. "I remarried last year to a good Christian woman. She has adult children and grandchildren, and they are so close. It took seeing that to realize how much I'd screwed up. I want to make it right, so you'll forgive me, but I don't know how."

Cooper paused at the end of the corridor and decided not to interrupt their conversation. From the window, sunlight spilled into the common room, filled with large potted plants and benches, where Lily stood with her father.

The man continued. "After Philip's death, I just lost it. I don't know how to describe it. I just couldn't deal with the memories, and every time I came home—"

"You had to look at me. The person who caused your

son's death." Her hands fisted by her side.

Her father's eyes widened. "What?"

"You left because you couldn't stand to look at me."

"No, that's not true. You weren't responsible for Philip's death."

"How can you say that? I left the gate open! You blamed me for his death, and then you went away."

Silence washed over the room. Cooper glanced back toward his office, not liking that he was eavesdropping.

Her father shook his head, his hands lifting only to drop back down by his sides. "No, I never blamed you."

"Liar! You yelled at me and said I killed Philip." She gulped in a mouthful of air just as her tear-filled gaze locked on to Cooper.

"I'll be in my office." Cooper shifted his stance on the crutches. "Lil, when you're done come talk to me."

"No," she said. "Stay."

Cooper nodded. Pressure spread throughout his chest. Lily had done this for him. Had ripped the scab of a deep, painful wound and now confronted the man who made her childhood miserable. He knew now he'd judged her harshly, that her inner strength and goodness far outweighed her faults.

Her father sank onto the bench and buried his face in his hands, beside him water trickled down the stacked stone wall. Heavy minutes dragged past. Finally, Mr. San-born peered up at her with watery eyes. "That day is a blank for me. I can't believe I would have said such a thing. You weren't to blame. I was. Please forgive me, Lily."

"What?"

"The day before, I'd noticed the gate was hard to close. I

was going to fix it, but I'd gotten called for work. There was a breaking story and…"

Lily braced a hand against the wallpaper behind her, a crease marring her brow. "Not my fault? All this time I believed you left because you were mad at me, that you wanted another family, and that's why you kept seeing all of those women."

Cooper wanted to hold Lily so badly he shook.

"No. I left because I was a selfish bastard." Her father gained his feet. "And I couldn't deal with everything. Your mom and I, we weren't good for each other. I'd sleep around thinking I could find the part of me I was missing, and she'd just let me cheat. Your mother battled with depression, and I couldn't handle that on top of my own guilt."

Lily straightened. "I know I contacted you, and I thank you for coming…but I just don't know if I can forgive you."

"I know." Heavy lines creased Mr. Sanborn's forehead. "Thank you for hearing me out. You are welcome to contact me anytime, even if you just need something." The door settled closed with his departure.

Lily stared at Cooper and inhaled a ragged breath. "I need a little time to collect myself. Can you meet me later at my hotel?"

Uneasiness pricked at his spine. "I'll give you space. Just don't shut me out."

"I'm not. Promise. Maybe we can go to dinner, like around six thirty." Lily mentioned where she was staying.

"All right. But first I need you to come here, sweetheart."

She rushed to him, and he wrapped his arms around her. He closed his eyes and savored the feel of her. Too soon she eased away, and a minute later she was gone.

. . .

Lily sat on a multi-colored upholstered chair in her hotel room and zipped up her high-heeled leather boots. A bedside lamp cast a glow across the king-sized bed with a cranberry and purple comforter. She glanced at the clock. Almost six thirty, Cooper would be here any minute. She stood and straightened her red clingy dress and proceeded to pace a tight circle. She'd had time to process what her father had said but decided to place this morning's exchange in the back of her mind. Tonight she needed to convince Cooper to give their relationship a chance.

She smoothed her chin-length hair, still feeling naked without the long strands she'd had since childhood. She glanced at the clock. Five minutes late. Maybe he'd changed his mind. She'd just released a tense breath when a rap sounded on the door.

"Coming," she said. As soon as she opened the door, her gaze locked with a pair of piercing blue eyes. Uneasiness and excitement ricocheted inside her.

"Hi, Lil." Cooper wore jeans and a button-down shirt that revealed a tempting glimpse down the column of his tan neck.

Earlier at his office, she'd noticed that he'd cut his blond hair, losing the sun-streaks, and it somehow made him look even more handsome. He leaned against a pair of aluminum crutches, keeping his weight off of his foot housed in a plastic boot.

"Come in." She stepped back.

He maneuvered inside.

As the door clicked shut, she faced him. Silence stretched out while they stared at each other.

"How are you holding up?" He shifted his weight on his crutches.

"Fine."

"Your father threw a lot at you today."

"Yeah, but it was for the best." She wasn't quite ready to forgive her father, but her anger at him had lessened. She flexed her hands. "I know I need a lot of work. It's hard for me to trust people, but I do trust you. I can't promise to get it right all the time, but would you take a risk and give us a try?"

A slow grin spread across his face. "You're all I can think about. I even dream about you. It's either make you mine or get fitted for a straightjacket." He clasped her hand and drew her to him. "You sacrificed so much by going to your father, and I'm touched beyond words that you put yourself through that for me. Lily, I love you."

Her heart fluttered. "I love you, too."

He pressed a kiss to her forehead, her closed eyelids, and captured her mouth. She stood on her tiptoes, cupped the back of his head, and deepened the kiss. She fought to grasp that she had Cooper, and he'd forgiven her, wanted her. Her hands eagerly caressed his hard body across the span of his chest, muscular arms, and lean torso. He moaned. His crutch hit the floor before he circled her waist and crushed her against him. He nipped at her jaw and slowly trailed kisses until he returned to her mouth. The contact shot delicious tingles across her skin. He licked the seam of her lips before his tongue slipped in and brushed in slow, long strokes against hers. Heat swirled in her belly, and her breaths came in rapid gasps. His hand caressed her breast through her dress, his touch driving her wild.

Seconds later, she pushed at his chest. Cooper lost his balance and fell onto the bed, his remaining crutch thudding to the floor. Lily climbed on top of him and propped her hands on both sides of his head. She paused and glanced at his injured foot draped slightly off the bed. "Did I hurt you?" Her words came out breathy.

He smirked, his dimple winking at her. "No, but you can hurt me a little. I don't mind."

His hand brushed against her hair. "Love the cut. Makes your cheekbones stand out."

"I don't. I feel naked."

"Keep talking like that, and we'll miss dinner."

"I don't want dinner. I just want you."

Heat blazed in his eyes. "Come here," Cooper rasped as he drew her into a fervent kiss.

She arched toward him, trailing her fingers across his shoulders. His other hand caressed her exposed thigh below her hemline that had crept dangerously high. She needed this man. Needed to feel him love her.

Cooper unzipped the back of her dress and tugged it down to her waist. He slid his hands up her back and unfastened her bra, flinging it across the room. He palmed her breasts. "You're exquisite. I can't believe you're in my arms."

His mouth teased her sensitive flesh.

"Make love to me," she moaned.

"Oh, I will. Patience. I'm just getting started." He rubbed the length of his lower body against hers, sending sparks skittering across her nerve endings.

Urgency nipped at her overheated body. "I don't want to wait." She eased back, and with a rip, all the buttons of his dress shirt went flying. Lily ran her fingers across his smooth, muscular chest. "I want you now."

"Damn! That was hot. I'm about to lose it."

"Good." She leaned down, bit lightly at the base of his neck, and licked a delicious line across his pec.

He moaned and peeled the dress farther down.

"Hold on." She climbed off of him to remove the clingy dress and her panties.

"I have one request. Keep those leather boots on." He shifted on the bed to shrug off his shirt.

She returned her attention to him just as he shoved his jeans to his knees. Her eyes feasted on his well-formed body sprinkled with hair. Hunger pulsated through her, making her shake. His wallet lay beside him as he fumbled with the plastic boot. He fell back flat on the bed, panting. "Lil—"

"Leave it. Tonight it's boots and sex."

A grin flashed across his handsome face as he withdrew a foil packet from his wallet.

He donned protection and seconds later, she seated herself on him and in a smooth motion, they were joined. His strong hands tightened on her hips as their bodies worked in perfect sync. Time stretched out. Her hypersensitive flesh felt every touch, caress, and moist kiss. She wanted to lock the world away and share intimacies with this man who had snuck in and captured her heart. Emotions grasped her so strongly she wanted to cry. She'd never loved a man before, and it frightened her.

Spasms of liquid heat radiated and burst inside of her. With a moan, Cooper called out her name. Together they captured their pleasure. Breathless and shuddering from aftershocks, Lily collapsed onto his chest. Drained of all coherent thought, her eyes drifted closed. Neither of them moved until a chill crept into the air-conditioned room. Cooper shifted her to his side and lifted the covers.

She snuggled against the crook of his arm, relishing the feeling of being with him.

"That was incredible," he murmured. "My vision turned white, and I was soaring."

A smile spread across her face. "You turned into a bird?"

His finger jabbed her in the ribs, making her squeak. He drew her close and nibbled on her neck. "I was trying to say I think you caused a blood vessel to explode in my brain. Don't *ever* get rid of those boots."

Epilogue

Surrounded by the warm night air, Cooper relaxed in the patio lounge chair with Lily cuddled by his side. From inside the mobile home park the scent of barbeque wafted through the air. In the distance, Fourth of July fireworks exploded above a glowing Vegas skyline. Everything seemed to be falling into place. His relationship with Lily had taken off in the last two weeks.

He'd returned to Vegas with Lily and after five days in a hotel, she had suggested he save his money and stay with her and G-ma. He loved Lily's feisty grandmother, who'd also extended the invitation. A grin tilted across his face as he recalled the day he'd moved to their third bedroom. Along with his suitcase, he'd brought a bag of fresh produce and had insisted on sharing with the cooking.

Well, in G-ma's typical blunt manner, she'd told him to stay out of her kitchen. She'd snatched the bag from him and washed the vegetables. Then the tiny woman with her short, gray hair had threatened him as she'd hacked vegetables with a butcher knife. "My Lily's a good girl. If you sneak in her room"—*whack*—"I make new recipe to cook you in soup." Cooper loved the thought of having a soup named in his honor, but not if he was the main ingredient.

"What are you laughing about?" Lily shifted in his arms. A flash of her creamy thigh peeked out from her yellow sundress, redirecting his attention to her lovely body.

"Just remembering my first night staying here last week." He smiled and nestled against her neck.

In response she moaned and gave him access to more of her smooth flesh to nibble. "Are you still scared of G-ma? Every time I check your door at night, it's locked."

"Are you trying to seduce your house guest?" he murmured. It was driving him crazy, but he'd kept his pants zipped.

Muffled voices came from inside the mobile home, and then clear as day, Lily's friend said, "G-ma, one day I'm going to hide that broom."

"I think Rae's regretting her offer to get another round of wine coolers from my refrigerator," Lily said, humor in her tone.

Footsteps crunched on the rock lawn as a vibrant blue firework sizzled and went haywire across the sky. "Hey." Rae stepped into view. "You two had better cut that out before G-ma comes out here and turns the garden hose on you again."

Cooper laughed. "That was a first."

"A word of advice." Rae handed him two out of the three wine coolers. "If someday you plan to join this family, don't ever get a tattoo."

He glanced at the crow tattoo on her shoulder, exposed by the spaghetti straps on her tank top. "Duly noted." He'd seen G-ma wield that broom when Rae had arrived earlier to join them for dinner. Funny as hell, but clearly Rae found it annoying.

He thanked Rae for the drinks, handed the chilled bottle to Lily, then opened his.

Rae adjusted the hem of her jean shorts as she perched on the other lounge chair. "So, Cooper, did you get the university gig here in Vegas?"

"I did." He took a sip of the wine cooler, wincing at its sweetness. "I'll start teaching biology part time for winter quarter."

Life was working out. The article "The World's Loss of Finding a Vaccine for Meningitis B" had been printed in the *New York Times*. There was so much public outcry and media coverage the Belizean government lifted the suspension, and Cooper could return in late July. Lily and her father had refused to let him go down without a fight, and now everything was falling perfectly into place. Soon he would have the cure. He and another scientist would only have one day to prepare for the research team from the University of Belize before they started harvesting and replanting. It would be bittersweet. Once again he had his dream in the palm of his hands, but he had to leave Lily.

"When are you heading to Berkeley?" Rae asked, staring up at the shimmering fireworks.

Cooper took another drink of his wine cooler and set it down. "Next week. I have to spend some time with my parents, clear out my office at the university, and vacate my apartment."

"A trailer on the other side of the park will be up for rent in a few weeks." Lily grinned. A plane flew overhead, and a breeze followed in its wake.

He pretended to think about it. "Tempting, but I'll have to pass. I'd like something close to the university, so I could ride my bike to work."

"How long will you be gone in Belize?" Rae took a long swig of her wine cooler.

Cooper liked Rae, but he noticed sometimes she had a haunted look in her eyes. He'd asked Lily about it once, and she shrugged and said she'd wondered the same thing herself. He was glad Lily had such a close friend. Leaving would be difficult, but they were independent people, and after this, he would stay put.

"He'll be in Belize for thirty days." Lily took a long gulp of her wine cooler and set it on the ground. Another firework lit the sky. Although she hadn't said anything, he knew Lily was bothered by his return to Belize. For the first time in his life, he was eager to be done with research, so he could spend time with the woman he loved.

"Well, I'm going to head home," Rae announced. "I have the morning shift tomorrow. Thanks for dinner." After saying their good-byes, Rae left.

"How'd your conversation go this morning with your father?" Cooper had been on his way out to turn in paperwork to the university when she'd answered the phone.

"Fine." Silence stretched out. Lily could never be accused of talking too much.

He'd learned early on with her that if he wanted to know something, he would have to ask. "Would you care to elaborate?"

She sighed. "We spoke for half an hour. I even chatted with his wife. Seems nice. He wants us to fly down for Thanksgiving and even offered to pay the airfare, but I told him I'd have to think about it."

"I'm game if you are. We can hang with my parents at Christmas." Cooper was proud of her effort to forgive her father.

A series of colorful explosions signaled the firework finale.

"I love Fourth of July." Lily rubbed her hand up and down his chest which was clad in a gray T-shirt.

Desire thrummed through his body. "It's quickly becoming my favorite holiday." He molded his hand over her firm backside and gave a squeeze. If he wasn't still on crutches, he could throw her over his shoulder, dodge the flying blade flung by G-ma, and take her into the bushes.

"It's been a while; you think your grandmother fell asleep again in her recliner?" His tongue traced her lips until she opened for him. Her fingers caressed his neck as she covered his mouth with a hungry kiss. Urgent need pumped into his blood. His hand closed over the swell of her breast. A moan escaped from her throat as she arched against him.

After several delicious moments, Lily eased back, her cheeks flushed, mouth damp and a little swollen. "Don't know what G-ma's up to, but I know this morning I saw her sharpening her kitchen knives." She gave him a wink. "You up for a little danger, bugman?"

Acknowledgments

Thank you to my husband, Scott, for his encouragement and for cooking all those delicious meals so I could have more time to write.

Many thanks to Rita Robles-Baker for her advice and tips on embalming procedures. We have to go for margaritas again.

Thank you to my editor, Laura Stone, for her many hours of hard work.

As always I appreciate the endless support from my local critique group: Victoria Montes, Teri Moore, Meg Halter, Tanya Spencer, Tanis Galik, and Gary Adams.

And special thanks to Samanthe Beck, Rebekah R. Ganiere, Robena Grant, Vicky Hankins, and Karen Johnson for taking the time to provide valuable feedback for this novel.

About the Author

J.L. Hammer is a California girl and enjoys living in her small mountain town with her husband and two children. She loves to write fast-paced novels filled with suspense, romantic tension, and gripping action. She is a member of the International Thriller Writers and the Romance Writers of America. When she isn't writing or lost in the pages of a good book, she loves traveling, listening to country music, or just enjoying a nice glass of wine. Visit J.L. online to discover her other exciting novels.

www.JL-Hammer.com
Twitter @HammerJL
www.facebook.com/HammerJL

Discover the **Vegas Vixens** *series…*

NOTHING BUT TROUBLE